Dear Peter –
Many thanks for your
interest in my ravings
Wm Keller

A Place like HOBOKEN

by
William Keller

ISBN-13: 978-1986939379
ISBN-10: 1986939375

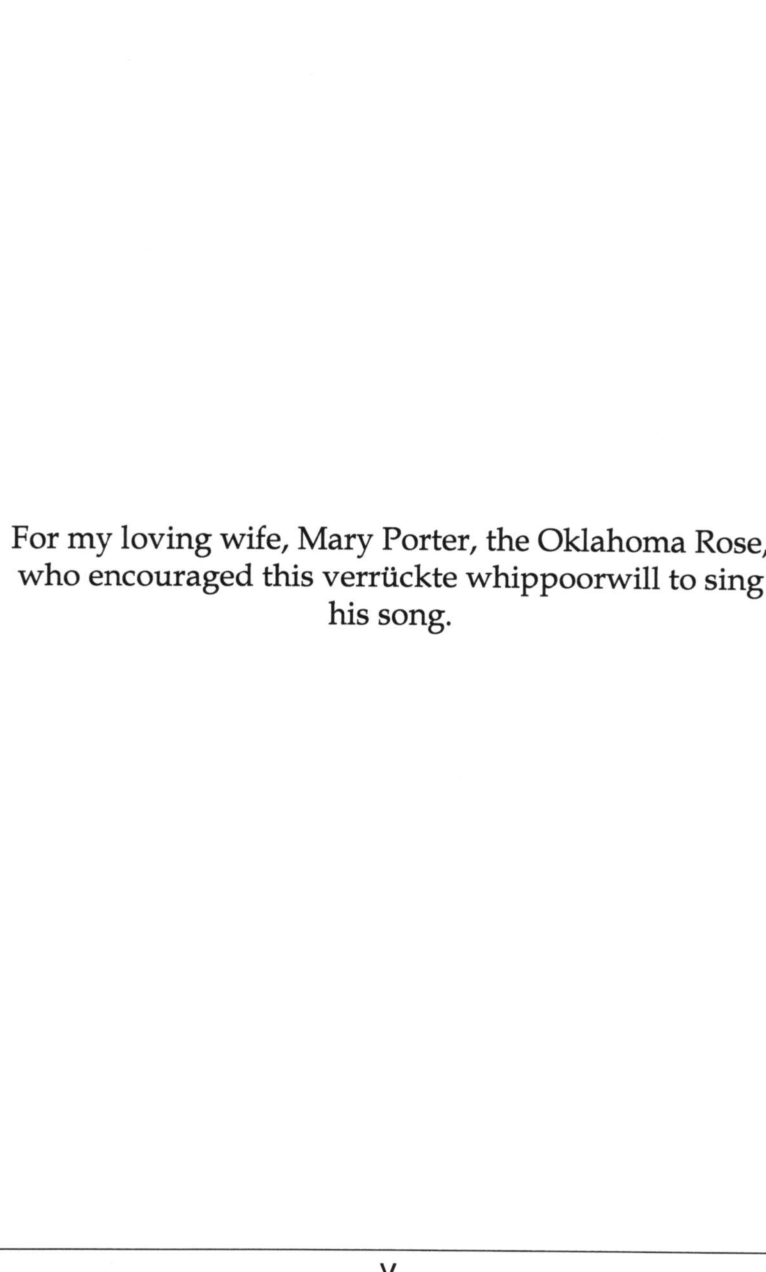

For my loving wife, Mary Porter, the Oklahoma Rose, who encouraged this verrückte whippoorwill to sing his song.

Hoboken Nocturne

or
Bye Bye Gingerman

In the twinkling nightspawn
of an early evening's bender
Mc Hugh
cloaked the ephemeral hue
of pool cue powder blue
dances
Dionysiac but shuffling off to Buffalo,
Terpsichore–tripping
with tuneless grace
to the jive time, ragtime,
mother-lovin' music of the spheres,
swingin' as he's singin'
ashen hymns of amorous praise
to a slew of nightingales many summers past.

Mc Hugh,
that shabby dream-bedwindled Mick
adrift now amidst the storybook images
of his iceman-cometh pleasure dome
and rappa tat tat
he tappy toes his dapper songs
along the Barbary Shore
where once he set the psychic threads aglitter
with the milk of love
in places like the Wunder-Bar
and no way he's gonna' hear
Time's winged razor
whizzing through the good-bye to Hollywood

nighty night,
that dark and empty fluid wherein
even the stars hang suspended,
cancelled perhaps
in a million light-years' deceitful lapse.

Still
behind the gossamer veil of summer's eve
a bevy of spiteful spirits
swarm to pantomime such deathless rhapsody,
for toothless songs or no
Time's a' wastin'
in the chill and barren caverns of the near beyond
and besides
Mc Hugh is blind
drunk.

No, no. Nanette,
no sense in crying over spilt milk
celestial or otherwise.
Mandrake's in Dreamland,
a hamburger for the Furies.

This poem is reprinted by permission having originally appeared in the April, 1987 issue of Irish America magazine

Preface

Wilhelm Müller's centuries old folksong "Der Lindenbaum" poignantly expresses a German's or, for that matter, anyone's love of place. For me that locale has always been Hoboken, a blue collar Paradise that now exists only in memory, not unlike the Garden of Eden – but without the harps and the angel wings. And to my mind, no one embodied the spirit of a place like Hoboken better than Dennis Weyouche (R.I.P.), a boisterous, somewhat eccentric young soul whose exploits I once extolled in my "Alas, Babylon" column for the Hoboken Elks Bulletin, with a readership of about three and a half. An excerpt therefrom – *in medias res*, as my high school Latin teacher used to say – appears below in hopes of setting the tone for the fictional stories to follow.

Originally "Alas, Atlantis" seemed a better title for my scribblings, largely because of something I once overheard – a marvelous, scornful legend spun by one of Hoboken's own grand dames. Someone we'll call Morticia as she was a funeral director's wife. She was an arch, fairly attractive Italian princess whose practiced hauteur proclaimed to all that living in the Corsage of the Garden State was aristocratic hell. Indeed, she had the conceit of a patrician but also a fiery imagination dipped in venom and wonder.

Hoboken, she opined, was actually the Lost City of Atlantis, with a Space Age 2001 intergalactic twist. The Gods, Zeus and such, greatly coveting the unique comic vitality of the Mile Square Miracle, plucked the city from its idyllic shores lock, stock, and many a barrel, and then set it diamond-like amongst the furthest constellations, in the silvery silence of deepest space – an American Oz. But the mighty ones soon tired of Hoboken's splendor, suddenly found the city rude and incorrigibly plebian. So they promptly hurled it back to New Jersey, tailing charismatic paths of glory.

Not surprisingly, the dazzling afterburn of such a legend falls on but a few undaunted native sons. Not the least of which is Dennis Weyouche – warrior, gurrier, history buff, and master of the bon mot. Presently toiling in the bowels of the Big Apple as a "sanitation engineer," the sometimes bellicose Mr. Weyouche also works as a clean-up man at the Elysian Café. Wherein his witticisms skitter along the bar like a well-aimed shuffleboard weight – that is, when he's not rummaging around in underground stockroom. He admits to guzzling the odd beer down there, but only from those cans which have already been dented. Café habitués claim he carries a miniature ballpeen hammer, but no one has actually seen it.

Understandably, many of Dennis's linguistic convolutions emanate from those dank recesses beneath the bar - *de profundis* but quite unseen. Bill Barron, the day man, once shouted down into the trap door behind the bar, "Are you all stocked up now, laddy, with the liqueurs and all?" Came the answer, "Yeah, everything 'cept that Aunt Jemima stuff." A Frangelico decanter greatly resembles a Mrs. Butterworth's bottle of maple syrup. Miraculously, everyone knew exactly what he meant and laughed. Similarly, unclogging a commode in the subterranean men's room, he announced to all what had caused the blockage: "Some oye took a Navy yard and shoved his skivvies down the sh*tter." Once again, all was perfectly clear.

Obviously, Professor Weyouche, an A-1 verbal alchemist, likes to mix the old and the new as can be heard when he growls (in a voice best described as the death rattle of a Tasmanian devil) that he is going across the street for some "squares" (a pack of cigarettes), but not before grabbing his "skimmer" or hat, for fear of the elements. In such a mind, shoes easily transmogrify into "wheels" and "hitting the silk" means going forth with vigor, as any paratrooper knows.

Wrestling a six pack under his arm, Dennis has been known to hit the silk in the splendid quietude of the early morn, trolling for beasties as he put it, oft-times finishing his afterhours wanderings with a few historical salvos at the Hotel Hildemann, the residence of his mentor and pal, John. And then homewards and perchance to sleep. As J.P. Donleavy once enjoined, "God bless the Gingerman" - Dennis Weyouche, the rightful lord mayor of Hoboken.

Table of Contents

MISCELLANY

VETS

Statue dedicated to the veterans of World War II in Elysian Park where Eustis Mullevoy envisioned troops marching unto glory in the story "Trailing Paths of Glory."

Confiteor

Of German-Irish descent, my real name's Brody Shultz, but it 'oughta be Ishmael, the lone survivor in *Moby Dick,* because all my relatives and friends have gone the long meander. The saying goes, "Only the good die young," but that's pure baloney. This side of Paradise saints *and* scoundrels, both the wheat and the chaff, get plowed under 'irregardless - even as a few revenants like me look on from their rickety porches, casements, and trellises.

Thus, as with the fella in that Irish song, The Old Bog Road:

I've discovered life's a weary puzzle... so I'll take the day for what it's worth and smoke my pipe alone.

A tad glib, I know, but ruminations of a similar stripe lead me to ask: when you awake in the dead of night, what do you think of during those hours of unsettling dreams and trepidation? Over what noisome particle of dread stuck between the eyeteeth of your consciousness do you obsess?

For all their heartfelt wonder, Ishmael's riffs on the immensity of the universe - the star flung galaxies on the one hand, mankind and the paltry unraveling of individual souls on the other - certainly didn't seem relevant to a blue bottle like me as ages ago I bustled about in that fervent little existence of mine. No crow's nest meditations for me. Goodness, though, how overwhelming such thoughts loom just now in the wee hours of the morning as the wind howls and a garbage can cover scuttles over the cobblestone streets below. It's that quintessential dread of an *alter kocker*. Inevitably, too, shame rears its ugly head.

For some the rub hinges upon what they've done. For others upon what they haven't done. Then I guess it's safe to say I'm gettin' a double whammy tonight because on top of my misdeeds I know somehow I should 'of sprung my father from that ghastly nursing home, but couldn't. Or maybe just plain didn't. Then, too, maybe bad juju's why I'm here all alone in the dark like him. No, not quite. As an M.D., he had it worse. He knew the body's inexorable decline as plain as day - from top to bottomus, as the Cowardly Lion used to say in Oz.

And, of course, regarding what I've done, that "cruci*fiction*" thing in prep school surfaces from time to time (so punned as we didn't actually nail old Ralphie Truetz in). Ralph was a weaselly character - bony, unsightly, and conniving. We were on a mandatory retreat and silence was the rule - except for an hour in the afternoon when we were allowed to wander about outdoors along the Stations of the Cross and monkey about. Round about the tenth station, Ralphie took to shying rocks at a pair of bluebirds.

Seizing the like as justification (Ralphie was easy to despise), three of us pounced on him and held him down. I found a large fallen tree limb, a two-by-four that held up a makeshift notice to keep-off-the-grass, and some clothesline that roped off a newly seeded area behind the grass sign. Knowing some lashings from Boy Scouts, I fastened the two-by-four to the tree limb as a crossbeam. Jameson, our ringleader, cut the excess clothesline into several three-foot lengths with his pocket knife, and we tied Ralphie's outstretched arms to the cross.

Mostly, when we hoisted him up, Ralphie cooperated by stepping nicely onto a nubbed up joint near the base of the fallen limb so that the ropes didn't dig into his wrists and puny biceps. As Jameson put it afterwards, he took it quite well.

Later that evening at Benediction, Rev. Tristan Speevy, S.J., just back from the missions, mentioned that he had traveled the world over - India, Africa, and the like. But, in his opinion, the greatest savages he ever encountered were right here in our midst. Sheepishly, 'me and a few other treacherous bastards in the pews offered up a reluctant, not so silent "Amen." Nonetheless, I could swear I heard Pontius Pilate wheezing in the background. In truth, however, it was only Ralphie.

Despite such youthful indiscretions, a nostalgia for my youth endures - rather like the Garden of Eden in the Old Testament. I loved growing up in Hoboken because back then it was a city teeming with eccentrics, some of them dangerous and edgy. For example, there was Casey Sikes, a vicious bitch who shivved her boyfriends, a drunk named Dennis Hogan who periodically tried to swim across the Hudson, and Sharpy Finnegan, the homoerotic bum who wandered through town making obscene facial gestures to the tune of "It's a Long Way to Tipperary."

Yes 'indeedy, for us Hoboken was microcosm of the lunacy at large in places like New York and Chicago;

so we knew what to expect when later we stepped out into the world. But Hoboken was safer, less mean-spirited; everybody had a job in a prosperity-forever town that abounded with German butcher stores, pizzerias, bakeries, pastry shops, Italian delis, and candy stores. Not to mention a few girls of easy virtue and Puerto Rican transvestite named Daisy Mae who was way, way ahead of her time.

Then along came the Vietnam War with trouble aplenty. If nothing else, it showed how easily a virtuous impulse can backslide into a wallow of petty grievances. Heeding what I considered an act of bravery, I volunteered my draft. My father insisted I'd done so only because my buddy Jameson enlisted in the Marines.

Be that as it may, during my training at Fort Knox on the Sheridan assault vehicle (essentially a small tank), I went AWOL on a Friday to attend my brother's wedding. When I returned Sunday evening, the muckety-mucks couldn't Article 15 me because they hadn't recorded my absence on Saturday's morning report. But a self-righteous Staff Sergeant Enos Ponder evened that score for the Army by placing me under the thumb of one Roosevelt Suggs, a sorry ass squad leader whose duty I had to pull for a month - right down to the platoon's graduation day when I had to replace him on KP, a delay which made me miss my flight out of Louisville and cost me a night of bliss with a zaftig blond on Bloomfield Street.

God forgive me, but to this day if I happened upon Sgt. Ponder at some hospice with him hooked up to a tangle of monitors, IVs, and a COPD nebulizer, I'd push that son-of-a-bitch down a flight of stairs, wheelchair and all, just like Tommy Udo in that film *Kiss of Death*. As to Roosevelt, he got his comeuppance the final day of training, qualifying on the assault vehicle's 152 mm cannon. Even our instructors admitted this piece of artillery was much too big for the tank that accommodated it; when you pulled the trigger, the entire vehicle rocked back on its tracks, forcing the gunner to jerk back too. We were warned to hold on tight "'cause surer than shit 'summa you dickweed peckerwoods're 'gonna slam your heads up against the sighting device when rolling forward again. Not that I really give a sh*t, but then I'll 'hafta fill out reams of goddam paperwork called a medical report." Shortly thereafter Buck Private Suggs was hauled out of the Sheridan with two black eyes and a broken nose. I never so much as grinned, but Schadenfreude coursed through my veins like honey.

Alas, vengeance's not the only thorn late night insomnia can spawn. Painful lessons abound therein. A year or so after my father wrecked his '62 Mercury in the Lincoln Tunnel, he, my stepmother, my brother, and I waited on a platform in the Port Authority Terminal for a bus to take us to Teaneck where my Uncle Hans was hosting a big family dinner. This was long before the installation of cubicles to shield commuters from the toxic fumes billowing forth from the idling buses.

We languished there for an hour or more, after which my father telephoned his brother, from a scuzzy booth in the waiting room below, to apprise him of our situation. Always amenable, Hans offered to pay for a cab – no small sum for a guy who drove a fish truck for a living; but my father, angered that Hans' mooching in-laws hadn't offered to fetch us with their station wagon, slammed down the receiver and ushered us onto a # 63 bus, which ferried our disgruntled posse homeward to Hoboken.

Rankled to the core, he didn't speak to his brother again until years later one frosty afternoon when Hans, the mere shell of his former self, arrived at my father's office with his wife. Hans, once with the heart of a warrior, was a shrunken man, cancer having eaten him half alive.

My father, a physician at St. Mary's Hospital, had him admitted lickety-split and eased Hans' sufferings with morphine; but it was curtains. My father's considerable skill as a healer went for naught. He was an unrepentant never-give-an-inch hardass and something of a stoic (as a doctor who dealt with sickness and death all the time, he almost had to be). At the funeral parlor's last viewing he leapt onto Hans' open coffin bellowing like an animal, keening indecipherable woe in a garbled version of the German of his youth, sobbing uncontrollably.

Amidst the flowers and the candles, my younger half-sisters were shepherded from this tumultuous unmooring before it poisoned forever their sense of well-being. It did so anyway. Thus it was that I learned how grudges become the nails with which we crucify ourselves. Doubtless, I'm fashioning my own as I reminisce. Seems no matter how carefully you step through the foliage, this evil pollen dusts your shoulders and your toes. After all, those ancients in charge of spinning myths knew well the persistence of evil, that which is much older than man – perhaps older even than Lucifer.

Deliverance

An unsightly cowlick no amount of Brylcreem could tame lent Terence O'Keefe's fiery red hair a disheveled appearance. But a gentle smile endeared him to his German grandmother with whom he lived as a little boy. He often accompanied her to Barill's, the corner saloon, to fill her growler with Ballantine XXX Ale. At Easter she bought him marzipan rabbits and once a marzipan statue of a Teutonic ogre known as the Kinderfresser who ate little children. She told Terence if he ate it, in a reverse psychology sort of a way, he'd never be frightened again. He believed her, and for a long stretch of time his life was, indeed, peaches 'n cream.

St. Peter's Prep in Jersey City required all seniors, even hooligans from Hoboken, to attend a retreat in the wilds of Staten Island. Thus Terence O'Keefe, a tall good-natured hobbledehoy with hands the size of Westphalian hams, listened intently to the Spiritual Exercises of St. Ignatius Loyola in a tiny chapel surrounded by rhododendrons and the fireflies of a peaceful night in June.

Fr. Hofnagel, a mainstay at the Jesuit retreat house, described in lurid detail the agonies Jesus Christ endured for the salvation of all – the sweating of blood at Gethsemane, the crown of thorns, the scourging, the nails, the lance, and the death-rattle cry of despair: *Eli, eli, lama sabachthani*. "And for this horrific sacrifice, my fellow penitents, we repay our Savior with vile transgressions and sin - ah, yes, with vanity, sex, gluttony, violence, calumny and lies," intoned the elderly priest amidst the flicker of votive candles.

He dabbed his glistening forehead with a handkerchief; much aggrieved, Terence collapsed in a paroxysm of sobs, striking his head on the pew before him. His comrades reached to help but with some hesitation. Terence rebuffed their efforts even as Fr. Hofnagel made the sign of the cross and murmured, "Well may you weep for us all."

Four years later, Sgt. O'Keefe stood atop a Sheridan assault vehicle in Vietnam and took the heads off two captured Vietcong guerillas with bursts from a .50 caliber machine gun as the wretched pair was led forth from the bush. They were the bloodied remnant of a force which had successfully attacked Terence's unit the night before and slit the throat of Terence's childhood buddy, Mickey Devlin, who had stood guard.

Terence returned to the States a broken man, a pariah who regularly indulged in LSD laced hashish inhaled from a hookah - not for any pleasure or relief it might have provided but rather for the punishment its hallucinations triggered within. Such was his self-imposed penance, for the drug's dissolution-of-self so liberating for some was every bit as terrifying for him. Its horror served as chastisement due, the very opposite of the Lord's Prayer and its "Deliver us from evil." He supported himself as an exterminator's assistant, laboring for Stanley Hokel, a gap toothed entrepreneur on Washington St. who greatly resembled the rodents they destroyed. For Terrence, the job was yet another gateway into retribution and the macabre.

A wiry man of contradiction and faith, Artie Shimmel, the pastor of the Church of the Chancy Whirligig, held that human existence was a transcendent experience regardless of which religion one usually espoused, for all such faiths intimated a continuance of one kind or another after death. Even hard-and-fast secularists like himself insisted *buonanima*'s (dearly departed souls) lived on in the hearts of their families and friends. And, he added, what did any layman, priest, rabbi, imam, or yogi really know of the details pertaining to heaven, hell, the wheel of life, or nirvana? Hence, Artie concluded, the wisest simply relied on love.

He delivered his sermons in a kind of rap, using a whacky mix of buzz words and stilted jargon- snippets of which he had purloined here and there:

> *At the beginning in an existential blur, / 'twas the willy-willies our Creator's fingers stirred / as the primordial gusts circled and whirred; / and whether you focus on Jesus, the Buddha, Mohammed / or even Freud's monsters of the Id, / drink deeply the joie de vivre, my brethren, that stream of energy. / Ah yes, even if you have sinned / and sway like a reed in the wind, / heaven forfend, / life is never as desolate as the Demon would contend. / Hallelujah, whomever you give the nod, / there ain't no fleas on the Lamb of God.*

He was something of a screwball – claiming, for instance, that Kurt Laemmel's smoked eels "put hair on your yarbles and a song in your heart." But when push came to shove, he had the courage and the tenacity of a Tasmanian devil.

He started out in a store front which had once been a Laundromat, then moved to an abandoned garage. He punctuated his "church" meetings with readings from sources as diverse as Genet and St. Augustine - not to mention poetry from Ginsberg on the one hand and John Donne on the other. Afterwards he positioned folding tables amongst the already standing chairs and served a simple repast prepared on a stove he had purchased second hand. A makeshift band featuring a hurdy-gurdy, kazoos, a Jew's harp, and a wash board sufficed as entertainment. Private donations kept the enterprise afloat.

Tyler Halliburton, III, Deshawn "Mookie" Bethune, and Yukio Kawasaki - a trio of suburban-born ne'er-do-wells who called themselves the Tri-racial Musketeers - emerged from Maxwell's after an evening of punk rock, coke in the jacks, and several smart cocktails. Tyler crossed Washington St. to buy can of lighter fluid at a cigar store and refilled the reservoir of his custom-made windproof Zippo lighter.

Shortly thereafter, yammering obscenely on their way to the parking garage where Yukio's BMW was parked, the Musketeers happened upon Terence, who slept in a hallway twitching spasmodically. Tyler flicked open his Zippo, lighting the flame; despite the matting and the filth, he spied Terence's carrot top red hair. In that puddle of sputtering light, Terence embraced a metal container, the contents of which had spilled across his chest. Terence often toted about his grandmother's growler as a talisman from the past.

Whistling "Danny Boy," Tyler emptied what was left of the lighter fluid on Terence, lit the bar receipt from Maxwell's, and tossed it on the slumbering form, proclaiming as he did so, "'Cause the world needs fewer shanty Irish dirt bags like him." Terence writhed in pain and terror.

The feckless trio fled the scene just as footsteps sounded round the corner - the footsteps of Artie Shimmel. When he beheld the crackling fire enveloping Terence, he took off his outsized overcoat and tackled Terence, beating down the flames with this garment as the two rolled about the pavement.

Terence recovered with only a few minor scars. Oddly enough, he claimed the attendant pain was just what he needed. Luckily, the stale beer spilt from his grandmother's growler minimized the damage to his neck and face. In any case, he was on the mend, so much so that he began attending Artie's "revival" meetings, the best of which was held in 4th St. Park.

Standing on a wooden milk crate behind the drinking fountain, Artie delivered an impassioned homily which the *Hoboken Reporter* referred to as the Sermon on the Fount. His audience spread out upon a hillock looking out on an expanse of the Hudson River where once Johnny Friendly ruled it over the deaf 'n dumb in the film "On the Waterfront."

Though listening intently, Terence watched as off to the west thousands of starlings wheeled across a gunmetal sky in dizzying murmurations before they settled down like confetti - probably upon the unseen meadowlands beyond. Artie's spiritual discourse alluded to Aesop's fable about the water pitcher and a thirsty crow. So deep was the pitcher and so low the water that the bird couldn't drink. Not to be denied, the crow dropped stones into the vessel to make the water rise and thus most cleverly quenched its thirst.

"Likewise, use your wits, your patience, and your determination to endure. For no matter how bleak the present, the opportunities for joy abide." Artie concluded. Stanley Hokel, one of Artie's disciples, set up a card table with coffee and donuts, which when stale, Stanley explained, made excellent bait for rats if smeared with peanut butter.

Terence wandered riverward down to the Wicked Wolf Tavern on Sinatra Drive to fill the growler he carried under his field jacket, the very same he'd worn in Nam. He thought it weird that the street he was on didn't even exist when he was a kid, back when the area was wharfs and warehouses. Then he moseyed back along the promenade behind the Little League field where, seated on the circular pedestal for the statues honoring veterans of WWII, he guzzled almost the entire quart of beer.

Shoving the metal container aside, he fell asleep propped up against a marble slab. When he awoke a small seagull swooped down from one of the monument's embedded rifles and peered into the nearly empty growler, pecking at it gingerly.

Grinning, Terence wished he had a pocketful of stones to lend the thirsty creature. To the west, St. Peter and Paul's church bells rang. Terence closed his eyes and, for a moment, he thought of the rats he'd poison on the morrow and the stash of hashish he had hidden behind some loose wainscoting in his room. But when he opened his eyes, memory flooded his consciousness with images of his grandmother and home.

Trailing Paths of Glory

One evening in May, a cafard descended upon the soul of Eustis Mullevoy - an inner trembling the morning sun did little to quell. He had an inkling the like would occur. For some weeks ago he had tended to the grave of his beloved Uncle Otto, the Marine paratrooper, in the Hoboken Cemetery along Tonnelle Avenue. It's a rarely visited site overlooking first the hurly burly of Route 9 and then the quiescence of the meadowlands beyond. Nearing twilight, the rusting iron fences and the tilted stones had lent his musings a prophetic tone. But trepidation or no, suddenly it was Memorial Day, a holiday from his job as a dockman at APA trucking in North Bergen. It was a time Eustis had set aside for visitations to living vets - if for no other reason than to banish ennui.

He glanced out the rear window of his basement flat; like a band of tinkers, grackles splashed in a puddle near the backyard fence where Mr. Gutterman was tending to his horseradish patch, digging up last year's roots before they lost any of their pungency and carefully laying in a bed of compost and wood ash for harvesting next spring. Eustis remembered how flavorful even a dollop of the Meerrettich tasted at *Der Alte Pflug,* a German restaurant in Schwabach, back when he served as a clerk for cavalry unit, fighting what he ironically called the Battle of Schnitzel.

Simultaneously, across the globe at Khe Sanh, his swamp buddy, Pax, had burrowed into the earth and cursed God as ARVA artillery pummeled his fellow Marines with punishing regularity. 'Twas always such, Eustis concluded, the bravest suffer terribly and the shabby just shuffle along. Oddly enough, Mr. Gutterman's son, Horst, sold Nazi paraphernalia in a corner store on 7th & Bloomfield. Reality, it seemed, was riddled with contradictions.

Later, out front, the sun set everything apart in startling detail. On the corner a swarthy Italian in restaurant whites called out, "A-dreep!" hawking such delicacies as capuzzelle, sweetbreads, and tripe from a little red van with bright yellow lettering that spelled out Zazzarino's - Hoboken's own autopsy on wheels. Thinking ahead, Eustis headed for Filthy Sil's (short for Silvio's) Army & Navy on the "other side" of Washington Street to purchase some used fatigues, the perfect apparel for slugging freight. After a leisurely stroll on the avenue, Eustis peered into Sil's storefront through the murky windows behind which merchandise was piled willy-nilly, but no one stirred. Eustis knew Filthy Sil's opened every weekday - holiday or no. But you never knew exactly when.

Just then a jitney pulled up, and Filthy Sil's exiting avoirdupois made the bus genuflect curbside long before buses were designed to do so. Carrying a bag of doughnuts, Sil shuffled towards his doorway in canvas shoes crushed flat at the heels. The laces were, perforce, untied.

A black schnauzer, perhaps drawn by the aromatic cloud that at times enveloped Sil, suddenly lunged and snapped at his Achilles tendon. The timid giant tried to leap away from the dog's ivory maw, his arms and ample flesh sloshing upwards - without, however, so much as a centimeter between his footwear and the pavement.

Torn between laughter and genuine concern, the owner of the snarling canine finally got his beast under control while Sil glared at his tormenter and sidled towards safety of his lair. Within, Eustis noted, the dim fluorescence and the fusty odors of wool and canvas contrasted with the Aegean splendors outdoors. In the meager twinkling of an indoor sty, Sil languished peacefully behind his counter where, to quote Hopkins, one might see "worlds of wanwood leafmeal lie."

Eventually, though, Sil inhaled stentorian gasps of air as, bathed in sweat, he wrapped Eustis's purchases in heavy brown paper and string. Bockedy package in hand, Eustis ventured forth.

The orange number 6 bus dropped him within walking distance of the Hamilton Park hospice in lower Jersey City where his former scoutmaster, Jim Keagan, suffered the last stages of cancer. Despite the languor of morphine, Jim greeted Eustis as cheerfully as he could, commenting then on the imaginary clowns and the circus animals he saw cavorting beneath the nearby ramps leading to Journal Square and the Turnpike. Feigning wonder, Eustis humored his friend who unexplainably fell into a remembrance of a horrific engagement during the Korean War when he and others walked along a firebombed convoy of enemy troops euthanizing screaming soldiers, some of whom had been napalmed together. Blessedly, Jim soon drifted off to sleep, and after a time Eustis bade him a silent farewell.

In the corridor, Eustis bumped into Major Dunne, an aged priest who helped out as a chaplain on the weekends. Eustis knew him from his unsuccessful foray as a college student at St. Peters where the Major once taught history. Like many former soldiers and Jesuits, Fr. Dunne was fond of Scotch, jiggers of which he poured for Eustis and himself in his office. Fr. Dunne's burly corpus sank into a tattered easy chair. Apropos of his chaplaincy at the hospice, he recounted a story from his days as a young priest when he heard the death bed confessions of elderly seamen along New York City's Barbary shore.

"By way of a general confession, I ran through the Commandments for one old Irish salt who knew well his days were numbered. Gnarly to the end, the old devil shook his head with gusto when I mentioned the sixth commandment. I asked, 'Surely in those exotic ports, and you in your prime, at least one painted maiden held way?' 'And what of it, Father,' answered he almost indignantly, 'didn't I always pay?'"

"Incidentally," the Major continued, "your buddy, Fr. Coleman, Fearless Fosdick himself, delivered quite a sermon last weekend in which he identified Christianity as 'the pantheism of human flesh'- in as much as we are all supposed to see the face of suffering Jesus in all those we meet. Not bad, huh?"

"It figures, Eustis replied. "He always understood the magic of even the stuff people just 'wanna believe."

When Eustis got off the bus on 10th & Washington, he made a beeline for the Elysian Park statue of the returning doughboys where Memorial Day festivities he had read about in the newspapers had already begun. His fatigues under his arm, Eustis jogged east past the former residence of James Rado and Gerome Ragni, creators of the anti-war musical *Hair*- the one, Eustis recalled, resembling Marty Feldman in a Medusa wig, the other Zacherley, TV's Cool Ghoul, on LSD. Though these lovely terraced digs exuded the laid back charm of the French Quarter in New Orleans, Eustis detested them every bit as much as he had the Karl Marx *Haus* in Germany. Commies and dissidents were all the same to him.

Further on, a little boy in a sailor suit danced about the iron fence surrounding the memorial, and to the west Eustis beheld a magnificent vermilion haze into which the sun was setting. The tri-colored bunting around the statue flapped in a breeze, and a ragtag band - some members uniformed, some not - played a rousing stanza or two of Battle Hymn of the Republic.

A lone voice, a contralto, took up the tune: "In the beauty of the lily, Christ transfigures you and me..." To Eustis, mesmerized for the moment, it seemed only fitting that ghostly columns of American soldiers should have been marching into that eternal blaze, into that rosy suffusion above the Heights. But as he gazed westward at the heavens, Zazzarino's little red van - which was trundling by at the moment - backfired and legions of starlings that had been roosting in the surrounding sycamore trees filled the sky with their dun colored wings instead.

The oratory was blessedly brief. As the ceremony drew to a close, Eustis strode towards the entrance to the park where a disheveled member of the VFW was distributing paper flowers to those who donated to the cause. Few afforded the burly coot as much as a glance as they sauntered by. But the toothless grin that lit up his stubbly face was more than genuine - a haggard visage not unlike Jim Keagan's. Choking back his emotions, Eustis stuffed a tenner into the yeoman's cardboard canister. Out of nowhere, he remembered his grandfather's definition of a coward: "Someone who wouldn't fight even when the Garryowen was playing." But he knew in his heart of hearts, such vainglorious notions hailed from the world of make believe where Taps was never blown. Strangely, though, the pall upon his spirits lifted.

Though half a city away, the hotdogs at Cal's were magnificent. The walk had done Eustis good, and Cal's onions were almost as good as Mr. Gutterman's horseradish - something he finagled from time to time.

RELIGION

"Stations of the Cross" or no, the littlest angel looks homeward from a niche outside the Church of the Holy Innocents on Sixth & Willow.

Stations of the Cross

Schlomo Hexel, aka Moe, was a bookie's runner of numbers - even on Holy Thursday. Once he was an obese, bowling ball of a man - that is, before he lost a lot of weight due to illness and the Scarsdale diet. This loss of avoirdupois plus a fleshy dewlap he'd always possessed lent him the appearance of a melted candle. At times, dressed in a frayed white shirt and a garish plaid suit, he resembled an elderly circus barker - a comparison encouraged by his rapid fire blend of witticisms and malarkey. But once his listeners side-stepped his outward appearance of folderol and buffoonery, they quickly discovered Moe was neither shallow nor clueless.

Like many a schmoozer, he had a *shtik* for those he kept at arm's length and quite another demeanor for those he knew well. For example, responding to the outrage of a mere acquaintance regarding criminal behavior featured in the newspapers, he'd often answer in knee jerk fashion with something treacly like, "Before we judge, 'ya 'gotta walk a mile in his shoes!" or, "There but for the grace of God go we all." If, however, he considered you a *mensch,* he'd likely observe, more honestly, "We all make choices, and over the course of a lifetime they bend us to their bidding. You make your bed, and there you sleep."

In either case, he'd then record your numbers and wagers on the back of receipts and other scraps of paper in an encrypted code all his own. He liked to encourage his bettors with tag lines like, "Don't shackle the shekels or they'll never flow." Finally, especially if dealing with a Christian, he'd add, "May the Jews (juice) be with you. But why drag religion into this?"

Besides corny puns, Moe loved to collect Hoboken gossip and stories of old to share with his variegated clientele - stories his pal Fiorello Rosicone, the manager of the Paradiso Funeral Home, often embellished with snippets he had culled from unthinking, slightly tipsy raconteurs who held court in his flower-laden parlor of horrors. Earlier that very morning Fiorello told Moe, "This Wolfie Gertz of whom you speak was an odd duck surer than sh*t. He became a Boy Scout leader's assistant, and for a time everyone sang his praises 'cause on winter camping trips he'd rub the feet of scouts whose feet got cold and sweaty - so the kids wouldn't get frost bite. Turns out he had a foot fetish and he was secretly getting' off while he was performing his works of mercy. Feats of clay, I'd 'hafta say."

Moe smiled wryly as from a treasured dispenser he popped a Pez mint into his mouth, a treat that kept his breath sweet. Fiorello continued, "Guess you knew, Johnny Hildebrand's funeral was only yesterday. You were missed. Funny guy. Hildy once predicted what with all the new condos and Hoboken's crumbling sewerage system, someday everyone would flush their toilets at the same time and Hoboken would vanish in twinkling of an anus like the Lost City of Atlantis."

"Ah, the butt of jokes no more," guffawed Moe, "Figures, though. 'Mosta the city used 'ta be swamp anyways. You're right, John was a 14 karat pisser - 'witta good heart to boot. Once, while in his cups, he envisioned a theme park of Hoboken's past for the benefit of the Yuppies. It would be a place where some of the city's iconic madness could be reenacted – like that crazy cop Hanrahan leapin' out of a tree so he could nab a guy goin' through a stop sign or a thoroughly soused Dennis Hogan ridin' that horse into the Hoboken House for a beer. Tongue-in-cheek, John claimed he only wanted to reconcile the born-'n-breds with the Yups. But as with all comedians, his imagination was tinged with malice. Delightfully so. As to his funeral, I passed. They're good for business but that one was too close to home for me."

The born-'n-breds to whom Moe referred were almost a separate species, and in Hoboken nicknames flourished like weeds in an abandoned lot – of which now there were precious few as every inch of the city was transformed into real estate gold. Moe's childhood gaggle of misfits called themselves the Zephyrs, after a line in a popular ditty praising Hoboken "whose the girls are the fairest / in any old town that I know / down where the breezes blow." Jewish on his mother's side, Moe came in for a lot a razing. The raggedy youths, with whom he hung as a kid, quickly transmogrified Moe's name into "Homo-'Sexal" via a less-than-laudatory Spoonerism – not that they knew what Spoonerism meant.

Most kids growing up back then expected at least one nickname. But his Uncle Irwin, who liked to tease, came up with yet another. As an amiable "yid," Shlomo was, for a time, bullied left and right. But no milquetoast, he soon developed more than a little skill with his fists- thus earning him the reputation of an hombre of sorts. Noting Moe's peripatetic tendencies (he loved to rove all over his beloved city) and his newly acquired steely exterior, Uncle Irwin dubbed him Shlepperman, adding, "You're so short and your his ass is so hard, it causes sparks every time you stepped 'offa 'wunna Hoboken's granite curbs."

This toughness served Moe well because from time to time - and even now - some foolish thugs tried to strong arm him for the cash he regularly carried. Moe was a big live-and-let-live kind of a guy, but occasionally the live-and-let-die came out as well.

He had a keen eye for opportunity, too. Many Catholics in Hoboken held to a Lenten tradition of visiting three or more churches in town to pray for forgiveness and to light candles for a brighter future. Moe theorized that many of these pilgrims exited their churches feeling blessed and that some foolishly associated such benevolence with Lady Luck - especially as regards the "Pick-Three" numbers game that was Moe's bread and butter. Thus Holy Thursday was one of the briskest squares on the calendar. The ultimate pragmatist, Moe excused his being a bookie's lackey on Holy Thursday, or any day for that matter with one of the pithier expressions he'd learned at Uncle Irwin's side: "Mach ein Leben!" - a rejoinder that translated into something like, "Everyone's 'gotta make a living!" Best of all were the wagers crammed beneath or behind religious statues which adorned some of the private residences along his route.

Station #I... *is condemned.* As was often the case, Mrs. Josie Sirocco's candy store downtown was Moe's first stop of the day. A harried soul, she bet the numbers every day. Her son Frankie was a ballbuster growing up - anything but malicious though. Just now he was in a heap of trouble for having tossed a ruthless bastard named Antoine Pagan off a rooftop. Antoine liked shooting a pellet gun at birds and people up there. Frankie was snorting a small quantity of coke behind the pigeon coop that Mary Ellen Hogan tended for her uncle when he saw Antoine backhand Mary Ellen across the face and tear open her blouse. Frankie was sweet on Mary Ellen so Antoine's fatal back gainer into the courtyard behind their tenement was well-nigh inexorable.

Frankie and Mary Ellen cooked up a story, partially true, involving her rescue and self-defense. But Antoine's toady Alejandro Judaeus, who had been promised sloppy seconds, had seen it all. After fleeing pell-mell down the stairs into the starry-starry night, he told the cops and the prosecutor whatever they wanted to hear. Alejandro played the race card nicely and blamed the whole thing on white boy Frankie's trumped up hatred of Puerto Ricans.

Mrs. Sirocco grasped Moe's arm and wailed, "Mother of God, Moe, 'dey 'gonna stick my poor boy in there with those perverted Rahway animals and my Frankie with his beautiful face. 'Dey'll eat 'im alive. Even a short stay would be a sentence of death." She wept.

Moe embraced her and cautioned, "You 'gotta keep your fingers crossed and hope, Josie. A judge 'hasta see Frankie was trying to protect an innocent girl from that dybbuk. If the public defender is any good, he should be able to prove Frankie was only defending himself and that Antoine slipped and fell in the ruckus. I know that lying gonif for the prosecution has a string of juvenile offenses against him, too." In his heart of hearts, though, Moe knew the namby-pamby judge might just as well wash his hands of the affair and let the prosecutor, one Joaquin Castillo, do his worst.

"From your lips to God's ear," Mrs. Sirocco replied wiping her tears on her shirt sleeve. Then changing the subject so as not to make a show of herself again, she added, "I heard you attended Alfie Hanrahan's funeral - the rich real estate guy. What was the food like at the fancy schmancy repast?"

Moe replied only half in jest, "Plenty of cold shoulder and tongue."

Josie covered her mouth and laughed as Shlomo grinned from ear to ear saying, "None so queer as folk - especially the Irish." Josie slipped him money in an envelope as he left.

Outside Moe scratched his head in worriment for he knew as Josie didn't that Mary Ellen was knocked up and the lawyer assigned to Frankie's case wasn't worth a bucket of warm spit. Deep in thought, Moe ventured out into the street between two cars but jumped back onto the pavement as an Uber cab skidded round the corner and honked angrily.

"Über mein arsch," cursed Moe as he hiked up his trousers now at least two sizes too large. He remembered only the other day telling Tony Malignaggi, the bookie for whom he canvased, that he didn't want to die by inches like his father in an oxygen tank. Instead, Moe told Tony, someday near the end he wanted to step out into Willow Avenue and get run over by a beer truck - preferably Heineken's, the green death." Tony didn't miss a beat answering, "And that'd be the first time the drinks were on you." Tony was a miserable human being, mused Moe, but highly

amusing every now and then.

Zack Haggard, a mean-spirited gossip columnist for the *Hoboken Picayune,* a throw-away weekly, once described Moe as a "three-card-monty flaneur." Haggard could have said "gypsy drifter," but he had literary aspirations. True to form, Moe strode riverward towards his favorite breakfast nook, the Spur, on the other side of town. The Spur was a hole in the wall eatery next to the Hotel Alphonse whose owner Freddie Torio once tried to steer clear of hourly rates and outright whorey, but then had to relent due to hard times. "Hey," reasoned Freddie, "like it or not, married guys and losers 'gotta have a place to conjugate."

In the tradition of Mugsy McGinnis and Archie Bunker, such a mangler of the language was Freddie that Moe never so much as lifted an eyebrow when he heard Freddie's malapropism. Freddie liked to play whatever room number was vacant that day. Two thirteen was often the choice as this was the nastiest of the chambers therein. With the numbered key in one hand and money in the other, Freddie would say, "Here's the tenner I owe 'ya!" in order to deceive the mostly non-existent eavesdroppers.

When dining at the Spur, Moe always sat at the counter in front of the sizzling grill as his bacon and eggs always arrived piping hot when he did so. Watching the short order cook, Moe thought of another - named Tommy - who back in the day served up hundreds of orders in the A.M. at Schaefer's opposite the train station without so much as burning a bun. Just a kid, Moe worked there as a busboy, and come lunch time he'd watch Tommy divvying up the tips. The memory of those precious coins spilling forth on the counter made

Moe think of a recent conversation he'd had with Georgie Phipps, the Grand Exalted Ruler of the Hoboken Elks, about how often enough the multitasking skills of minimum wage people filling orders at places like McDonald's and Burger King surpassed those of the big shots who ran those companies that raked in millions.

Wiping his mouth with a handkerchief, Moe realized just sitting around wasn't making him any big bucks either. Although, on his way out, just by chance, he picked up a few wagers from customers - one of whom, a dirt bomb named Albie Jension, accosted Moe as Albie exited the tiny men's room with his fly unzipped. Albie, who often went commando, frequently won with the numbers 666 and claimed to be a warlock. His 'maloik was feared by many. Some, of a superstitious bent, might have divined evil prophecies in Albie's exposed genitalia. But Moe insisted such hocus-pocus was but part of the numbers game - and the game of life. So, too, was coincidence.

Indeed, Moe knew miracles and debacles happened, just not every day. Witness the train car number 932 as it dangled above Newark Bay, the picture of which appeared in the *Jersey Journal* story about four cars that fell between the jaws of an open drawbridge back in 1958. A great score for a few, and disaster for others. Human nature being what it is, everyone and his brother played that number, but many a bookie fled to avoid paying hordes a fortune. Moe's boss, Tony Malignaggi, helped fill the void that the diaspora of shylocks had caused.

Outside the Spa, Moe found one of the avocado pits which the newspapers reported some lunatic had been swatting out into various neighborhoods from randomly chosen rooftops via a golf club - oft times shattering windows or conking people off the head. The Skyliners' tune "Pennies from Heaven" came to mind. Moe pocketed the avocado pit as a bad luck charm.

Station #II... *carries His cross.* Several blocks away Moe found a portly gentleman, Señor Jesus Valdez, seated in his customary place outside the Freakin' Rican, a Latino bar that catered to, oddly enough, hipster Yuppies as well as Hispanics. The nattily attired Jesus had his chosen numbers and his money folded up in a match book ready to go. He handed it over to Moe between the index finger and the ring finger of his right hand. Both appendages were stained a jaundiced brown from the marijuana that he used to offset the effects of glaucoma.

"So," said Moe toying with the fuzz on one of his ears, "Hay-suess, how's it hangin'?"

"Moe, you vulgar Heeb. Sometimes I think you only pretend to be lowbrow.'

"Nice of you to say so. But really, Señor Valdez, how you doin'?"

"Well, you probably heard my eyesight is pretty much shot. I can't design jewelry anymore, so I sold my share of the business to Manny Keon, my penny pinching partner of some twenty years - for a song, as it turns out. I hadn't much leverage; to be honest, I was never much for finances. That said, I moved to a smaller, more affordable place - comfortable enough all the same.

"But knowing I'm slowly going blind is a cross to bear, amigo. I can't read my beloved Cervantes, Lorca,

José Saramago, Octavio Paz, or Gabriel Garcia-Marquez. So I listen to what I can find on CDs. I can't drink anymore either because of the diabetes. Vino was a great consolation to me."

"Especially that stuff your brother makes, a liquid form of sunlight tinted red," interjected Moe. "Tastes good, too!"

"Always the joker. Interesting, though, you should describe Pepe's wine in that way, since we experience the wonders of this earth largely through what that shanty Irish visionary James Joyce called the modality of light. He, too, went blind. The Bible says the Creator separated light from darkness on the first day, and now half of creation is lost to me."

"Angelica still look in on you every now and then?" asked Moe.

"If I thought you'd be offended, I'd call you a rutting swine, but I know you revel in such pig's play and earthly delights. Yes, to answer your impertinent question, we're still an item - discretely so."

"Pig's play, very good!" Moe continued, "As to such *Schweinerei,* should you ever go completely blind, you can cast your nets wider and haul some truly ugly mamas aboard 'cause you wouldn't give a rat's ass what they look like."

Jesus nodded his head in approval, but Moe noticed there were tears in his eyes. Moe couldn't tell if that was the glaucoma or had his folderol turned a bit too grim.

As though in response to this uncertainty, Jesus covered his eyes with both hands and reminisced in a halting fashion. "When I graduated Hoboken High, me and several other guys got scholarships to play football out in the Oklahoma Panhandle. I was a lot skinnier then. We were pretty much yahoos out there. One weekend round Easter time we threw a big party and held an ugly girl contest - scouting out every nook and cranny for unsuspecting beastly females. I can only imagine what went through the minds of those poor girls at our nasty little soirée. I'd totally forgotten the like until today. But I'm sure it's one of the things I'll regret to my dying day - yet another item to confess down that long and lonesome road you and I must go."

Confess, thought Moe. Yes, Moe knew he would, too, as in addition to playing the numbers every day, Jesus attended daily Mass as well.

Jesus stood up smiling and explained, "This morning Angelica is going to wash my feet and dry them with her hair - figuratively speaking."

Moe took off his battered fedora and said, "I'll keep it under my sombrero, *mein* dude. Sounds as though you're taking all this grief in stride - like the Stoics."

"All this grief," repeated Jesus dismissively. "That's rich, given some kid is sleeping under bridges in Buenos Aires and taking it up the ass for his daily bread. As to Marcus Aurelius and that lot, they took pride in their acceptance of man's fate. I wave no such banners, and I still have a smidgen of faith in my Savior. I don't know if He'll accept one so lukewarm, but I cling to life quietly - now and, who knows, forever.

"Here's Angelica now, dressed to the nines," observed Moe.

"As the Spanish saying goes, 'A woman without jewels is like a night without stars,' " said Jesus kissing his fingertips by way of farewell.

Station #III... *falls for the first time*. Shortly thereafter Moe slipped into several taverns wherein the pickings were plentiful, especially as regards football betting tickets that required you to predict at least four winners with or without the point spread. Buoyed by such bounty, Moe sidled up onto the Avenue where he encountered Vladimir Tarabocchia jogging up towards Frank Sinatra Drive in his sweats. Perspiring profusely, Vladi stopped for a red light and greeted Moe, one of his biggest fans. "If it isn't Max Bialystock in the flesh. Just call me Bloom!" Both were *Producers* fans.

Moe beamed despite the huge hematoma that stood forth on Vladi's forehead like the deformities sufferers of the Proteus Syndrome endured. A highly ranked welterweight, Vladi, aka the Yugoslavian Yeoman, had only last week absorbed a terrible beating at the hands of Ramon "Straight Razor" Calderone at Madison Square Garden.

Razor dropped Vladi in the tenth round with a wicked overhand right. Vladi had never been on the canvas before, and Calderone was way ahead on all the scorecards- out jabbing Vladi and pummeling him with hooks and uppercuts for most of the fight. But with little or no chance of victory, Vladi arose and finished the ordeal with his left eye swollen shut. Not to mention an ugly gash on his side caused when he slipped and fell through the ropes at the very end of the bout.

"Hell of a battle, Bloom," offered Moe.

"Yeah, but how you keepin'?" asked Vladi.

"Makin' the rounds as usual?"

"Yep. And I seen you made the rounds yourself, kiddo, on HBO."

"For sure, all ten rounds with little to show for it 'cept this giant mushroom on my head." Vladi laughed. "Can you believe it, when Calderone stopped by my locker room to see if I was okay. In the commotion some scumbag stole my embroidered robe. But I did make enough to send my daughter to Catholic school so those dickweeds bustin' a sag with their bling and their tattoos and their $100 stolen sneakers can drool over someone else."

The light changed and Vladi was off pawing at the air as he sped across the thoroughfare. Standing in front of the Chatterbox Bar, Moe, whose hearing was extraordinary for an *alter kocker,* overheard two unsavory characters loitering nearby. Said one musclebound gallant, named Boodles Cavonella, in a T-shirt of dayglo orange, "I lost a 'lotta money bettin' on that 'Yugo Montenegro ham 'n egger. A beatin' or not, wouldn't surprise me none if this Slavic bum took a dive for an extra thirty pieces of silver."

Said the other, "Hard to believe the fix was in given the hammerin' he took. He could easily have packed it in during round ten. You're talkin' through your ass." Though a Jew, Moe had seen *Kings of Kings* in the movies, and the squabbling duo reminded him of the New Testament story about the two thieves crucified alongside of the Christ - the one mocking, the other proclaiming His innocence and His worth.

Purely by chance, Dr. Malachi O'Heir, once Moe's classmate at Demarest High School, hurried along

Washington St. carrying his telltale little black bag. By way of comic relief, Boodles, suddenly reanimated by the sight of the physician, railed as though truly outraged: "Not for nothin', Doc, but you know those suppository things you gave me? For all the good they did, I 'cudda shoved 'em up my ass." Moe stifled laughter as best he could.

Not to be outdone, the doctor asked Moe if he'd ever heard Rodney Dangerfield's complaint that someone put Krazy Glue in his Preparation H? Thus ignored and subtly rebuffed, Boodles slunk back into the saloon muttering imprecations. Changing his expression to one of concern, Doc touched a few darkling blemishes on Moe's neck and told him to get them checked out.

"Ah, my barber tells me they're 'prolly just the ordinary barnacles of life."

"Could be," Doc allowed as he shrugged his shoulders. "Then again, maybe they'll be measuring you for the shirt with no back. Like your pal Fiorello, the funeral director, likes to say, you could be a long time dead."

"Oy," groaned Moe, for Doc was rarely wrong in such matters. Then quickly changing the subject to an aspect of life dear to his heart, Moe riffed: "Doc, you bein' Irish 'n all, I 'gotta tell 'ya I was lolling around in the public library the other day. You know the way we used to scour the dictionary in grammar school looking for dirty words, I found a collection of filthy limericks, very scholarly, too. Wouldn't you know it, there was a humdinger 'bout Hoboken 'wimmenses, as Freddie Torio calls 'em. Went like this:

There once was a girl from Hoboken

Who claimed her cherry was broken

From ridin' a bike

On a cobblestone pike

But we know it was broken from pokin'.

"Such is the stuff of the immaculate deception," chaffed the good doctor in parting. "And I believe I knew her. She was only a German's daughter, but, oh, what a heinie!"

Station #IV... *meets his mother*. Later Moe sauntered past St. Peter and Paul's and down behind the Little League field for a view of the river. Briny aromas awakened the memory of pilings permeated with creosote back in the days when the Cunard luxury liners docked there. In his mind's eye he could see Marlon Brando staggering from a ramshackle floating office as the bloodied hero Terry Malloy mumbled seismographic profundities to the deaf 'n dumb during the filming of *On the Waterfront*. Moe smoked a Camel and pegged a few errant rocks at a seagull before ambling back towards the church. Out onto the steps he saw Sister Cecil Rose emerging through a pair of classic wooden doors adorned with sinuous designs, a fiery gold in color.

"Ah, Sister, 'I haven't seen you in a pig's age,' said the friar to the rabbi.' Any action for me today?" he asked in the best imitation of a gigolo he could muster.

"Moe Hexel, you incorrigible old rooster," she declared.

Continuing in his irreverent vein, Moe teased, "I'll take that as a no. Ah, but do you have any inspiring tales of piety for a Good Samaritan like me today, something to offset centuries of crusades and pogroms, hmmmm?"

Sister Cecil put her fragile, freckled hands in his and whispered, "Believe it or not I do, and it's something that shaken me to the core. Come into the church and I'll unburden myself to you."

They slipped back through the majestic doors into the foyer and then back farther amongst the pews. Devotional candles flickered in the sconces, and stained glass windows spilled colors roseate and blue upon the stone floor which was oddly soothing underfoot. Behind them, Moe could hear the murmuring hum of the confessional, and Sister Cecil began her tale of woe.

"One of our sisters, Sidney Elizabeth, had a son, the product of a rape by a stranger when she was a just a teenager, a child her parents urged her to give up for adoption. She agreed and signed an agreement never to contact the boy. He grew into a sturdy fellow and as a young man he began to search for his biological parents, a quest he continued for years."

Sister Cecil Rose gently struck her breast with her right hand and pressed on, "The young man, Lance Corporal Christopher Geist, finally found her. They met right here in this church with her eyes bathed in tears of delight. He was dead a month later in Afghanistan, and Sister Sidney has been a basket case ever since – 'a sword pierced her soul' as it says in the Gospel of St. Luke."

"Not my part of the Bible, Sister. But nothing's 'gonna make something like that right. Sometimes, I figure you know well, the best you can do is just listen-which, unfortunately, Job's neighbors and friends in the Old Testament would never do."

Sister Cecil quivered with emotion but eventually regained control of herself. Back out on the front steps, she slipped Moe $2 and gazing out at the New York City skyline piped up with, "Seven eleven straight, just like always." Moe gushed, "That's my girl!" and shambled forth.

Station # V... *Simon of Cyrene helps carry His cross.* On River St. once again, Moe glanced at his Longines watch, a gift from the local pawnbroker Tevya Mendel after Tevye won a bundle on the Knicks. Right on time, Smoky Miggs ascended from the depths of an air conditioned sports bar called the Urban Entrails. With his weekly wager wrapped up in a receipt from Müller's delicatessen and, secured by a large red paperclip, Smoky inserted it into the lapel pocket of Moe's suit jacket after checking the immediate surroundings for unwanted onlookers. Moe could never quite figure out how old Miggs was because, as with many a schwartze, his scars and wrinkles and calluses gave his dark complexion the leathery look and resilience of beef jerky.

"So what's up?" asked Smoky, his gold tooth gleaming in the brilliant sunshine, much of which suddenly spilled across the Hudson like heaven's own honey.

"Same old same old for a tired ass hustler," rejoined Moe. "Whaddia know?"

"Didja hear 'bout last night's holdup on Garden St.?" queried Smoky, his bloodshot eyes popping forth like those of the boogieman.

"No," rasped Moe, " 'bout nine P.M. or so this sore throat freaked me out 'cause last time it led to bronchitis. So I took Tylenol and then a Xanax on 'accounta I was havin' a panic attack. That knocked me out till ten this morning so I haven't seen any TV or checked the newspaper properly 'cept to double check the number."

"You, a panic attack? That's like Satan getting' a chill. Anyhow, you know Patsy Schlagel, that roly-poly lummox of a cop everyone our age compares to Toody, the goofy flatfoot of *Car 54, Where Are You?* fame? Well, he stumbled on a stick-up on 8th Street. Some rat-faced mook (his 'pitcher was in the papers) raced 'outta the liquor store after pistol whippin' old man Cooney and robbin' the till – not to mention the odd bottle of Ripple. Patsy, in uniform, seen the gun in the thief's hand from 'cross the street, drew his .45, and yelled, "Hands up, sh*tbird.' Hot stuff, Moe. And this from a guy 'everbody thinks is a doofus.

"Be that as it may, the skell shot Schlagel in the shoulder and, wouldn't 'ya know it, Patsy dropped his pistola. So happens, though, a ballsy Cubano by the name of Raphael Buendia was passing by. Seeing the armed perp advancing on the downed officer, he hurled the softball bat and the cleats he was tottin' at the gunman, who then flinched just long enough for Patsy to retrieve his weapon and wing the fleeing lowlife in the keister. Trailing blood, this hum job headed for the hills, and Hoboken's Finest snagged him quicker 'n you 'kin say Jack Robinson down around the Projects in front of that devotional display to Jesus, the Saints, and the Holy Mother on Jackson St."

"Outstanding, Miggsy, *mozel tov* in the extreme," exclaimed Moe. " 'Lotsa people lean in to help a brother, but lending a shoulder to a stranger is above and beyond. Makes Raphael what my people call *ein held.*

He'll be the toast of the town for a while and all the horny mommies at the El Coqui will be swarmin' 'ovah him for a week or more."

"Yeah," laughed Smoky, "Sho-nuff, he 'wuz *all* pumped up. Wouldn't 'wanna been his girlfriend nohow last night. Not for nothin', Moe, but sayin' this rat-faced bandito headed for the hills reminds an old Hobokenite like me of Councilman Louie Francone's claim back in the day that the swarms of rodents in his ward were actually brown rats from Jersey City that invaded Hoboken 'offa the palisades."

"Yeah," agreed Moe guffawing, "and when questioned as to the size of the intruders he proclaimed, 'Meeses, mices, what's the difference? They all grow up to be rats.' "

"The stuff of legend."

"Amen," seconded Moe.

"Any truth to the tale that when he showed up late to a council meeting at city hall his fellow councilmen were going at it tooth and nail over the Civil Rights Bill? Louie told them, 'Ah what the hell, just pay it.'"

"Pure baloney," Moe surmised, "with more than a whiff of myth."

"What now, you 'da Studs Terkel 'a Hoboken?" scoffed Smoky good-naturedly.

Moe was about to say, "More like the Wandering Jew." But, realizing it was unlikely Smoky would be familiar with that nasty bit of folklore, he replied, "Nah, I ain't no historian - like those uptown hotshots at the Hoboken Museum. All the same, like the 'Oirish donkeys put it, 'May the road rise up and kick you dead in the arse.'"

"True that," answered Smoky. And then with slightly less sincerity, "Keep it real."

Station # VI...*Veronica wipes His face with a veil.* Two blocks later Dee Dee (Dion) Dolan, aka Sh-Boom because of his terpsichorean renditions of the jitterbug and his fondness for the Chords' doo wop tune so-called, honked his horn and double parked his Chevy Fairlane. "Goin' my way, Moe?" he chirped in his high pitched birdlike way. "I 'gotta pick up the Mrs. at the hair salon."

"Hallelujah, you're just in time. My dogs are really barkin'," admitted Moe, nestling in.

"Didja see Jimmy Clancy's article 'bout old-timey Hoboken in the latest *New Jersey Magazine*?" asked Dee Dee. Moe shook his head and stroked his nose as Dee Dee rambled on, "Guy says Hoboken in the Fifties was the greatest place on earth to grow up in - kids galore, all kinds 'a ethnic crazies, the 'ginzo feasts, and everybody worked. And, Clancy said, the gleeful lunacy of the place not only kept one well entertained but simultaneously prepared 'ya for the grand shenanigans of the 20th century yet 'ta come. Remember Daisy Mae the flamboyant trannie? Even then 'ya 'hadda keep you knees loose 'cause in the 'backa 'ya head 'ya knew it was all a cod."

Moe nodded his head and grinned. Out of nowhere a dachshund with a prosthesis but no leash hobbled out into the street with its Yuppie owner in pursuit, thereby causing Dee Dee to slam on the brakes. While Dee Dee and the pooch's owner (a tetchy guy in cargo shorts and a Grateful Dead tee shirt) exchanged curses, Moe noticed a more promising ruckus taking place over by the Veterans of Foreign Wars.

"Curiosity killed the cat, but I 'gotta check this out," Moe informed his pal between Dee Dee's alternating spurts of obscenity with Dachshund Man. Exiting the car in a gingerly fashion, Moe pointed at Dee Dee and warned the scrawny Yuppie, "Don't mess with him. He's got a metal plate in his head." Tickled pink, Dee Dee tossed the rest of his diet Coke, cup and all, at them both and sped off. Moe brushed droplets of moisture off his sleeve as the Yuppie seethed and his three-legged wiener dog barked ferociously.

As to the fuss in front of the Veterans of Foreign Wars hall, Moe learned from onlookers that kids had been playing box ball at the intersection and their Spaldeen hi-bouncer rolled into the sewer. Not to be denied, they rolled aside the sewer cover but couldn't reach the ball- even after fashioning a scooper out of the wire clothes hanger they kept handy for that purpose. So they lowered the lightest player, Dustin Diderot, down into the sewer by his ankles. However, halfway through the operation, they lost their grip after the skinny kid almost slid out of his loose fitting jeans. He fell headfirst into the foul abyss, thrashing about in the debris and the fetid fluids of that subterranean prison.

Fortunately, because their ball had thumped up against his basement window more than once, Mr. Elwood Sekt, a librarian who lived across the street, saw the whole thing. Rushing across the street, he leaped into what the newspapers subsequently called "a silo of filth" and with considerable difficulty rescued the youngster from "its putrid depths." Another Good Samaritan, Otto

Frosch, took off his trousers to use as a lifeline, his tidy whities flapping in the noonday breeze. Moe arrived just in time to help haul first the child and then Mr. Sekt to safety. Soon an ambulance arrived, its siren blasting and its lights flashing.

During the commotion, Veronica Klaus, an artist who lived in a loft on Observer Highway and was only passing by, inveigled her way into the midst of this melee. As the EMS people tended to the boy, she wiped Elwood clean of the blood, grit, and slime covering his face with a silken scarf. Elwood, still sodden, accompanied Dustin to St. Mary's Hospital.

In less than a fortnight Ms. Klaus incorporated the scarf into a semi-abstract collage of mixed materials backed by funereal crepe tinged here and there with mauve and lavender, a work she entitled *Cosmic Energy.* Though she later won awards for her creations, she never sold that work. Its central image haunted her until her dying day but she couldn't really explain why. She liked to say that cosmic energy ran through all great works of art and that all an artist did was expose what was already there. She was, however, like many artists, a bit full of herself, comparing as she did her treasured collage to the Shroud of Turin.

Moe asked Otto, standing in a flimsy gown the EMS crowd provided him, who the woman was. Otto, a knowledgeable man about town and a trustee at the Hoboken Historical Museum, said she was a semi-famous artiste named Veronica Klaus, no better than she should be. Otto was Moe's occasional client, and suddenly for reasons known only to himself, he launched into a verse from a Max Raabe tune that translated as follows:

Veronika, spring has sprung
The whole world is bewitched.
Veronica, the asparagus grows
Veronica, the world is green
So let's dash off into the woods
As even grandpa says to grandmama
Veronica, spring is sprung.

"Sex springs eternal," Moe cried out by way of approval. Years later when he read of Fraulein Klaus's invoking the Shroud of Turin to describe her collage, he recalled his days as a roadie for a rock band called the Powdered Gonads. One starlit evening in Tallahassee while unloading a duffle bag filled with heavy band accoutrement - cymbals, mics, cables and stands, he mentioned that this raggedy bag had taken quite a beating of late - all tattered and torn. Scruff, the drummer, replied without missing a beat, "Yeah, it's the Shroud of Tourin'!" Of such amusement was Moe's memory adorned.

After his brief vocal performance, Otto pulled his wallet from his trousers which, enveloped in crud, were nearly ripped in two. Then he dug out a twenty-dollar bill, more wet than dry, and declared, "I was 'gonna put this double sawbuck on Who's Ye Daddy that's running in the fifth at Aqueduct this weekend. But given my present condition I 'wanna bet the filly, In My Skivvies, instead. Can't miss."

"Done," said Moe as he left humming Otto's "Der Lenz ist da," the very same song Moe remembered his Yiddishe grandmother singing sixty-five years ago. "The girls all sing tralala!"

Stations # VII & # IX *...falls for second and third time.* Moe backtracked to Ninth St. and headed for the hills himself, towards the Light Rail on Jackson Street. Along the way he stopped at Wu's dry cleaners and hand laundry. Moe chuckled to himself that a good hand job was tough to find these days. Might make for a catchy ad were it not so risqué.

When he heard the oriental chimes announcing the arrival of a customer, Wu, who liked to bet the ponies and baseball, greeted Moe with a face as bright as a bronze coin. Handing Moe an envelope from under the counter, he shook his head and chided, "You scallywag draining me dry." Seeing Moe empty handed, he rambled on almost as a chant, "No laundry today. Hamper not full? You like funny story. Good one happen last Monday. Frenchy guy leave bundle of shirts. Note inside say: 'Sh*tty on shirttail. Use more soap.' I reply with note: 'Use more toilet paper.' End of story."

Lame as it might seem, such appealed to Moe who had an affinity for schmutz due to the delight he took in what was familiar, be it smudged or no. Laughing, Moe figured Wu probably fabricated the incident or heard it on the radio; but doubt lingered in his heart of hearts. For Moe knew that Hoboken people - both old timers and the nouveau genteel - were wondrous strange.

Farther west, Moe boarded the Light Rail. Gently rolling along, he recalled how, as children, he and his posse would hop boxcars until Georgie Biers lost both his legs one summery afternoon. Just one slip away from tragedy - then and now. Moe got off at Second Street. Tiring, he lumbered over to Observer Highway where under a railway trestle he devoured a pair of Louie

Scarpelli's hotdogs with mustard and onions. Both frankfurters disappeared like herring down the gullet of a pelican. Pigeons pecked about Louie's mobile stand searching for the leavings. Moe dabbed his mouth with a bandana and dozed in one of the rickety captain's chairs Karl provided his customers.

A train rumbled overhead and the fragrance of Louie's much vaunted coffee wafted forth. Awakening, Moe noticed Remus "Unc" D'Angelo ordering a chili dog.

"Unc," marveled Moe, "I had no idea you were partial to the tube steak!" A contemporary of Moe's, Remus' father (a flighty soul, who in addition to his job as a school custodian, painted folksy murals about town) named his twin sons Romulus and Remus. But Remus' pals nicknamed him Uncle after Zip-a-Dee-Doo-Dah Uncle Remus in the Disney film *The Song of the South*. They then shortened his sobriquet to Unc. Romulus became just Ron.

"Oh yeah, Moe," Unc replied, "Best swamp dogs east of the Alleghenies. Truth be told, they're my inspiration to write some days - like Popeye's spinach, only for the imagination not the brawn."

Louie's balding pate shone in the afternoon's glare revealing an unsightly, mottled surface from which hither and thither sprang feathery outcroppings not unlike those on a scallion. The hideous nature of Karl's skull had achieved a comic notoriety about town as the lumps and crannies thereupon would have triggered orgasms in a phrenologist. Trash flew about the thoroughfare but not near the hotdog wagon as Louie swept periodically and deposited the refuse into a bright and shiny plastic barrel that read, "Keep it tidy sayeth the Almighty."

"What you workin' on lately," Moe queried Unc. Unc was a fairly successful writer whose stories had appeared in *Sewanee Review* and *The New Yorker*. He was, as one critic put it, Hoboken's O'Henry.

"A couple of good ones," Unc answered. "One is about a vigilante who hunts graffiti artists at night using infrared goggles and a crossbow. The second is about a writer who is forever working on two stories at a time because one of God's angels promised him he'd never die in the middle of composing one. I got the idea from the Italian film *Yesterday, Today, and Tomorrow* where Sophia Loren has to remain pregnant to stay out of jail."

"And how's your brother, if you don't mind my pokin' about in the thorns" inquired Louie stirring up a new batch of his paprika flavored homemade onions.

"You both probably know Ron's been in rehab three times, twice in the last year," responded Unc. "It's no secret musicians are prone to coke and heroine. It's part of the milieu. Artists and creative types just seem to get caught up in a yearning for ecstasy more easily than regular folk. And, yes, Ron is gay, but that's not why he's hooked. He's an addict because, once experienced, the euphoria these drugs induce is well-nigh irresistible. They're the next thing to being in heaven. In Ron's words, frailties fall away and for a short while every nerve ending in your translucent body tingles with a life force akin to an electricity you can actually taste.

"But the stint he did in prison pretty much cleaned him up. He makes his visits to a clinic regularly, and he plays in a straight edge band called the Disciples.

When I watch him perform and he's in a groove, the harshness of his features vanish and he's transformed - plugged into something timeless. His pain and his anxiety dissolve, and for a moment or two he just is."

"Sounds like James Baldwin's 'Sonny's Blues'," ventured Louie gently prying open several hotdog buns.

Both Moe and Unc looked up surprised, and Moe admitted, "Who knew you were a student of literature, Louie!"

Louie responded, "There's a good deal about me you nor anyone else knows about me. I guess you could say I'm an enigma with a brain. A fish monger 'cud call me a fillet of soul."

"Now *that* I can use," exclaimed Unc whipping out a notepad, "'cause turnaround is fair play, said the handsome beau proposing 69 to his date at the prom."

"Too clever by far," observed Moe and then reminisced, "but 'fillet of soul' and Bill Haley's 'Shake, Rattle, and Roll' with its one-eyed cat peepin' in a seafood store put me in mind of the blind guy who'd tap tap tap past Apicella's fish market on First Street. Smiling as he inhaled, he'd drawl, 'God morning, girls.'" It was an old joke, but all three were delighted.

Moe considered mentioning, too, the octogenarian passing the lingerie section of Macy's and saying, "Thanks for the mammaries." But just then Boodles Canonella roared by on a motorcycle, probably stolen, and jeered, "Nice head, Louie. Hey, Unc, give some to Ron." Quick as mongoose, Moe reached into his trouser pocket, and let fly with the avocado pit he'd picked up earlier as a talisman. The pit sailed in a storybook arc and found its mark, glancing off Boodles' helmetless noggin with a thunk.

Wobbling to a stop, Boodles dismounted and considered charging in retaliation. But Moe, Unc, and Louie stood as though in phalanx. So Boodles just cursed a blue streak as he puttered off into the bowels of lower Jersey City. "Still got it, Moe," rejoiced Louie, "just like you and Lenny Lips playing outfield for the Red Wings." Nonetheless, Moe wondered how he had missed that seagull down behind the Little League Field.

Station # VIII ... *meets the women of Jerusalem* The three Musketeers bade each other farewell, and Moe wended his way crosstown until Third and Clinton where he stopped at a patisserie called Celeste Delizie. As with Proust's madeleines, the shop's fragrance conjured forth visits as a kid to De Bari's pastry shop whose pasticciotti were like manna from heaven - creations of exquisite lightness that contrasted the heavier fare he usually favored. The little bell above the door at Celeste Delizie reminded him of the sanctus bells he heard at the funeral masses he'd attended over the years.

The elderly proprietress, Signora Leticia Della Fave, scurried over from behind the glass display case and folding her hands on the marble counter purred, "Buon giorno." The wrinkled skin on her still attractive visage and hands was every bit as delicate as the flakey surfaces of the heavenly pastries she baked. Moe ordered three sfogliatelles and gobbled one down on the spot. A dab of orange flavored ricotta lingered on his upper lip like Adolf Hitler's moustache.

"Simply divine," raved Moe.

Laeticia's deep-set eyes shone. "I can remember

the days when every bakery had its specialty - Schoening's the crumb cake, Hans Jesse's German pastries, Herald's the seven-layer cake, and Marie's Italian bread."

"All those *and* the hamantashen my father brought home from Brooklyn," Moe enthused.

"Brooklyn or no, Dom's bakery still makes the crunchiest, lightest loaves on earth," praised Signora Della Fave, as she gently lifted the pince-nez that left pinkish ridges near the top of her nose. "Remember," she asked, "those whacky questionnaires that purported to separate true Hobokenites from the Yuppie impostors, the lists your friends wrote? Such fun. It hinted at all those places"

"Not to mention," Moe replied, "the litany of oddball eccentrics and crazies who seemed to flourish back then - Powerhouse Arnold, Yankee Bob, Sharpie the homoerotic bum, Filthy Sil the clothier, Flukey O' Hara the barroom brawler, and Tommy Tears who appeared in *On the Waterfront* with Marlon Brando."

Laticia handed Moe a napkin, and he wiped his lips and nostrils before sidling towards the door. She mouthed a silent "*Ciao*" in answer to his "*Sei gesund.*" Overhead the bell tinkled once again.

Near the park sparrows roistered in the sycamores as Moe approached Our Lady of Perpetual Sorrows in front of which wooden barricades separated two opposing groups of noisy protesters - mostly women. Those on one side held up signs proclaiming, "Love is not a sin." Those on the other side brandished placards that read, "Sacrosanct isn't sexy." Recently, the bishop suspended Fr. Yancy Farrell, a young curate, from public ministry after social media revealed he was gay and that he had taken a lover. The scandal was all over the news.

To make matters dicier still, only last Sunday the elderly pastor, Fr. Winowski, delivered a fire and brimstone homily angrily condemning homosexuality per se along the lines of Liviticus and various New Testament texts. Now the press was in attendance, including Zack Haggard who doubled as a half-assed reporter when he thought an assignment might yield some gamey material for his column.

A handful of the faithful on either side of the wooden barricades witnessed to their beliefs in a prayerful, taciturn manner while the more apoplectic demonstrators bellowed and frothed. Among the former, Sister Cecil Rose hailed Moe as he shuffled on by. She introduced him to a youthful parishioner, Timothy Hodle. By word of mouth, Moe knew he was an idiot savant whose knowledge of birds was encyclopedic.

"Only last week, Mr. Hexel, 'ah 'seen 'a American kestrel right here in the park – a male falcon with those telltale blue wings and 'doze *bad ass* (Sorry, Sistah!) tomical teeth sharper 'den 'da curvy needle a doctor uses to stitch 'ya up. She knows I love this church 'cause it's got that bitchin' (Sorry again, Sistah!) paintin' of the Paraclete in the form 'ova dove above the pulpit. That and Fr. Farrell always makes time for kids like me."

"As a young man I was a birder myself. What's the state bird of New Jersey?" asked Moe.

"'Datz easy! The eastern goldfinch," yipped Tim. "Even as a kid my 'mudder 'youst 'ta read me Ogden

Nash's 'pome 'bout the pelican whose beak 'cud hold more 'den his belly can. Sometimes she'd sing a naughty Irish song 'bout a girl who wants 'ta see the cock-a-two at the Zoological Gardens."

"Great stuff," Moe agreed tousling Tim's already unkempt hair and biding them both farewell.

Moe then drifted past clots of people he didn't know until gaunt, but smiling, Mrs. D'Angelo grasped the sleeve of his jacket and parodied, "Ah, Moe Hexel, if I could but touch the hem of his garment."

"Great Caesar's ghost, if it isn't the suckling she-wolf herself!" Moe acknowledged with a grin. "Say, didn't your twins, Romulus and Remus, go to school here?"

"Never mind that suckling business, Mr. Wisenheimer, but indeed they did. And they were altar boys, too, till Fr. Winowski caught them battling it out *Ben-Hur* style in the sacristy. Story goes Remus whirled a thurible in one hand like a mace and dragged an alb in the other hand as a gladiator's net. Romulus wielded a three-foot candle snuffer and fended off blows from the thurible with a golden patin. If it wasn't so embarrassing, I 'wudda wet myself laughing."

"Mrs. D'Angelo, please!" scolded Moe feigning indignation.

Mrs. Sirocco was there, too, milling about with her rosary beads on the other side of the barricades. She greeted Moe, and across the way one of the more irate protesters shouted that Fr. Winowski was a "homophobic Judas who should burn in hell." Normally a timid soul, Mrs. Sirocco fired back, "Let ye who are without sin cast the first stone. We'll give 'ya Barabbas instead!"

Moe shook his head at that one, and Josie tried to explain, "Fr. Winowski was the only one who put in a good word with some people he knew in the prosecutor's office for my boy Frankie." Off to the right, a fat man with a pasty white face sat calmly in an aluminum lawn chair like a marshmallow crammed into a silvery thimble. The homemade poster he held forth warned, "The Pope should stop telling fairy tales." Somewhere the Brothers Grimm and Mother Goose were laughing, thought Moe. He squeezed Josie's shoulder and glided on.

Reconnoitering sharklike nearby, Zack Haggard buttonholed him and queried, "You 'ole King Solomon, working both sides of the rabble?"

"On the contrary," Moe amended. "Just passin' through 'n earning my daily bread. Grossinger's Jewish rye if I had my druthers."

Smiling slyly, Zack asked, "Apropos of this folderol that unfoldeth here, did 'ya hear the one about the two elderly poufs off on a spree in Dublin?" Intrigued, Moe lent him an ear. Zack began, "As they strolled along the quays of an evening in October, Liam, old as he was, jumped up onto the stone wall above the river and danced the light fantastic like a tightrope walker at the circus or the country fair. But he stepped on the hem of his overcoat and tumbled into the Liffey. Sean leaned over the granite barrier and watched his partner go under once, then twice. Struggling mightily, Liam called aloud, 'For God's sake, Sean, throw me a buoy!' But he finally disappeared for good beneath the murky waters below. Sadly, Sean bowed his head and sighed, 'Ai, that was Liam – game to the end.'"

"Well told," Moe applauded after an appreciable pause. "But 'ya might 'wanna work Brendan Behan's phrase 'carnival knowledge' into that jest." Moe suggested this by way of one-upmanship as he jockeyed his fedora about in dramatic fashion making ready to leave.

"Always 'gotta have the last word, huh?" Zack complained.

Moe's silence in parting sufficed as a rebuke. An old lady in black, a habitué of the church, fainted when Fr. Farrell appeared. Were it not for the hour, Zack would have conjectured "she had drink taken." No matter, awash in controversy, he had his juicy story even before the handsome young priest uttered a word: "Charismatic Outcast Soldiers On / As Weak Kneed Parishioners Cringe."

Station # X...*is stripped of his garments*

On Washington St. Moe, with his hands in his pockets, considered for several moments the day's extraordinary outpouring of suffering, tinted though it was with triumphs here and there. He gazed at his watch and realized the Elks Club was beckoning. Once there, he noted that the Stevens frat boys hadn't painted the balls of the Elk statue blue for several months now. Too warm for said jest by a half, Moe assumed.

Smiling and seated, bartender Howie "One Bite" (longer version One Bite, No Chew) Menjou, (so called for his propensity to consume meatball parmigiana sandwiches with considerable dispatch) hailed Moe as he descended into the bowels of the Grill Room & Bar. One Bite suffered from a facial tic that made it appear he was winking periodically - an oddity that rendered his moonfaced features ridiculous. His outsized ears flared outwardly like a pair of wide open taxicab doors.

Moe discretely pocketed about ten football tickets - wagers Howie had collected previously that day. After which transfer, Howie launched into a raunchy tale of boozing and casual sex at his basement hovel on Garden Street. "Last night I was asleep on the couch after polishin' off a six pack of Rolling Rock when my roommate Unc D'Angelo squires a shapely, giggly chippie into our tiny one-room abode. The night light over by the bathroom was on. Unc was boinking this sprightly creature on 'wunna our rickety beds across the way, and her cries of ecstasy awoke me. I opened one envious eye like a Cyclops in heat and, still supine, relit the roach on the coffee table in front of me. She noticed the glow and cried out, 'My 'gawd, your friend's watchin' us doin' the dirty!'

But Unc, desperately approaching the vinegar stroke, reassured her, 'Nah, sweetheart, he's just smokin' n his sleep. Does it all the time.' Can't say she bought the like, but it calmed her down. In any case, the roach went out and it made for some crazy dreams."

Elated by this tale, Moe fingered the golden Star of David that shone forth on his clavicle and reciprocated, "One Bite, horny as I was in my salad days from reading Philip Roth and Norman Mailer, I 'shudda been called the satyr of David. A rutting swine rolling in the splendor of the grass. The vanity of vanities, but so much fun - the nasty sheets at the York Motel notwithstanding. They were every bit as encrusted as the hulls of ships I had to scrape in the Navy." At such moments, Moe's glistening pendant served as but the remnant of a noble faith superseded by secularism, ham sandwiches, and psychology.

Back out on the *Strass,* a Yuppie stepped on Moe's shadow as a car radio blared forth a McDonald's commercial, "You deserve a break today...." Suddenly Moe was a mite peckish, and he decided in a flash that a couple of brats *mit kraut* would be just the thing for lunch. Maybe, too, a side of *pommes frites* as he was feeling quite continental. So he wended his way to the Pilsener Haus on 15th Street, a goodly hike from the Elks.

Walking along Willow Avenue, he gazed at the viaduct ramp that led heavenward towards Union City and the Heights. He recalled daredevil toughs of his youth, much braver than he, swinging by a hawser attached to the girders beneath the ramp. Howling obscenities, they swung pendulum-like from a dusty cliff so as to alight upon a cement stanchion some twenty feet away. The stanchion towered some fifty feet above the cobblestone thoroughfares below. He wondered what lunacies these knuckleheads embraced later in life and if any of them were still alive.

He knew that one, Gerhard Stickel, had become a paratrooper during Nam. Make or break you, some said. But just one slip and you were finished or crippled for life. Then again, without at least a touch of that holy hell within, you'd be a stone douche forever.

Outside the Pilsener Haus, a Doberman and a German shepherd snarled at each other as they strained against the heavy leashes of their masters, young men whose smiles revealed teeth every bit as white and menacing as their dogs. Moe, that cautious bon vivant, paused motionless not wishing to redirect the ferocity of these beasts.

Thus frozen, he reflected upon the documentary *Mando Cane,* an unnerving condemnation of mankind he had seen some forty years ago. Because he was hungry and one of the dog owners was cursing in Italian, it seemed as though the passion, pain, and carry-on he had seen and heard that eventful Thursday had been rolled up and baked into something as commonplace and comical as a Stromboli. The image of that comestible and of the Italian puppeteer in *Pinocchio* flashed through Moe's consciousness - as though it all had been turned into something darkly humorous as in a sinister prank. In the end, Moe concluded such was but the quintessential commedia dell'arte that was Hoboken. Come to think of it, that was human existence itself.

His meditation completed, Schlomo lumbered into the cavernous innards of the Pilsener Haus, a brick factory converted into a beerhall. He bellied up to the bar, behind which two huge built-in fans whirred about like the propellers of a submarine. Above, largely unnoticed, ersatz sacks of hops lay moldering on black dusty shelves. At one end of the bar, the likeness of an unyielding Prussian gendarme gazed down at the customers. At the other end an aloof Viennese aristocrat in a top hat stared out disapprovingly at nothing in particular.

Rearward of Moe raucous diners swilled steins of frothy amber and smeared dark brown mustard on pretzels as big as their heads. A recording of Lolita's song, "Seeman, deine Heimat ist das Meer" wafted through the din. The touch of the marble top bar was cool and soothing. Moe ordered a liter of Berliner Weiße with a splash of raspberry syrup along with a serving of bratwurst from the grill.

Dieter the barman, a garrulous young Peruvian with blond hair and blue eyes, told Moe he just read that Dunkin Donuts was introducing a new almond flavored bun to commemorate the grand opening of its store in Frankfurt, Germany. Dieter showed Moe a magazine ad in which this frosted item insisted, *"Ich bin nicht ein Berliner."*

"Sehr komisch," applauded Moe after a long pull on his beer, which left a bubbly moustache on his upper lip. Scanning the revelers over his left shoulder, Moe spied Evaristo Amorante, a squirrely character who venerated a wrestler with a name similar to his own - Enzo Amore. As expected, Evaristo broke out into his own mock (unintentionally so) heroic bit of introductory braggadocio based, of course, on the hilarious outpourings of his hero: "My name is Evaristo Amorante; and I'm a rootin'-tootin' fig Newton, a two-fisted Hobokenite made 'a dynamite - sweet as hell in a motel but a deadeye dick in a fight or a spat. And you can't beat 'dat! Botta-boom. Realest guy in the room!"

Since Moe was a wrestling fan, New Jersey's own Balls Mahoney leapt into his imagination, followed closely by the deeply troubled Mick Foley's Mankind who delivered existential soliloquies to a hand-sock puppet. In turn, Mankind's melodramatic introspection segued into memories of the grief-stricken Silver Surfer of Marvel Comics fame, comic books Moe read growing up in Hoboken, if anyone could be said to have grown up in that city of Oz.

Despite the clamor around him, Moe savored both the beer and his well-earned solitude - until he looked over his right shoulder where Seppel Kemmer, the owner of a local delicatessen, had abandoned a host of empty steins. Less than steady on his pins, Seppel lurched towards Moe, and Moe knew his peaceful Synagogue of Self would soon be disturbed. Seppel's blue eyes blazed forth from a mass of frizzy hair and a scraggly beard.

Unbeknownst to anyone, Seppel Kemmer had been a medical doctor in the SS. Concerned for his safety, his older brother Seigfried, a higher up in the administration of personnel, got Seppel transferred from a field unit to a concentration camp called Natzweiler-Struthof in occupied France. There he scrutinized arrivals at the camp during the final year of the war.

Reading the handwriting on the wall, Seppel gradually amassed a knapsack full of francs, pounds, and some American currency. When the time was right, he abandoned the camp in civvies confiscated from prisoners. Using forged papers, he eventually made his way to Marseilles where his cousins, second generation French citizens, ran an import/export business. They believed blood was thicker than water and bribed smugglers to transport Seppel across the channel to England. Eventually, with help from his cousins, he found work as a scullery knave on a freighter bound for Hoboken, almost as a stowaway.

Weeks later under the cover of darkness, Seppel scurried ashore like a frightened rat and slunk past Hoboken's Barbary Shore, a strip of taverns and tenements that paralleled the wharfs and piers along the Hudson. For a time, he found employment that didn't require identification, anything that paid and allowed him to keep a low profile, such jobs as a dishwasher at Schaefer's restaurant, a clerk at Karl Lupinski's jewelry store, and a waiter at the Swiss Townhouse in Union

City. There he met the homely but good natured woman Elvira who worked alongside him as a cook.

They lived together in common law and opened a deli called Yankee Doodle Strudel whose smoked eels and Senfgurken rivaled Elvira's potato salad and Rouladen in flavor – not to mention her tasty variation upon the aforesaid pastry. Seppel registered the business in Elvira's name so as to fly under the radar of watchdogs in charge of taxes, Social Security, or immigration. A trusting soul, Elvira thought his motives were but modesty and an acknowledgement of her culinary skill.

Seppel leaned against the bar where, with surprising dexterity, he slid $30 up into Moe's sleeve, enjoining Moe to put him down for triple zeroes.

Moe nodded sagely but queried, " 'Kinda early to be this tipsy, no, Herr Kemmer?"

"Nein," slurred Herr Kemmer. Then asking in return, "What more 'cud *ein alter kocker* like me ask – a blessing perhaps or an egg in mein beer?"

"Well, it's just that good German beer or no, you look petty glum," Moe observed.

"Just so, mein perceptive *Teufel,*" Seppel admitted, his eyes suddenly swimming in tears. After a prolonged silence, he resumed in a slow, deliberate manner, "I just finished reading a newspaper article about Oskar Gröning, a 94 year old ex Deutsche soldier who was convicted of war crimes for serving as a guard at Auschwitz. Though a member of the SS, he hadn't actually killed anyone, but the jury found him complicit in mass murder. Strangely, he refused to apologize, saying apologies for such atrocities were meaningless. He didn't ask to be forgiven – only judged, accepting whatever verdict the jury decreed.

"This weighs heavily on me," Seppel confessed, "especially when I drink and I drink at lot. I've never told anyone this, not even my wife, but I was doctor at a concentration camp."

Moe regarded Sappel with a calm that belied the rancor stirring in his breast. In the background Marlene Dietrich warbled "Lili Marlene."

In softened tones, almost dreamily, Seppel proceeded, "I evaluated the health of new arrivals, and I'm haunted to this day by the memory of the first inmate I examined, Jacob Gottesmann. Naked he stood before me most stoically. Though physically frail, he seemed to exude a kind of strength I can't really describe. Later he was tattooed # 175801, and my assistants rolled dice for his elegant civilian clothes – like something out of a Victor Mature movie. All the years I've played the numbers with you, Herr Hexel, I've never played either 175 or 801 and I've never won. A small vindication, wouldn't you say?"

Moe pursed his lips in silence and stoking down the fury within asked, "Why me, Herr Doktor?"

Seppel stood erectly and, hugging his shoulders, responded, "Well, for one thing you're a Jew, a man of the world, one with a human heart. So you may well understand how oppressive are the sins of the past – even if you don't want to. Sigmund Freud, your own modern day Moses, said the problem with guilt is that it forces you to live in the past. For me the past is alive with personal terrors – those I experienced and those I caused. At bottom there is a need, even for a fraudulent Lutheran sinner like me, to be shriven, to unburden my wretched soul. Ah yes, I know well what that word *shrieve* means. It's from Coleridge's "The Ancient Mariner" – that grey-beard loon. This poem they taught us in the Fatherland. Now it's clear why."

Breathing heavily, Moe assessed his client's woe. "Part of me's certain you should be in the belly of a shark with an ice pick in your spleen – shivved not shriven. Then again, there's a Jewish expression, 'Lass es gehen.' Sometimes it's for the best."

Moe put his fingertips to his forehead and continued, "I think you met John Hildebrand at the Elysian Cafe, God rest his soul. A witty devil, he once skewered a pretentious woman he overheard whining on and on about some distant cousin's uncle who had perished at Dachau. Never shy, John intruded, saying in that ironical manner of his, what a coincidence. He too had lost an Uncle Max at the very same camp when that intrepid warrior Max fell from one of the watchtowers dead drunk. It was extremely crass and offensive, though funny in its own twisted way – especially if you knew John. Sadly, the woman didn't, and this business of yours is no laughing matter either, possessed as it is with an immediacy and a severity all its own. But I ain't no B'nai B'rith Wiesenthal man, especially after all these years. I certainly won't be your accuser, if only 'cause I don't 'wanna be drawing attention to my, shall we say, less than savory livelihood. No, Seppel, if it's punishment you desire, you'll have to find it elsewhere."

For several moments Seppel stared vacantly into the dual fans which turned round and round. Edith Piaf's voice trilled, "Non, Je Ne Regrette Rien," and the waiter came with Moe's brats. Seppel staggered off in silence whilst Moe sampled the sauerkraut and tamped down the fury he was experiencing within.

Shortly thereafter Moe's hunger was sated, and that wiliest of souls gradually reclaimed his equanimity. "'Ole Seppel," he quipped, "will just 'hafta appeal to a higher authority: Hebrew National perhaps." Jokes, even poor ones, were safety values for Moe. Leaving the premises, he noticed a huge oil on canvas that graced the far wall of a separate little dining room and bar. Clad in white, the butcher in this portrait stood behind a chopping block over which lay the carcass of an enormous pig looking for all the world like a naked woman- both ghastly and inviting. The adjective *gothic* occurred to Moe- regarding both the painting and the rueful events of the day.

Stations # XI & XII ...*is crucified…and dies*

Still in something of a quandary, Moe boarded a crowded bus on Willow Avenue, and sufficiently jostled, he stepped lightly from the groaning vehicle and ducked into Lou's Tavern on 8th and Washington Street. At which location he garnered a goodly sum of football betting tickets. Meandering back out onto the pavement, Moe brightened further when he heard the rich, woody tones of a clarinet emanating from a frat house somewhere up on Hudson Terrace. A jazz combo was setting up on a patio for an outdoor soirée. A Sidney Bechet fan, Moe moseyed thereto and resting on the running board of an antique roadster he listened to a burly, bespectacled musician play "Promenade aux Champ-Elysées" with grace and authority. Moe felt the vibrato right down in his toes.

Ivy and wisteria covered the wall adjoining the frat house patio. In June when the wisteria bloomed, the shimmering mixture would transform the side of the building into a pointillist's work. As it was, the greenery was lush and refreshing. Farther along the block, Moe spied the house a rich guy named Claudio Pontrelli remodeled - all stucco, columns, and statuary in a style Moe dubbed 'guinnie posh.

Quite by chance, Freddie Torio, the hotel manager, appeared. He wore a striped sports jersey, one which emphasized his potbelly. Gesticulating as he jabbered away, he looked for all the world like some minor league third base coach - washed up and slightly irrelevant, which, of course, endeared him to Moe. Freddie asked, "Why you listenin' to this stuck-up stuff. My kid plays bass in a punk rock group called Shit or Go Blind. I'll tell 'ya, the electricity crackles like grackles when they get 'ta wailin', my fine feathered friend."

"Whaddia take me for, Big Bird?" asked Moe.

"Definitely not no dodo, dough-ee-oh-dough-dough," observed Freddie quoting a Looney Tune cartoon *Porky in Wackyland.* "Still you was always somethin' of a loon, but not as 'brassiere as some, like that dingleberry Dee Dee Dolan who brought his date to the prom in a garbage truck as a kind of a goof."

"And how 'bout Charlie Castillo dyin' his hair and usin' mascara. Like nobody noticed!" countered Moe.

"Yeah, I would echo 'doze 'sediments. He was a complete 'narcissorist," Freddie concurred. "'Deres a 'pitcher of him in our high school yearbook kissin' a mirror. Plus he thinks who the f**k he is."

"To say nothing of One Bite Menjou", amended Moe, "taking his pet rat to the annual blessing of the animals downtown on the Feast Day of St. Francis – just to bust balls. I'm told Fr. Vindigni went gaga. Like your kid's band, the poor old priest didn't know whether to sh*t or go blind."

Freddie tapped the ashes off his Tiparillo and concluded, "Well, I 'gotta go play pinochle at the Elks. 'Hatta leave my car way up here 'cause the parking in this burg's like tits on a bull. Then you got these phony baloney handicap spaces. 'Ya watch the Jack Be Nimble driver get 'outta the car 'n do a 'coupla handsprings and somersaults before enterin' his house. Needless to say, the crippled aunt he used to drive so she could shop at Safeway died decades ago. So now not only do the dead in Hudson County vote, they take up 'goddam parking spaces as well."

Chortling inwardly, Moe thought perhaps Freddie's financial footing was a bit shaky (such was common knowledge) because his real talent lay in vituperation not hotel management. On second thought, there wasn't much profit in tantrums either. Freddie took his leave in any case. Moe wandered off first south and then downward on Fourth St. until he reached Leforgia's homemade-candy store.

Therein he purchased a bag of chocolate covered marzipan which he nibbled gingerly – channeling all the while the *Geltscheisser* marzipan figurines his mother lavished upon him from time to time. Best of all, back then, was devouring the chocolate coin rolling forth twixt the *Geltscheisser's* naked buttocks. Stripping away the gold colored foil was a ritual unto itself. As always, Sinatra music wafted from the confectionery in the rear of the tiny store, and Moe toddled forth – first down Fourth St. and then around the corner on Bloomfield

Street where he spotted detective Montague "Monty" Molloy skulking in the shade of dogwood tree.

"So, mein 'comp," asked Moe, "what brings a *liaisons dangereuses* shamus like you to a lily white oasis like this?"

"Ah, 'ya nosy parker, you might well be surprised by the carry-on in this benighted neighborhood," Monty retorted. "For instance, every so often there's a scabrous 'bombie named Grits Oglethorpe who ambles about crying, 'Where do I go when even Hell doesn't want you?' and then exposes himself."

"I'm happy to say I never bumped into him. Then, too," Moe recalled, "only last Christmas didn't some unwed twizzle leave a newborn in a nativity manger outside the church on Christmas Eve – umbilical cord and all?"

"And wrapped in an old YMCA towel as a swaddling cloth," said Monty. "That, my friend, was a girl who 'cudda used what 'wunna my Greek girlfriends used to call a doula. And maybe a medulla oblongata as well, 'cause by law you can turn infants in at any police station, no questions asked."

"Now, now, judge not lest ye be judged," Moe cautioned with a smile.

"*Lest* is it," Monty remonstrated. "Goin' high hat on me, huh?"

"Yeah, maybe. But who's this Abdullah Obligata – the father?"

Molloy eyed Moe suspiciously. "Be that as it may," Monty resumed, "there's nothing near as intriguing on the agenda today. I'm on surveillance - bored to death keeping tabs on Eduardo Mercado, the Filipino from San Pedro Cutud who, I'm sure you know, had his compatriots crucify him last Good Friday - with nails, Baby Cakes!"

Moe nodded, "Yup, down along the palisades, just a stone's throw from the remnant of the old incline. Apparently, this grisly business is quite common in Brazil and the Philippines."

"Just so," Monty confirmed. "Not so well known is that Boodles Cavonella, of all people, happened upon Eduardo hangin' there in agony and called the cops anonymously - but not before he pelted Eduardo with rocks and bottles and gouged his thigh with a broken broom handle that he found in the weeds. Boodles was always a piece of work. I remember him as a kid running cock fights down in the project cellars. He'd eat the loser in the chicken cacciatore his mother made."

Moe offered Monty one of his chocolates, but Monty declined saying he had something sweet and crunchy tucked away for later.

"Anyways," Monty rattled on, "to make a long story short, last year's salvific gore caused quite a stir-most of it negative. Eduardo was charged with creating a public disturbance. Fortunately, that went nowhere-mostly because, I'm sure you read, Eduardo had promised to be crucified every Good Friday 'cause his daughter was cured of polio back in the Philippines, a miracle of sorts.

"But religion," Monty continued, "always complicates matters, so this year we're goin' proactive - cramping Eduardo's style, as it were. Me or another detective'll be prowlin' around out here today 'n tomorrow eyeballin' his crib. By a fluke, a uniformed officer lives in an apartment facing the yard behind the tenement house where Eduardo lives so we're covered front and back. If Eduardo leaves, we follow."

Captivated by Monty's revelations, Moe pressed him for more, "Any juicy tidbits of a more recent vintage- citywide, I mean?"

Monty often fed Moe bundles of info about the outlandish goings-on in Hoboken, stuff that eluded the newspapers and social media. Warming to the subject, Monty obliged, "There's always quality dementia afoot in this town. Like early, early this morning, too late to have made the papers, some hum job in the Clock Towers put an icepick through Mr. Winkie (his penis) thinking it was a deadly snake - an anaconda, or so he said once the hashish wore off."

Moe guffawed, and emboldened by Monty expansive mood ventured further, "As long as we're on the subject, word has it that you're the best hung Caucasian this side of Paradise. Freddie Torio claims if you line up nineteen washers on a workbench, you've a fair approximation of the *Schlange's* size."

Lowering his gaze, Monty corrected, "That business about the workbench is but extraneous detail. 'Better than average' should suffice."

"Even so, inquiring minds 'wanna know," Moe insisted halfheartedly. "Like they used to say on the quiz show *What's My Line?*, is it bigger than a bread box?"

Only slightly miffed, Monty caviled, "Let's put it this way, you wouldn't want it for a wart on your eye.

In truth, Moe had little real interest in such folderol as his Uncle Hyman had been a mohel. Schlomo was full up with jokes about the profession. One in particular stuck out in his mind: "'It vunt be long now,' said the mohel to the anxious parents at the bris." Malloy's wife was another matter altogether.

"How's the Mrs.?" asked Moe nonchalantly.

Remedios Malloy was a fiery young creature whom Monty married when she was just seventeen with the body of a goddess, a girl who could make men - Christian, Jew, or Muslim - get down on all fours and howl at the moon like rutting dogs. She was a trainer at the Luxor Baths & Training Emporium, a place that became popular with health conscious, electronically obsessed yuppies and with old school Hobokenites who enjoyed a good *schwitz.* In the locker room, Monty often teased Moe about the unsightly scars and declivities left by the removal of a kidney long ago, saying they were result of Moe's being shot in the back fleeing some jealous husband a la Sam Cooke.

As to Remedios, Monty replied, "Fine and dandy. In fact, she's expecting. Little one should be right on time for the upcoming census - a plus one for Hoboken," he joshed. "She's vacationing in P.R. with her older sisters who'll keep a sharp eye on her."

Schlomo smiled and thought of the old saw, "It's a wise man who knows his father." He wondered, too, how long a jovial devil like Monty, his outsized Johnson notwithstanding, could keep a lusty soul like Remedios satisfied. Across the way, a curtain moved in one of Eduardo's windows as the sun, though setting, threw ordinary objects into sharper relief. Just as suddenly clouds obscured the sun, forcing the multiform shadows to dissolve like water into a sponge. Leaning against a black wrought iron fence, Monty held up a hand by way of an apology and answered his phone, nodding periodically after an occasional *yes* or an *okay.*

He put the phone away and explained, "Got some bad news from the EMS guys. Jesus Valdez collapsed in the arms of his *'goo-mahd* Angelica about an hour ago. A brain aneurysm. Doctors say he'll be lucky to last the night. I know you and him were pals - from the Luxor Baths 'n all. They called 'cause Angelica and Remedios are cousins."

Moe removed his fedor and hung it on a gate post. Then he took a tattered yarmulke from his pocket and sat on a nearby stoop with his arms crossed, muttering what might have been prayers in Hebrew. Monty stood in silence. After a time, Moe explained such was his take on sitting *shiva* in the modern age - "for a goy no less."

Then he folded the yarmulke back into his trousers and, rubbing the back of his neck, avowed that Jesus was what the Italians called a *buonanima,* someone who did right by those he loved and by many he did not. Wearily he arose and, shoulders hunched, he lumbered off to what he called his "virtuous couch." Monty finished off a candy bar he had squirreled away in his jacket and recalled a TV ad in which a camel insisted, "I want a Clark bar."

Stations XIII & XIV *...is taken down from the cross... and laid in a tomb.* The following Monday friends and a spattering of surviving family members gathered at the Paradisio Funeral Home for Jesus' wake. Off to the side, Angelica sat moribund and silent in an armchair of black brocade. Though small in number, the floral displays enveloped Jesus' coffin in a cloying sweetness. Smiling serenely, Jesus lay therein grasping a set of fiery red rosary beads. The murmur of muted conversation continued, it seemed, the call and response of the just completed vigil service.

Dee Dee Dolan: Freakin' wakes give me the creeps.

Moe: A necessary evil, I'd say. But, for me, they're good for business.

Dee Dee Dolan: I remember my old man's. Just the one day after Labor Day. Tiny blurb in the papers didn't amount to much. Dad had been ill for quite a while, very much out of circulation. Most of his friends had already died or moved away. Just the family mostly. As closing time approached, me, my sister and assembled family, bummed out by the tedium, stood near the funeral parlor's entrance. We were about to call it a night when an emaciated figure entered, hat in hand - a mere skeleton of a man with a gaunt and stubbly visage and long silvery thinning hair.

It was Walter Knapp who lived across the street from the Hoboken House on 10th & Park where in better times my father liked to drink. Older than Methuselah, Walter's thirst was boundless; yet he somehow kept a harem of unsightly creatures with nicknames like Rip-in-the-tit (her garments were oft in tatters) and the Swan (because of her eerily long white neck) reasonably sated. In any case, sober as a judge that night, he offered his condolences and, with considerable decorum, marched forward to kneel at the coffin to say a Pater Noster or two. When Walter finished, he approached us mourners and buttoning his long black raincoat announced, "Yup, that's him." The resultant laughter dispelled more than a little gloom.

Freddie Torio: "A dreary business at best. But sometimes wakes make 'ya think of happier times. I remember once Jesus and me stopped at the Chauncy's Tipsy Rover for an adult beverage or two and we seen Chauncy sittin'at the bar lookin' 'kinda glum. He was reading an obituary in the *Hoboken Picayune* 'bout a teamster named Malachy McHugh who drank Four Roses whiskey at the Tipsy Rover nearly every day. I told Chauncy I had no idea he'd be that *aggrieved* (cool word, huh?) over Malachy's passing and Chauncy answered, "Aggrieved my ass. I've got three cases of Four Roses downstairs and nobody else drinks that shite."

Moe: Yeah, and I can finish the story 'cause I was there for the *denouement.* After Malachy's funeral, a bunch of his shanty Irish buddies came in with Jesus and Freddie to hoist a few in Malachy's memory. Chauncy was finishin' up a pastrami sandwich and straight away he ducked into the loo to wash his greasy hands. In his absence Jesus whipped out a fifth of Irish whiskey from under his jacket and, quicker than someone kissin' a duck's ass, he dumped the remains of a Four Roses bottle down a sink behind the bar and filled the empty bottle with Erin's usquebaugh.

Chauncy came back and at our request poured everyone a tumbler of the aforesaid whiskey - over which we raved. We made him try some. After his eyes lit up, we forever thereafter proclaimed it a miracle - the transmutation of Four Roses into Tullamore Dew, the blush upon the rose as it were. Needless to say, the like had little or no effect upon the rot gut which persisted down below in the cellar."

Freddie Torio (nonplused) How come you 'gotta be so quick 'ta kiss a duck's ass?

Moe: 'Ya 'gotta blow the feathers away.

Dee Dee Dolan (laughing) Sometimes I wonder if God knew what he was doing when he created humans.

Fiorello Rosicone: You're right, though. Jesus Valdez could be a mischievous devil, for sure. We went to Prep together. We had a German teacher named Dr. János Ronay, a Hungarian who was in many ways a real innocent, totally clueless as to the vagaries of the average Prep knucklehead. Like for instance, one day during class Doc overheard Jesus whisper "douchebag" to the dipsh*t sittin' behind him. Doc asked what in God's name the word meant so often had he heard it bantered about. Undaunted, Jesus explained that such was a colloquial term of endearment comparable to "my little darling" or the like. Eager to engage his students in the following class, Dr. Ronay asked them with great enthusiasm, "Well, my little douchebags, sollen wir ein bisschen Deutsch sprechen?"

Poorly muffled guffaws ensued. Blessedly, no one at the wake took any notice.

Moe: Shenanigans aside, Jesus knew what was important and what wasn't and 'ya couldn't find a more loyal guy. His amigo Lazslo Cernik wouldn't be alive today 'cept for Jesus' bone marrow donation.

Dee Dee Dolan: Also he didn't get all frazzled when things went wrong. I remember at one of the Elks' Crippled Kiddies Christmas Parties lots more people showed than we anticipated and our crew pretty much ran 'outta food. Everyone in the kitchen was jumpin' through their assholes trying to skimp on what we had. But cool as a cucumber, Jesus stumbled on several boxes of *strozzapreti* pasta tucked away in the pantry along with some cans of tomato sauce. Then he found a tray of meatballs in the fridge, leftovers from a previous Monday night gathering. Using a blender, he ground the meatballs into what became, after a little oregano and garlic, a half decent Bolognese sauce. Our guests had 'pleny, and he never broke a sweat.

Fiorello Rosicone: Reminds me of something a Fr. Pangborn said in religion class at Prep. Trying to elucidate the importance of the term *Yahweh* to the Jews, Pangy admitted the notion of a flesh and blood savior was much more accessible than the immensity of the Almighty. Witness, he urged us, little Moses Ginsberg, the tyke whom Christ summoned forth with a few loaves and a pair of paltry fish. "Thus," said our portly Jesuit, "was the first Jewish delicatessen born."

Such greatly amused Moe, and he suggested they amble outside for a breath of fresh air. Fiorello stayed behind to attend to the needs of the Valdez family. Dee Dee lit up a cigar and, after sighing, expelled perfect little haloes of blue grey smoke out into the evening air. Just then a pink Cadillac rolled softly by, its radio blaring forth a garbled, discordant tune. His serenity disturbed, Dee Dee asked, "What in f*ck's name was that abortion?" Moe, an aficionado of many musical genres, replied, "The Crash Test Dummies' *God Shuffled His Feet.*" Freddie Torio observed, "I 'wudda shuffled my feet, too, if I was headed for Calgary." Oddly, everyone knew exactly what he meant.

Postscript

Life continued much as it had before, but for some, the preceding events put a new slant on things. For instance, in no particular order, the avocado golfer graduated to actual golf balls, sacrificing oddity for distance. He sent a Titleist DT TruShot through the front window of Wu's Chinese laundry. Wu's insurance covered the damage. A month later, Albie Jension wasn't so lucky. One of the phantom's golf balls damn near killed him, striking him on his forehead and leaving a bruise that resembled the tattoo of a demon. Zack Haggard of the *Hoboken Picayune* called it "empyrean retribution."

Otto Frosch's horse, In My Skivvies, came in twenty to one. Dustin Diderot, the kid he helped rescue from a sewer, threw a no hitter for the Elks Little League team that summer. Yancy Farrell, the priest who admitted having a male lover, left the clergy and opened a German style *Konditorei* in Hoboken, a cafe the Yuppies adored. He also taught comparative religion at Hudson Community College's night school.

As Johnny Hildebrand might have foretold, a water main break on Observer Highway beneath the train trestle put Louie Scarpelli's hot dog stand out of business for almost a week. In a comeback attempt, Vladimir Taraboccia won a twelve round split decision over Horatio Boom Boom Ali, Smoky Miggs's grandson. Smoky summed up the outcome as follows: "Them judges gives the white man a leg up 'evey time." Sepple Kemmer, still secretly guilt-ridden, lived to be ninety.

During her vacation in San Juan, Remedios Molloy posted a Facebook selfie of herself in a red dress and a pair of catch-me/f*ck-me high heels. That likeness, indeed, made several of Monty's fellow officers get down on their knees and howl at the moon like dogs. Monty seethed. On the plus side, Monty became a mentor of sorts to Raphael Buendia, the hero in the Patsy Schlagel melee who eventually passed the entrance examination to become a policeman.

In keeping with Dr. O'Heir's prognosis, Moe had to have a handful of melanomas excised from this face and neck. After the surgery, Monty wondered if the person standing before him was really Moe because all of a sudden he had a face "like a plate 'fulla mortal sins." Accordingly, Moe pulled his shirt up and dared Doubting Thomases like Monty to put their fingers into the slits left behind by his age old kidney operation. Monty declined, insisting à la the Smothers Brothers, "There 'cud be pumas in the crevasses."

Romulus D'Angelo's band, the Disciples, banged out a huge hit entitled "All Aquiver You Make Me Shiver," after which Romulus descended into an interminable maelstrom of sex, drugs, and rock 'n roll. Perhaps strangest of all, Dee Dee Dolan bought a life size statue of the Risen Christ and with his cousin as a cameraman transported it suspended from a hot air balloon in a flight over the Phillipsburg area. Why? One, because Dee Dee is screwball. Two, because the Demarest High Redwings used to play Phillipsburg in football every year. And three, because he loved the opening scene in Fellini's *La Dolce Vita* wherein a helicopter whirlybirds a similar statue of Jesus to St. Peter's Square.

Sadly, Mrs. Sirocco's fears regarding her son's fatal run-in with Antoine Pagan proved correct. Frankie was convicted of manslaughter in July and sent to prison where he was stabbed to death after coming to the aid of a transgendered inmate during an attempted rape by two inmates, one of whom was Alejandro Judaeus, the miscreant whose testimony sent Frankie to jail. Incarcerated on an unrelated charge of breaking and entering, Alejandro wielded the murder weapon, a blade deftly fashioned from the top of a soup can.

Round about Christmas Mary Ellen Hogan gave birth to a child she named Francis Emanuel. A small but festive christening party, paid for by Mary Ellen's family and by Mrs. Sirocco, was held in the back room of the Tipsy Rover bar.

Though still garbed in black, Mrs. Sirocco took especial delight waltzing about with the baby in her arms. At Moe's urging, three of his buddies - Monty, Dee Dee, and Freddie - convened at the Tipsy Rover to make monetary offerings and to tipple in the baby's honor.

After paying their respects, the foursome clinked glasses of whiskey. As men are wont to do at such gatherings, they swapped dog-and-pony stories tinted with bombastic folderol. Monty revealed that he had obsessed over the tune "You Belong to Me" while Remedios was sojourning in P.R. Accordingly, Freddie broke into a verse of said song, mispronouncing the line, "Send me photographs and 'silveneers,'' just as those Jersey City boys the Duprees had in the Fifties.

Seizing on this gaffe, Dee Dee observed, "People in Hudson County, Moe, definitely got their own way of saying things. Take for instance the words kinnygarden, secatary, the viadock, poccabooks, burgulars, cockaroaches, natkins, and the chicken pops." Moe concurred, saying his cousin's first wife (a gum snapping woman from Weehawken with the soul of a barracuda and more than a little wit) hated snow with a passion. Moe said she told him she'd rather bang a tribe of Zulus than get caught in what she called a 'blizzid.

Freddie changed the subject so as to avert any possible references to his numerous linguistic faux pas. "Maybe 'youse remember that when Chauncy's dad, Thomas Aquinas Mulcahy, died, Chauncy perched an eight-by-ten glossy of the flinty old 'bastid over the cash register 'cause that's who Chauncy inherited the business from. And as y'all 'prolly know, every so often One Bite Menjou fills in as bartender. Word has it that he's fairly liberal with the blowbacks and that, after accounts at the close of day, the 'pitcher above the cash register cries real tears. Several habitués of the tavern have tried to get the like certified as a miracle, but to no avail."

Such drollery was much to Moe's liking, but he had to be off on his rounds. Outside, Garden Street was resplendent with sunshine and contrasting shadow. So inspired, he meditated for a moment or two on newborn infants and death. Then, improvising on a tune from Disney's *Pinocchio,* Moe warbled, with more than a little braggadocio for an easy-going mensch such as he:

"Hi-diddle-dee-dee

as to the Alpha and the Omega,

it little matters to me."

For no apparent reason, one of Smoky Miggs's timeless maxims coursed through Moe's consciousness: "The stars fell on Alabama, but we all just home boys here." Popping a Pez into his mouth, Moe leafed through his codified notepad of numbers and was reminded that Sister Cecil Rose won $500. On the other hand, Albie Jension, the warlock wacko who played 666, won just as often. Life's a puzzle, Moe mused. That's why people gamble.

The Devil and the Deep Blue Maelstrom

Italicized excerpt from the Book of Job rewritten for a different time and place: *Upon an astral plane behind which could be heard the music of the spheres and the whirring of the willy willies, the Prince of Darkness glanced at the lowly Principality of Hoboken through a momentary opening in a maelstrom of angry clouds and spake unto the Lord Almighty: "Although these odious humans, whom you prize above the angels, were created in your image and likeness, I foretell that they, if jostled from their cocoons of comfort and electronic gadgets, would even quicker than the lightning in yonder storm devolve into the serpents, rats, and maggots with whom they have so much in common."*

Smiling wistfully, the Lord God was intrigued; and Beelzebub continued, "So as a trial, render unto me the fate of all in that fusty city below and thus test my prediction that these verminous beings will, in the twinkling of an all-seeing-eye, curse each other and Thee." Sighing, the Master replied, "If the winds, the moon, and the tides converge as to wreak havoc upon those below, so be it. What will be will be."

Sean McAlevy, a reporter for the *Hoboken Picayune*, yawned even though a kerfuffle had broken out at a tedious Board of Ed meeting in Hoboken - a highly partisan disagreement concerning some venal arrangement gone awry. Overturned furniture revealed disgusting wads of dried chewing gum adhering to the underside of a conference table. Order was soon restored, but the story Sean had been sent to cover still didn't add up to a hill of beans. Sadly, he prayed for something, anything extraordinary to write about - be it jubilation or perdition.

Later, breathing in the urban miasma of a mild October evening, he bumped into his neighbor, Jethro Gamp - named after Jethro Tull, a limey band in the Seventies famous for such tunes as "Cross Eyed Mary." Gamp was a bartender's "mop" at the Tube Bar in Jersey City - tapping kegs, stocking coolers, and slopping out the men's. One of Gamp's fondest memories was being present when the owner, Red, began getting obscene prank calls from two whack job musicians, the hilarious recordings of which Howard Stern helped make famous.

Jethro was, despite the depravity of his everyday existence, an insatiable reader - and a thoroughgoing rogue, one quite adept at getting others to pay for his extravagances. In no time at all, he'd convinced Sean to drive them both to Krejewski's, a go-go bar in Secaucus where the ever corpulent Smokey Burgess and his Tomcat Troubadours were "'gonna crank out some ass kickin' country music on the slide guitar."

Krejewski's inner décor was orange and black because Halloween was just around the corner. Smokey was on a break while a curvaceous siren filled the void with some nifty pole dancing, gyrations she punctuated with an edgy line of patter. Her caustic remarks, delivered through a smile as fraudulent as it was wide, lent the entire performance a delightful hint of irony an effect she enhanced by plucking a rubber skeleton from her snatch at the conclusion of the set. Mesmerized, Jethro exploded into paroxysms of mirth.

Another Hobokenite, Tevye Hinckle, slumped in his stool next to Sean and Jethro - quite unamused. "Know what? Son-of-a-bitchin' doctors told me I got MS bad. Said I'm 'gonna wind up a vegetable - 'prolly all covered in bed sores. Life's a bitch and then you die. Never won no awards or seen my name in lights. But I'll bet ya' 'herda this Hurricane Pandora that's 'sposed 'ta be comin' our way! Well, I plan 'ta ride its freakin' tidal surge 'inta Hoboken like the Silver Surfer, man. Already got a jet ski hid in an abandoned shed down alongside the river 'ta get me out there. You guys know my brother Aaron, all modest 'n humble pie. But I'm Tevye, the Fiddler on the Roof, baby, and I'm goin' out in a blaze of glory."

"'Kinda fits in with what I've been reading," rejoined Jethro. "In his book, *Leviathan,* Thomas Hobbes says human existence is 'nasty, brutish and short.' Far as I'm concerned, that's it in a nut shell. The guy wrote during a period known as the Age of Enlightenment. Mention that to the average schmuck in here and he'll assume you were talkin' about PSE&G. Put another way, short circuits in their frontal lobes pretty much put the kibosh on any 'kinda luminescence upstairs.

"'Anyways," Jethro continued, "these yahoos notwithstanding, books really can give you a pretty good handle on life. Although hotshot writers like Camus claimed that suicide was the *only* philosophical question. Be that as it may, stow the hemlock for now, buddy boy, 'cause there's still plenty of poontang and booze to be had."

Only half listening, Sean burped. Gamp eyed him narrowly and responded, "Camus' pal, Jean Paul Sartre, took things a bit further in his play *No Exit,* insisting that *hell is other people.*" Yawning, Sean harrumphed. Gamp cautioned, "No offense, dude, but he just might be right."

Already half in his cups, Sean quipped, "God damn the Existential Man!"- channeling Steppenwolf's Pusher Man as he did so. To which Gamp replied, "No sense draggin' the Almighty in here, bunkie. Nietzsche proclaimed Him dead long ago. Good riddance, if 'ya asked me."

Shortly thereafter Jethro left with the slutty dancer, and Tevye, overcome with self-pity, left in tears. Bombed out of his mind, Sean somehow made it home after he bounced off a guard rail or two.

Two days later Pandora's tsunami-like tidal surge inundated Hoboken, just as the weather men said it would. Sean, eager to witness the city's destruction first hand, ventured out into the chaos in his roommate's kayak, which he launched from the building's front stoop. Beyond the scudding white caps of the Hudson River, Manhattan's towers of mortar, glass, and steel arose like the Lost City of Atlantis. Flickering halos of light glowed through spitfire lines of horizontal rain. Overhead, angry low lying clouds thundered charcoal gray as though tombstones and plinths had tumbled one upon the other. The smell of ozone from arcing electricity mixed with the briny odors of the incoming sea.

The western rim of the city was lit up by what looked like green lightning as one transformer after another exploded. Straying perilously close to the PATH entrance, Sean held onto a lamppost for dear life as torrents of raging water cascaded down the steps leading to the tunnels below. After a time, the deluge leveled off. Sean paddled north on Hudson St. where, shining a flashlight this way and that, he beheld Tevye impaled on one of the angle irons that supported the Clam Broth House's sign - a Hoboken icon which, twisted and partially separated from its moorings, had rotated in such a way as to suggest an obscene middle finger. Approvingly, the Banshee winds continued to howl.

Meanwhile, downtown, Tevye's brother, Aaron Hinckle of the Hoboken Ambulance Corps, pounded his head upon the steering wheel. His cargo, an elderly woman, groaned as swampy gases and raw sewerage bubbled up in the waters surrounding his stalled vehicle - bilge through which Aaron had just waded. His fury and his disgust were such that, had he been home, he would have destroyed everything in sight - the bric-a-brac, the grandfather clock, perhaps even the menorah. This because a fiery impulse, barely recognizable as thought, raged through his being: 'This sucks a fireman's balls. F*** this *Gott verdammte* (his Yiddish was oozing through), scumbag, senseless *Scheisse* now and forever.' But the words never actually escaped his lips. Although rancor still held sway in his heart, out of nowhere it seemed, he heard Rabbi Edelweiss quoting *Ecclesiastes* to his congregation at the United Synagogue on 1st & Park some thirty years ago: "Remember, my dear friends, even in the filth of some wretched hovel, 'The sun also rises!' "

"And so it shall," Aaron murmured after a second, though lesser jolts of hostility coursed through his veins; "so it shall - once I get out of these s**t soaked clothes." For effect, Aaron repeated the rabbi's quotation, "The sun also rises!" a bit louder. From the rear of the ambulance his assistant, Roscoe Harms (a black, born-again Pentecostal) chimed in with, "Amen, brother, just like the Son of God do 'evy Easter come the spring."

Smiling broadly, Roscoe then called for help on his cell phone. Aaron's radio crackled twice before shorting out for good. Ever so reluctantly, silence begat resignation - despite the people in darkened tenements beckoning for assistance like ghosts in a Tim Burton cartoon. Fifteen minutes later, volunteers arrived with a rubber raft to ferry Aaron's patient to safety. The ambulance corps soldiered on.

Above, the Lord God addressed His dusky angel who, still riven by pride and shame, stormed about the celestial canyons: "Thus, you see, my Prince, love is the cohesion that binds all together – just as, in the physical universe, charged electrons attract molecules one to another. Oh, to be sure, evil abounds; but love, redemptive love, is as perennial as the grass." Maddened by what his adversary had chosen to extol and what to forgive, Satan smoldered. Off in a shadowy alcove, he urged his minions to redouble their efforts in the furtherance of misery even as he hurled countless imprecations out into the eternity of the stars – a medieval slurry of menace and Angst.

Seven Deadly Sins

The following tale is set back in Hoboken's golden age of blue collar folderol. Apologies are, however, due Hoboken purists for my conflating things and times in a manner not consistent with history. As justification I cite Shakespeare's ***Julius Caesar*** *in which Brutus harkens to a clock (Big Ben perhaps!) that struck three. Needless to say, no such machine existed in ancient Rome.*

Tuesday: Detective Harvey Quatsch finished up some paperwork on a pair of kayaking Yuppies who drowned after their craft was torpedoed by a huge current-driven length of timber in the Hudson River. Harvey, who was reading the classics at the time, worked the word *hubris* into his report, observing to his partner, Georgy Metz, that he could have told the aforesaid dipsh*ts the Hudson River was a treacherous sort of a waterway. Twenty years ago, didn't his childhood friend, poor Billy Boynton, perish when he dove from the Maxwell House piers, aka Bare Ass Beach, into those same murky waters and his head got stuck in an industrial sized milk container submerged therein. Anyway, once Harvey'd dotted his i's and crossed his t's, regarding the unfortunate mariners, he had a several days of vacation time all to himself.

Wednesday, Diamond # 2 at "the cricket," long before it became JFK Stadium. The sun beat down on the dusty field like a Chernobyl death ray despite the lateness of the hour. The members of the Zephyrs softball team frolicked about with plastic cups of frothy beer like hordes of insects as when first the overhead light's flicked on in some vermin ridden downtown kitchen, hardcore roaches immune to the exterminator's lethal spray.

Meanwhile, Wilhelmina Birdsong, all tits and frizzy red hair, slurred her displeasure with Jubilation Tremblay-Cournoyer (real name, Jude, of Haitian descent) in a near poetic stream of obscenities for allowing her Angora pussycat, Nay Nay, to escape, never to be seen again, via an open window leading out onto a fire escape and the labyrinthine world beyond.

Jubilation was always fussy about (1) that hyphen in his name and (2) his Mohawk. He was considerably less so about other things. Slouched as Jubilation was in a rickety lawn chair, Mister Winkie hung forth from Jubilation's Izod shorts like a garter snake in corn silk. Jubilation was known to bleach the shrubbery surrounding his nether parts.

Glancing their way, Wilhelmina gagged and then exclaimed, "Look at this 'scheevy lounge lizard scumbag. There's a logo 'fa 'yiz all!" Most of the players ignored her best they could, pretending she was but a hologram from Hell. So she hocked up a bolus of phlegm and, together with the liquorice upon which she was gnawing, spat an ebony loogie across the "Zephyrs" banner, which hung proudly above a cooler of Bud.

It was, therefore, hardly surprising that when Wilhelmina had her throat slit on **Thursday**, Jubilation was arrested for her murder. The discovery of a linoleum knife with her blood upon it in Jubilation's locker at the maintenance depot on Observer Highway didn't help either.

Friday: Casper Tiddle had positioned himself at the bottom of the main stairwell in City Hall, so that he might, craning his long neck amorously just so, stare up at the seat of some tart's desire as she descended step by languorous step in a micro-mini. Possessed of bulging lips and a scraggly moustache of blond and brown, Casper swept a sweaty hank of hair behind an ear, closed his eyes, and smiled. Quatsch touched his elbow and, apropos of nothing, noticed several of Casper's discolored teeth listed left and right like neglected tombstones. "Shame on you, Cassie boy, cautioned Harvey smiling half-heartedly. "Next you'll be barking at the moon."

"Good one, you 'ole flatfoot, Harv;" said Casper as recognition dawned. "But offhand, fee fi fo fum, I'd 'hafta say she was a planetarium blond."

"You mean platinum, like the drapes and the carpet don't match?" asked Harvey as the aforesaid hottie sashayed by.

"'Zackly. Truth be known, I 'wuz always a horny devil, a regular Lothario my granny used 'ta say," whispered Casper by way of an apology for his none too subtle ogling. "Even growin' up I wanted to bang the White Rock Girl, Betty Boop, and Little Bo Peep."

"Little Bo Peep?" queried Quatsch.

"Yeah, I seen her in that movie *March of the Wooden 'Sojers* 'wit Fat 'n Skinny. 'Them goodie two shoes 'wimmenses 'yousta get me hot."

"Dude, 'musta been tough then you not bein' the most handsome guy in the litter, if 'ya don't mind my sayin' so."

"Nah, what you say has merit, Harv. It droppeth as the gentle rain. Indeed, I 'hadda whack it up against the sink from time 'ta time. But when 'da real thing finally 'come along, say in the Fabian theater or down by the sewerage plant, it 'wuz like 'da 'Fourtha July – bing bang, pyrotechnical up the wazoo be you Dorian Grey or the Creature from the Black Lagoon. Then too, 'ya know, tastes change as 'ya get older. The sexy cartoon stuff went south. Not for nothin', but now I like Greek broads 'da best."

"A regular Don Juan of Astoria, huh? Anyhow, best steer clear of those Rooskie sluts in Brighton Beach. They're a ruthless lot – 'specially when you're tryin' to play hide the salami. Or should I say kolbasa?"

"Don't worry 'bout that, 'cumpy, Stolichnaya ain't my 'cuppa tea. Besides, it's not like I'm 'gonna take these babes home 'ta mom." The stereo in a passing red hot Cabriolet blared forth a current hit, "'Gimme Me an Artie Shaw, Sweetie Pie," a few lines of which echoed in the spacious lobby having wafted through the big front doors.

"Alas," joshed Harvey, "whatever happened to classics like Lee Andrews's 'Long, Long, and Lonely Nights'?"

Casper shrugged.

"Long as I got 'ya here," continued Harvey, "'lemme ask 'ya if you know anything about this Jubilation throat slittin' thing. I'm not the investigating officer. Kevin Riggs is. Me and him share some history a while back. He reneged on a bet, said we never shook on it, so my nosin' around's bound to look like spite. Tough sh*t. I just don't want to see an innocent guy, even someone as squirrely as Cournoyer, pay for what someone else did. Makes the whole department all look bad. Plus, it's just plain wrong. And if I can put my finger in this deadbeat's eye, so much the better."

"That's all well and good, but I heard they found the murder weapon in 'Jewbee's locker," Casper interjected.

"Yeah, one that wasn't even locked. Plus, this dingbat 'Jewbee told his public defender that he read about some 'cafone in Jimmy Breslin's *The Gang That Couldn't Shoot Straight* who got away with murder by just saying absolutely nothing. So, even though he didn't kill anyone, he's doin' the same."

"Not the smartest guy in the world, I'll grant 'ya," offered Casper. "If he's got an alibi, even a half-assed one, he 'oughta cough it up."

"Unless there's somethin' else he's hidin', someone else he's protecting," countered Quatsch.

"You're well out of my depth there, Harvey. All I can say is talk to his old music teacher, Mr. Flann. He might be able to put you in touch with some hipsters that rubbed shoulders with Wilhemina and Jubilation. A widget to stir things up, so to speak. School's out by now, so you might catch him at the Elks. If you don't snag him at the Lodge, I know he goes to Mass in Weehawken every Saturday night - penance for swallowing half the world, I 'spose," added Casper with a sneer. "Jesus, the man has an ass the size of Milwaukee."

"Everyone plays the hand he's dealt, but the Devil shuffles the cards," answered Harvey ending the discussion on a philosophical note that startled Casper into a moment of silence, after which Casper, renowned for his non-sequiturs, countered with, "Russian roulette if you asked me."

On his way to the Elks, Harvey ducked into the Jewish War Vets' on Washington Street to confer with Schatzi Schlägel as to his picks for the next day's races at Monmouth. Schatzi won more often than Harvey, as from time to time jockeys and stable hands fed him inside dope on "sure things." But Schatzi still placed considerable trust in Harvey's intuition and expertise. Not a bookie himself, Schatzi placed bets for Harv.

As Harvey strode within, Schatzi sat next to a phone and a tumbler of Four Roses examining the *Daily Racing Form*. His slicked back streaks of graying hair, his long elegant nose, and the fleshy wattles that hung from his jaws lent him the appearance of an elderly pelican – a vision somewhat belied by the enormous cigar he puffed upon. Schatzi's leisurely pace of life was made possible by a no-show job he had acquired during his years of trusty service and silence as an accountant for an embattled Teamsters' local.

"How's it hangin', Harvey?" asked Schatzi scratching an ear. "For your information, I haven't heard nothin' to contradict Dog's Breakfast, that long shot you're so fond of in tomorrow's featured race at Monmouth."

"Much obliged," answered Harvey, as he slipped Schatzi a hundred as a wager on his dark horse hunch. Schatzi remained seated, for as a rule it took a crowbar to separate his bony posterior from his cushioned armchair. Most days Schatzi would finish the bottle in front of him and still not get soused – pacing himself as it were. Babbling all the while about his plans for tomorrow is how he acquired his second nickname, Mañana – a sobriquet only his fellow Vets were allowed to use. Needless to say, these plans rarely, if ever, morphed into deeds.

"By any chance, you 'seen Flann lately?" asked Harvey.

"Yeah, he was waddling about the Wilton House earlier today. Mostly, though, he leaves before now."

Irwin, the Vets' unofficial bartender, a comical fellow with Dumbo ears, piped up, "'Hey, Mañana, you tol' me to remind you to call your brother Abe 'cause it's his birthday."

"Thanks, Irwin," answered Schatzi, "but he's 'prolly eatin' now. I'll call 'im later." Grins all around, Harvey headed north. Schatzi took up the *Jersey Journal* to read an article about the treatment of festering boils, something from which he feared he might one day suffer.

Hoping to speak to Flann, Harvey checked in at the Elks, to no avail. Then he wandered off home but not before he beheld card shark Eddie Ritzic seated upon a commode in the men's room with his trousers down around his ankles and one of those paper Burger King crowns upon his head. He was out like a light, and Harvey woke him with what members thereafter referred to as "the royal flush."

Saturday, early evening: One block south of a go-go bar known as the Zoo, adjacent to the bridge from Weehawken into Hoboken, stood a tenement house. Its windows overlooked the aforesaid stretch of elevated roadway, a tangle of rusting railroad tracks, and the river beyond. The ground floor of this edifice housed a tavern called Earthquake McGoon's, a name lifted from Al Capp's comic strip in the funny papers. It was a lively pub with an eclectic choice of music on the jukebox, a juggernaut of a fan overhead, and a huge mural of Li'l Abner and Daisy Mae on the far wall.

As was often the case, a horde of youthful Yuppies danced to a hip hop tune beside the glowing Wirlitzer 1015 music machine – the words to which hit included the verse: "Don't care if ya' got the seven year itch or if I caught 'ya unawares. / Pull up 'ya panties, bitch, 'cause I'm 'gunna throw ya' down the stairs." The enthralled Terpsichoreans resembled nothing so much as a swarm of spermatozoa wriggling between the bubbles in a glass of champagne.

Closest the stained glass door, one depicting a rose and a Baby Ruth, several ne'er-do-wells buzzed about Susanna, aka Girly, Mulcahy – a curvaceous creature thirty years of age in a see-through blouse and stone washed jeans. She wore a red bandana tied about her slender throat, affording her a western flair.

Seated further down the long, well-worn mahogany bar, nearest the cash register sat Silas Garner- the diminutive owner of the Hotel Victoria on River Street in Hoboken. McGoon's was his home away from home – with fewer moochers looking for an easy touch. The ceiling fan droned on, and Silas cast a covetous glance at the flirtatious carry-on of Girly's emboldened suitors, one of whom had his hand squarely on her rump.

Silas's ground floor saloon and eatery did quite

well, much better than McGoon's, particularly on pay days as the bar cashed checks - with, of course, the understanding that you'd tip the bartender and buy at least one round of drinks. Rarely, though, did anyone actually rent the hotel's rooms above, for most had been parceled out free of charge to down-and-out homeless tramps who agreed to take out life insurance policies with Silas as their beneficiary. Silas looked upon these arrangements as a mutually aggrandizing form of social welfare - not without some justification.

Similarly, Silas had for decades maintained a reasonably large apartment on Hudson St. in a building that had recently gone condo. With the aid of a crafty lawyer, he ixnayed numerous offers to buy him out. Standing firm upon his rights as a tenant, he eventually acquired ownership of this apartment condo for next to nothing. Regarding his personal life, he'd been married once, but such hadn't turned out well. He vowed "never to be skinned again."

To be fair, however, matters of amour rarely run smooth. Just then the gorgeous Tatiana Polyakov, a recently divorced mail order bride, sauntered into McGoon's. Both Susanna's suitors made room, shamelessly spazzing out like tabbies on catnip. Tatiana, upon whose collarbone shone a golden crucifix, smiled as the perfidious swains paid court to her rival.

Girly seethed, for the tide had definitely turned. Sensing an opportunity, Silas asked Girly if she'd like a drink, but she was too angry to reply, choosing instead to hurl herself into an old timey barber's chair which was positioned near a bay window aglow with lurid neon signs. She crossed her shapely legs, lit a cigaret, and pumped her right foot as though she were churning butter.

Seemingly unflustered, Silas challenged the less charming of the two hipsters to a game of eight ball. What with the clatter of balls and a sizeable tip upon the bar, the remaining bon vivant escorted Tatiana to the door - chuckling like the man who broke the bank at Monte Carlo. However, disappearing like a will o' the wisp, the ever lissome Tatiana never heard her featherlight Gucci wristwatch hit the floor. But Girly did, and as she scurried over to pick up the money she herself had left in a sodden pile on the bar, she ground Tatiana's watch into smithereens, pretending all the while she'd no knowledge of the watch's presence underfoot.

Silas had seen it all and beamed. Staring Girly dead in the face, he mimicked a cat's claws and exclaimed, "Meow!"

Narrowing her flashing eyes, Susanna asked, "You know any girls who, mirror mirror on the wall, don't 'wanna be the fairest of them all, especially that Tatiana Twatnitzski?" She cocked her head to one side and added, "We all have our shortcomings - like, hmm, for instance, your thalidomide arms and your bottomless pockets, you beady-eyed gnome. Word is you still have your communion money or was it Bar Mitzvahed you were?"

Silas shot back, "As my aged mother used to say to my aunt, 'Put some color on your face, Rose; you look bad enough as it is.' Oh, and Skanky, can 'ya hear me? Go down around the Projects where the competition isn't so keen."

Over her shoulder, a departing Girly rejoined, "More than you can afford at any price, you cheapskate douchebag. And don't go sniffin' my barstool after I'm gone."

"Nah, I ain't 'inta sushi," scoffed Sidney's in reply.

Paradoxically, off duty Detective Harvey Quatsch was "on the job" Saturday evening round about five o'clock as he listened to one of Fr. Fedor's masterful homilies at St. Lawrence's Church. To Harvey this poking about in matters pertaining to the dark side, like Wilhelmina's murder, seemed entirely fitting in as much as the church was located in a section of Weehawken known as the Shades. Lounging in Fr. Fedor's modernistic church took him back to the days when, ages ago, he'd stumble over to Mass straight from a session of go-go rama at the Zoo, located just around the corner - the better some fourteen hours later to nurse the inevitable heebie-jeebies of a Sunday morning.

Oddly enough, even a tainted, half-hearted participation in the liturgy seemed to provide some modicum of grace with which to endure the day-after screaming meemies, contingent upon his weekend pub crawls - something, anything to suggest human existence wasn't as topsy-turvy as his stomach and head. Besides, he loved Fr. Fedor's spin on sin and redemption. Be that as it may, Harvey had already located his prey, Percy Flann, several rows back. So for the moment, he could slide back in his pew and listen, breathing in all the while the scent of incense and votive candles.

"Some see Catholicism as a numbers game," intoned the Jesuit priest, his silvery locks carefully combed. "There are, of course, the four cardinal virtues:

courage, temperance, prudence, and justice. Just for the record, they have nothing to do with the baseball team in St. Louis. St. Thomas Aquinas spent considerable ink on the three theological virtues of faith, hope, and charity in his *Summa Theologica* – making for a total of seven. You may remember from your Catechism the seven gifts of the Holy Spirit. Lucky sevens come up at least twice more as there are seven corporal works of mercy and, though nobody likes to talk about them anymore, seven deadly sins: avarice, gluttony, envy, lust, wrath, sloth, and pride – the last of which I'll touch upon this evening, the sin of Lucifer, a fallen angel who would not serve.

"I've heard a fair share of deathbed confessions in my line of work, but none so pitiful as that of my friend, let's call him Stanislav Lecowitch. He was a man of considerable virtue but totally lacking in humility, taking as he did inordinate pride in the sensuous life he'd led – especially as regards his pugilistic victories over men and his mastery over women. Even unto the last, poor man, he refused to renounce the earthly joy he took in both. According to Stash, the mayhem he had caused seemed to justify his very existence. I mention this flaw because I have his permission to do so and, more importantly, because Stanislav's recalcitrance serves as a cautionary tale for us all.

"So beware, fellow dreamers, of the romantic notion that outrageous behavior is one-in-being with some Zorba the Greek Pantheistic Life Force. Such is a lie – the vanity of vanities, as the Bible puts it. Cast aside, too, you foolhardy pilgrims, the gambler's trust in earthly delights and magic numbers. Rather bow your heads and pray, for the Peace of Christ is eternal – clearly not a mere game of chance. And for those who think religion is but fairy tale, recall if you will the myth of original sin the effects of which reality confirms 24/7."

Quatsch lit a candle for his deceased parents at a side altar, all the while keeping his sights on Percy, who stuffed rosary beads into his shirt pocket as he waddled down the center aisle. He wasn't hard to follow. Minutes later Quatsch watched him tiptoe away from Tobias's Tube Steak van, daintily avoiding the puddles of an overnight deluge.

Once on dry terra firma, Percy leaned against a telephone pole, itself more than a little askew. He inhaled two puppies smothered in onions and sauerkraut. His considerable girth made it appear that Percy's avoire de poir had caused the pylon to list. Quatsch approached. Licking two fingers, Percy greeted his former student with only a toothy grin for his mouth was full. Percy was fond of Quatsch as back in the day Harvey had stirred many an assembly with his tenor saxophone.

"Ah, Mr. Flann," exclaimed Harvey, "always a pleasure, as our dearly departed Mayor Tom Vezzetti used to say. If there's one thing you know better than music, it's where to find the tender vittles."

"Indeed, my rebel-rousing soloist, just so. Truth be known, however, I much prefer Cal's on Observer Highway when it comes to the succulence of a swamp dog. 'Ya know, Harvey, for a gourmand with ethnic cravings, Hoboken was always next door to Nirvana – Fiore's for that milky, textured 'mutz, Hans Jesse's for those deutsche pastries, the Blue Point for its mussels in marinara sauce, Kurt Laemmel's for smoked eels, the St.

Anne's Feast for those zeppolas drenched in powdered sugar, Gustoso's for its crusty *panis angelicus,* the Clam broth House for those outrageous corned beef sandwiches on rye, Benny Tudino's pizza, Herald's chocolate layer cake, Biggy's ice cold clams, and the yum yum man.

"If you think about it, the history of Hoboken is contained therein. God forgive me," Max continued in near rhapsody, "for years I'd wander downtown to 'Migaleen's candy store just for a whiff of the pasta 'vazool she always had simmering in the background. It transported me back to my childhood like the madeleines in Marcel Proust's *Swann's Way.*"

"I'm surprised you omitted Helmer's steak sandwich, Mr. Flann, but you really lost me there with that business 'bout the swans. I've had a tasty goose or two in my time, but never one of those long necked devils. And who was Madeline?"

"Fancy schmancy stuff from some Frenchy novel. High brow folderol you'd have little patience for. Anyhow, what can I do 'ya for?"

"Actually, I'd like to pick your brain about this Jubilation thing. I guess you know he's being held for offing Wilhelmina Birdsong. Unofficially, I wondered what's your take on this killing, you having dealt with them both during their stints with Hoboken High's marching band."

"A nasty business entirely," answered Percy dabbing at his delicately pursed lips with a paper napkin. "I'm sure he's no angel, but it doesn't sound much like Jubilation though, does it? Actually, Jewbee's quite fond of women. They fuss over him unceasingly, mainly because he's gayer than laughter and desires nothing so much as their company. As to Wilhelmina, I'm told she could be a bitch on wheels when she was on the blow. But like Jessica Rabbit, she wasn't really evil, she was just drawn that way."

Percy waited for a laugh, but hearing none continued, "More like Ferlinghetti's 'Coney Island of the Mind' meets Fellini's *Juliet of the Spirits*." Nonplused, Quatsch threw up his hands and shook his head - though amiably. Sighing, Percy clarified, "A honky tonk ditz if ever there was one, rather than a 14 karat demon."

"I'd say you were on target about Jubilation, in any case. Not his style at all. Besides I'm told his weapon of choice is the stiletto, nothing so plebian as a workman's tool."

"*Voilà*, my friend, got it in one. There's little Jubilation'd do without a certain panache," Percy answered as he glanced towards Tobias's van, longing for another tube steak. "You could do worse than to ask around in Excalibur, that raunchy gay bar down by the cricket. And while you're at it, put a new reed in your sax and jam with us fogies sometime soon at the high school. If he's not tickling the ivories at Frankie and Johnny's, Antoine Benoit joins us every now and then. He's pretty good."

"Fair enough, Percy, and adieu," said Harvey somewhat disingenuously for Harvey hadn't touched his sax in years. Meanwhile Flim Flann (for such had been his nickname back in the day) trundled off to the hot dog stand once again. Chuckling, Harvey turned towards his car, which he had double parked beside the bridge leading into Hoboken; but before he'd gone very far, his cell phone rang.

"Real quick, 'ya lucky goyim 'bastid, Dog's Breakfast came in at 20 'ta one," Schatzi exclaimed.

"Manna from heaven! Shalom, you 'ole Hebrewski kabbalah man," Harvey cheered. But his glee was short lived as his windshield was lathered with the droppings of monk parrots, interlopers for which the area had recently become famous.

One brazen minty-green creature remained perched upon an overhead cable as though to claim responsibility for the mess. His compatriots warbled merrily in their nests high above amongst the electrical transformers across the way. Lovely little creatures with noisome habits – just like us humans, Harvey mused. He headed for McGoon's for some paper towels.

Exiting in tears and a mighty huff, Susanna bumped into Harvey just outside the stained glass door, whereupon Harvey observed, "If it isn't Girly Mulcahy, 'wunna my favorite people on earth lookin' like she's got a colossal case of the ass."

"Right on the money, Sherlock," she snapped dabbing smeared mascara from her eyes. Harvey recoiled; and she softened her tone, "That skinflint Silas Garner really rubs me the wrong way. I envy you bein' a cop 'n all 'cause if I had a 'pistola right now, I'd send him straight to hell."

Inwardly, Harvey knew well his own capacity for wrath, having only months ago drowned William Sipes, the child molester, in the long slip behind the Erie Lackawanna train station – a passionate act not easily reconciled with Fr. Fedor's idea of mercy and repentance. But in truth Harvey was abuzz with contradictions. Just then, even as he smiled upon Girly, sex, death and religion graced his silent ruminations with a touch of poetry: "If ourselves we truly knew, it's on the cusps of guilt and joy we'd be torn in two."

Fortunately, Girly was no mind reader. Thus, only half in earnest, he said instead, "So happens I keep an untraceable Saturday night special strapped to my ankle, lest some dead unarmed perp should require one. Yours for the asking." offered Harvey. "I take your meanin', however; pricks like Sy give new meaning to the expression penis envy."

Girly thought about his gun proposal for a moment or two, but then conceded, "No, Harvey, you know I'm only rantin' 'n ravin'. What say we retire to Hoboken and slake our thirsts at the Elysian Café?"

"Suits me to a "t," agreed Harvey; "my car's parked right here alongside the bridge."

"Illegally!"

"Only way to go. But first I 'gotta get a rag or somethin' from McGoon's to tidy up my shit encrusted windshield."

"Skip it," suggested Girly, "this kerchief'll do just fine.

Zipping past Dykes Lumber Company on Park Avenue, Harvey observed, "'Ya know, the only bad 'parta of drinking in Hoboken is it's a lot like a village. Everybody knows everybody's business."

"You're tellin' me," said Girly. "Last Wednesday I took my dog for a walk on Jefferson St., and I saw a chartreuse Citroën cruisin' past Excalibur, the gay joint just behind the baseball field. That gnarly looking coot who plays piano at Frankie and Johnny's was at the wheel. When me 'n Maximillian (he's the cutest little Doberman 'pincher) got a block over to Madison St., a weirdo with a Mohawk slid into the front seat of the Citroën like he was a CIA undercover man. Mother 'a Jesus, I thought, what a parlay those two make!"

"'Ew whee, Girly, if you only knew" Harvey replied, grinning from ear to ear, "the jackpot and the daily double all in one."

Subsequently, the youthful couple was quite festive at the Elysian. Later still, well hidden beneath the viaduct, Girly frolicked in Harvey's arms all through the night.

Sunday afternoon, a second floor apartment above Yacullo's candy Store on Washington St.: Antoine Benoit's gaunt facial features - sunken cheekbones and a pronounced Adam's apple - contrasted with a thoroughly disarming smile. Tall, thin, and meticulous in his attire, Antoine sat at a roll top desk examining a series of photographs he had singled out for a show at the Hoboken Historical Museum. Among them were portraits of a counter girl from Schoening's Bakery tying up a box of crumb cake with string pulled from a skein dangling overhead, a Fifties hood, Gerhard Stutz, scowling at the camera in his Rock of Hoboken leather jacket, Vincenzo De Pasqual, the aged codger who used to set off the fireworks at the St. Ann's feast, gazing at the truncated fingers of his right hand whilst lighting a cigar, and the cabaret singer Jimmy Roselli belting out "Mala Femmena" at a 'Muffi wedding at the Union Club.

Benoit's methods and his use of film with a high

ASA lent his atmospheric portraits a grainy appearance that only added to their allure as the very essence of his subjects seemed to ooze through the pixels. Puttering about his hobby on the weekend took Antoine's mind off the tedium of his nine-to-five job as a clerk in the tax department upstairs at city hall. He lifted a tumbler of water to drink, but the glass coaster stuck to it and fell just as Harvey knocked upon his door.

Harvey introduced himself as a policeman and asked if he could come in. Antoine ushered him over to rickety looking antique chair just inches from the pictures on the desk. "Entryway downstairs was ajar," Harvey apologized.

"That's often the case," explained Antoine.

"Not for nothin', but those pictures are impressive – 'kinda like Walter Penn's stuff," Harvey noted, eyeballing Benoit's work.

"Ah, you know something of the craft!"

"Not much," Harvey rejoined, "but my older brother was something of a shutter bug."

Antoine elaborated, though timidly, "The effect I occasionally achieve has as much to do with the developing as it does with the actual taking of the photos. I converted that closet across the room into a dark room."

Harvey looked away when Antoine said "closet" and then launched into the following: "You know, I asked around and it seems that, other than playing piano at nightspots from time to time, you're a quiet, unassuming guy, the sort of person who takes his pleasures far from the maddening crowd. People like that, people who've worked hard to keep a low profile, often obsess over what others think of them. So much so that when the chips are down they need a little nudge to do the right thing."

Antoine tugged at the collar of his dress shirt, but the expression on his face remained as inscrutable as the Sphinx's. Harvey forged ahead, "There was a time when silence might have been justified. Nowadays, though, fewer 'n fewer give a rat's ass about such carrying on. Every summer I go fishin' on an out-of-the-way beach in South Amboy, and often enough there's a bunch of nitwits oohing and aahing over some unusual driftwood as it lies glistening in the sun 'n surf. Then it dries out and suddenly nobody even knows it's there. Look this square in the eye, Antoine, and it's little more than a tempest in a teapot. A crack of thunder, a flash of lightning, and before you can say 'f*ck all,' the boogeyman's gone with the wind. Worth considerin', dude."

Antoine reached for the glass coaster he'd dropped before, and Harvey concluded, "I knew 'Jewbee's mother, a friend of the family. Since you're a musician 'n all, I thought I'd tell you, by way of haphazard comic relief, 'Jewbee's namesake was a character in *L'il Abner*, a musical comedy by Johnny Mercer. Jubilation T. Cornpone was a Confederate general famous for bein' first in war, first in peace, first 'ta holler, 'I quit!'" With that Harvey took his leave.

Antoine Benoit placed the glass coaster, still intact, upon the edge of the roll top desk. Drumming his fingers on his desk as though noodling *Rhapsody in Blue* on a baby grand, he gazed out onto the Avenue where a multicolored swarm of very ordinary people bustled about attending to their chores.

Monday morning at the Spa, a greasy spoon catty-cornered to the Victoria Hotel: Casper Tiddle sat in a booth opposite a buxom brunette named Chloe Kotsiopoulus, who sipped her coffee demurely. Casper finished the last of the prunes in his bowl when Detective Quatsch sashayed into the diner with a newspaper under his arm. "Hey, Harv," exclaimed Casper, "seems that Liberace guy in the water works manned up and took the heat 'offa 'Jewbee with an alibi. Holy shit, hard 'ta believe that wizened old scarecrow even had a pair."

"What," ejaculated Harvey, "you of all people never 'herda Benoit balls?" Chloe tittered.

Postscript: Arnold Dax - Wilhemina's on again, off again lover - was later identified as her murderer but never captured. His own mother, the librarian, once observed, "Were you to trespass into the noirish environs of my son's heart and soul, you'd want to be packing a flashlight and a gun." When in his cups, Detective Riggs referred to his elusive nemesis, Arnold Dax, as the "Scarlet Pickerel."

In as much as the trivial and the profound often vie for our attention with an unsettling uniformity, the final standings of the softball league, alluded to at the beginning of this story, are offered below. The Whoop-dee-Du's won the championship and celebrated with Alphonso mangoes (sacred to the elephant god Ganesha), fruit which was enlivened by massive injections of Grey Goose vodka, a potation much beloved by the French. Tossing the rinds up in the air, the Du's taunted the losing pitcher on the Italian team chanting, "Cosmo Tedesco, rump bump bumpa ba!"

League Standings by Ethnic Origin:

Hindustani	Whoop-dee-Du's	12-3
Italians	Sal Minellas	11-4
Whiteboys	Zephyrs	9-5
Yugos	'Ewbotz	8-6
P.R.'s	Meeta Meetas	8-6
Blacks	Darktown Mooncrickets	6-8
Germans	die Schadenfreude	5-9
Irish	Cornbeef Amadáns	4-10
Jewish	Schlomo's Schnorrers (aka the SS)	1-13

Gryphons 'n Hillies

Their feathers spattered with shite, a squadron of gryphons soared out of the crimson sunset behind the palisades like shrapnel exploding from an inferno - skimming then over the lowland streets of Hoboken in search of young girls they'd enslave to their master, Magnifico, whose real name was Fidel "Ojos Humeante" Valdivielso. A splendiferous figure, this Latino cigar mogul also provided unblemished chickens for devout voodoo worshippers and Cubalayan roosters (comb and wattles removed) for rapacious cock-fight aficionados. But that which enriched him beyond all telling were the cigars rolled by what he called his "little Veronicas" - innocent ten-year old gamines swooped up from "that mile square preserve down below." The flavor of these diademas and panatelas bordered on the ambrosial. The thin wisps of smoke, rising from their tapered forms, were in fragrance like unto the frankincense that once upon a time Catholics favored during Benediction of the Blessed Sacrament.

Periodically, when Magnifico's cigar business expanded, Joaquin de Niero, a sardonic dwarf dressed as the sorcerer's assistant in Disney's *Fantasia,* sent his frightful gryphons aloft much in the manner of Wotan commanding the Valkyries. Although mercenary to the core, de Niero wasn't a true acolyte to Evil. But he did like to assume sinister airs in connection with his captaincy of the gryphons - prompting him, whenever he had an audience, to muse: "Olaf Roemer calculated the speed of light. But who, other than Magnifico and Lucifer, knows the speed of darkness?" In between missions Joaquin garrisoned the gryphons batlike in the belfry of the long since abandoned St. Michael's Monastery on Summit Avenue.

In response to these free-flying raids, Methuselah Oblongadavita, a Sephardic Jew of mixed parentage, organized the Zen Bowmen, a band of archers who patrolled Hoboken rooftops hoping for a shot at de Niero's celestial kidnappers - those supernatural beings with dirty faces. The slowest of these aerial raptors were from time to time brought low. Piecing together their dying utterances and their infirmities (curses, ungodly supplications, scars, and broken wings), Methuselah, who had lost a daughter to their talons, concluded that they were, in fact, the last of Satan's fallen angels. Methuselah reasoned that God's own seraphim (the tried and true ethereal creatures still in thrall to their Creator) would have been impervious to the ordinary slings and arrows of outrageous fortune. Also, real angels do no harm. If they did, they'd become demons.

Grief-stricken but undaunted, Methuselah quickly became a hero in town. Hoboken kids, especially the boys, imitated his archers by firing shards of linoleum from homemade carpet guns at grackles, starlings, and other noisome invaders.

Actually searching for the abducted girls, as some like Methuselah were wont to do, was a perilous undertaking. The palisades were guarded by Ancient Order of the Hillies, a gang of white trash marauding hooligans, many them with elfin ears, who were famous for stoning any trespassers upon that territory between Hoboken and Union City - an escarpment they called their own. Even railway "bulls" and the police were fair game for their missiles. Consequently, facial scars and eye patches became common fare in the blue collar town Frank Sinatra once fled with his boyish savoir faire.

Albrecht Qual, a deacon at St. Peter and Paul's Church and a counterman at Kurt Laemmel's deutsche deli on Hudson St., was, nonetheless, determined to find the missing children one way or another - which was hardly surprising as his two nieces had likewise been whisked away by de Niero's demons. Since both girls spoke fluent German, he persuaded WITZ, a local radio station for landsmen like himself, to broadcast rescue messages *auf Deutsch* in the hope that his lovelies might be listening.

As it happened, they were - because Magnifico had music piped into his captives' workplace in an effort to keep them content if not happy. Accordingly, each of his Veronicas got to choose a favorite radio station during different parts of the day. Naturally, the nieces selected WITZ. So, along with enjoying Will Glahé's "Liechtensteiner Polka," they eventually learned that they weren't forgotten and that they should await instructions. Needless to say, none of their captors knew what they knew *auf Deutsch*.

Best of all, luck was on their side. Once a week every girl was allowed a special treat as part of Magnifico's self serving "benevolence." Both nieces had, even as tots, developed a craving for headcheese, a typically German comestible consisting of what amounted to sliced pigs' jowls encased in a translucent gelatin of fat. Very few delis purvey such exotic delicacies, for, as one might expect, the demand is quite limited. Thus one day when an Hispanic dude entered Kurt Laemmel's and ordered two pounds of headcheese sliced thin, clearly not a staple of the Caribbean, suspicions were aroused. The ever wily Albrecht gave Helmut Koschig, a frequent customer who was purchasing a loaf of *kommisbrot,* the eye. Smooth as silk, Mr. Koschig followed the interloper up to Washington St. and onto a # 22 bus bound for Union City.

As a waiter at the Swiss Town House restaurant in Union City, Mr. Koschig was one of the few Hobokenites the Hillies still allowed to enter that city by bus. Most such passengers were frog-walked back across the border on Park Avenue in Weehawken and warned never to return. A master of the schmooze, Helmut had been grandfathered in as a "harmless" old timer. Meanwhile, Albrecht put out an advisory to his nieces via station WITZ. Should they be permitted outings, supervised or otherwise, they were to leave behind a trail of headcheese niblets – if, indeed, any such delicacies came their way.

Like the Hound of Heaven, Helmut stalked his prey to a quiet neighborhood not far from Sears & Roebuck's, but the swarthy Cubano finally realized he was being tailed and vanished like a spirit without a shadow. Even so, Helmut was sure Magnifico's safe house was nearby, so he quit for the day.

The very next morning Ernesto Pizzicato, Magnifico's effete but efficient chief of operations at the cigar factory (in fact, a converted three storey tenement), took the Veronicas out for their daily promenade by way of exercise. As always, his charges walked in two straight lines, holding hands like the little Parisian girls in the children's story *Madeline*. But Renata, the older of Albrecht's nieces, dutifully dropped crumpled up bits of headcheese as they marched homeward. She had gotten Albrecht's message loud and clear.

Later that afternoon, on his lunch hour, Helmut borrowed the boss's dachshund Fritzie - a Teutonic pooch that greatly favored headcheese over Kibble 'n Bits. Helmut found Renata's trail of headcheese easily enough; but, a la the tale about Hansel and Gretel, birds had eaten all but a speck here and there. No matter, because Fritzie was on the scent like a shot, trotting straight to a tidy brick building with a well kept lawn out front. Old as he was, Helmut clicked his heels, and Fritzie piddled on the wrought iron fence.

Word of mouth flew like electricity through an electric grapevine. Out of nowhere, like the snakes spawned by Medusa's blood in far off Africa, a multinational force arose. Armed with cudgels, pool cues, and Louisville sluggers, these yeomen warriors stormed the palisades hell bent upon avenging countless outrages from above - a Children's Crusade, so to speak. Spearheaded by a pride of chupacabras, a Puerto Rican contingent humorously dubbed Pendejo's Volunteers, charged into the fray before all others, much as Hannibal used elephants during his Alpine sorties into Rome. Consequently, an entire cohort of Hillies fell away like sugar cane beneath the Volunteers' machetes. These efforts were augmented by a fiery coterie of Italians who called themselves the 'Geeta Mort, a ragtag corps led by the slightly crazed but courageous Enzio Multifarious.

Elsewhere brickbats from on high clanged harmlessly upon garbage can covers below. From the Projects, Methuselah's longbows slew Joaquin's dive bombing gryphons one and all, just as the English had slain the French at Agincourt in 1415. A group of aged deutsche militants, known as die Alte Knochen from the Altenheim in Shützen Park, executed a brilliant rearguard flanking maneuver and ravaged the endgame forces which Magnifico held in reserve. Many in this German brigade were former Hoboken residents armed with ceremonial swords from WWII.

By noon a pitched battle ensued with Magnifico's regulars, devil to devil and man to man, as swarms of Hobokenites overwhelmed their opponents like rioters liberating the Bastille. Even before the tide had turned, Joaquin, foreseeing the inevitable, absconded into North Street Park and hid in a trash can like a spider in a thimble.

Soon thereafter Magnifico, a consummate realist, fled in a red Eldorado convertible loaded with loot. At last, his imprisoned Veronicas were set free to tumultuous applause. (*Historical footnote: This climactic battle led to the annexation of Union City and the establishment of the "Principality of Hoboken and the Upper Regions," a fiefdom unrivaled in its egalitarian bonhomie and grit.*)

Immediately following this victory, Albrecht, his face besmirched with the excretions of gryphons, kneeled before OLG's statue of Our Lady crushing the head of the Serpent and placed a bunch of hyssop there. Then, in the manner of Abraham, he closed his eyes and envisioned his beloved nieces as adults naked in the arms of their future lovers - girls every bit as lovely as the women about whom he'd read in fairy tales and myths, wondrous creatures who frolicked in the twinkling of God's eyes. Their offspring were, it seemed, as countless as the stars. Though chaste and childless, Albrecht smiled as Yahweh must have when He created sexual desire and love in the Garden of Eden.

Nonetheless, in the darkness beyond, a Satanic few grumbled about the absence of those cigars. The gates of Hell yawn forever.

LOVE GONE AWRY

Stained glass window adorning the residence at 645 Bloomfield Street, artistry which depicts elegant cobs like those at Spring Lake, N.J., in the story "Swan Song: A Midsummer Night's Scheme."

Bírds of a Feather

Sean Finn McFeeley was nicknamed Sinn Féin (a nationalist political party which is pronounced "Shin Fain") because he had the map of Ireland on his face. He achieved legendary status in Hoboken at the age of sixteen when on a bet he streaked from a beer bash on 5th and Garden to his home on 12th and Hudson. It was St. Patrick's Day, and Sinn had a hole in his "Kiss Me I'm Irish" T-shirt. As was the custom, Joe Joe Baccalá put his finger into the hole and rent the flimsy garment asunder. Enlivened by such frivolity, other revelers, the van Everdingen brothers Horst and Willem among them, joined in and tore Sinn's chinos from his corpus, rendering said trousers next to scandalous. By way of compensation, Joe Joe then offered Sinn $40 plus a brand new "Póg Mo Thón" (Kiss My Ass) T-shirt if he'd run home stark naked.

Not one to shirk from a challenge, a glassy-eyed Sinn hied forth with vigor if not perfect equilibrium. After all, he had drink taken; and he'd have made it home unscathed, too, if he hadn't stumbled in front of the Maxwell House guard shack - thereby gaining the attention of an otherwise somnolent sentry. Apocryphally, some wags claim Sinn tripped because he stepped on his outsized pecker - the Irish curse in reverse, as it were. But, regarding the like, it's important to remember that the people who spin myths often embroider.

Be that as it may, the guard called the cops who,

having little else to do, pulled up at Sinn's residence only moments after Sinn had scampered up his front steps two to a stride- but not before he advised several startled neighbors who were languishing there that he'd explain all subsequently. Needless to say, they gave him up to the police immediately.

Fortunately, back then such youthful indiscretions were easily swept under the carpet, and Sinn strode into manhood without officially blotting his copybook with a sex crime. But that sprint in the buff remained in the collective subconscious of Sinn's blue collar town, for his mad dash that St. Patrick's Day was Hoboken's equivalent of Phidippides' fabled marathon run.

Ozzie Fogel, whose hunger for confrontation was insatiable, owned a salmon-colored cockatoo named Dufloid. It was a mangy looking creature that squawked, "Ay, caramba! Check this douchebag out!" at the slightest provocation. Dufloid often traveled about perched on Ozzie's shoulder - as he did one summer evening at the St. Ann's Feast. A passing Puerto Rican accidentally sneezed on the temperamental bird, and Dufloid uttered his classic putdown once too often. The offended Hispanic wrung his neck on the spot.

Outraged, Ozzie put the guy in a headlock and dragged him over to where the zeppoles were sizzling in a vat of bubbling oil in an attempt to immerse his face therein. Upending a huge bowl on a table, both fell to the floor in a shower of confectionary sugar and then stood up sputtering in disbelief like comedic actors in whiteface. Mickey O'Flaherty, a motorcycle cop assigned to the Feast, kicked them both in the slats and sent them on their way.

Ozzie took Dufloid home in a discarded hatbox and found out where his killer, one Fernando Miranda, lived with his cat Pepe. Ozzie was a B&E expert. A week later UPS delivered Fernando's dismembered tabby in the selfsame hatbox Dufloid had briefly occupied. Offing cats was another of Ozzie's specialties. Every March he rounded up about fifty of them in burlap sacks so that he, and a band of enthusiastic urchins, could chase them into the Hudson in an event he called the Rites of Spring.

Night Train Lorraine, so called because of her irrepressible energy, was for a while in love with Ozzie-which, despite his drawbacks, was not that hard to believe. Ozzie was a handsome man with a jet black widow's peak and a pencil line moustache to lend him a bit of panache. He owned a strip joint and spent liberally. He could be uncommonly witty, too. Introduced to a German actor by a waitress at Helmer's restaurant, he responded, "Ah, yet another Westphalian ham!" to the delight of all except the performer.

Like Lorraine he had a lust for life, but he was a controlling soul, constantly trying to rein Lorraine in. For a while she reveled in her safety under Ozzie's wing. Eventually, though, she rebelled, for he was insanely jealous and none too faithful himself. In truth, he had much to be suspicious of as Lorraine was a knockout - possessed of smoky eyes and a set of maracas that would make Tito Puente weep.

A flirtatious creature, she had dated Sinn Féin in high school and from time to time still wore a moonstone pendant he'd given her, one that glowed milky white with a tinge of blue. But the two remained just friends. Bumping into Sinn and his chums on their way up to

Transfer Station in Union City where Ozzie had his go-go bar, she confided in Sinn that she was meeting someone new that very day on the last voyage of a ferryboat called the *Binghamton* – something that was sure to become a gala event in Hoboken's history. Sinn didn't say much about her assignation because he didn't like to meddle, and they went their separate ways. Sinn's cousin who worked at Miller's Abattoir on Tonnelle Avenue drove the crew up to Ozzie's go-go bar, a place called Boom Boom Geoffrion because Ozzie was a big hockey fan.

When they sauntered through the front door, the girls were already swinging around on poles like nymphomaniacs trying out for the Olympic gymnastics team. Flailing breasts and twerking buttocks appeared and disappeared surrealistically in the mirror behind the stage. The beverages went down like silk, and the boys marveled at the signed photos of such Hoboken notables as Frank Sinatra and baseball players like Honey Romano, Johnny Kucks, and Bill Kunkel on the lounge's walls. This made sense since the area was once known as West Hoboken. To add to the merriment, the boys donned some outsized green plastic hats and bowties Ozzie had left over from St. Patrick's Day.

Round about one o'clock, however, Ozzie made an impromptu decision to attend the *Binghamton* shindig himself, but he had to wait for his replacement to arrive. Sinn and the lads drank up and left. They knew what they had to do. Joe Joe and the boys went to find a cab, but none were available. Joe Joe staggered off to borrow his sister's Fiat on the other side of the Boulevard.

In the meantime, Sinn set off running through North St. Park, past the Doric apartments, and down the palisades. He flew down the precipitous path grasping at what he could so as not to tumble ass over teakettle. In so doing he tore his shirt on the branch of an ailanthus tree. He then rambled hell-bent for leather past the bamboo factory, past the Pietá outside OLG, past Kramer's clock on 2nd and Washington Street, past the Clam Broth House, and on into the cobblestone plaza in front of the ferries.

The area was mobbed, but he found the lovebirds in the Erie-Lackawanna waiting room holding hands next to a smiling bootblack who busied himself making his shoeshine rag pop and sing. Though breathless, Sinn warned the trysting pair of Ozzie's impending arrival, and they fled to Journal Square where *The Graduate* was playing.

Moments later Joe Joe and the boys screeched to a halt in his sister's Fiat still clad in the derbies and the bowties - lending them the appearance of clowns in the Big Apple Circus. Sinn sounded the all clear whereupon they began pousetting wildly like Okies at a hoedown. Apropos of nothing, Sinn got off a pretty good one-liner: "When attacked by clowns, always go for the juggler!" However, eyeing the tear in Sinn's shirt, Sinn's comrades fell upon him with gusto, and, once again, he was stripped of his habiliments. Fortunately, he lived nearby.

Aboard the ferry, a ruckus broke out when a disgruntled Union Hill interloper poured the remains of his Budweiser beer into a burly musician's sousaphone during the playing of the Red Wing fight song. But that was nothing compared to what would have happened if Ozzie had discovered Lorraine with her new lover. His name - Fernando Miranda.

Swan Song: a Midsummer Night's Scheme

Though Fiona O'Faolain's dad played the horses and drank at Tahn's, her home was awash with books and she became an avid reader. Piety abounded, but, oddly enough, so did joy and charity. The O'Faolains were a family often touched by the grief of others. An uptown lovely, Fiona was an only child, which might explain the naiveté of her early years. She was a spirited soul whose effervescent imagination many a yahoo bedewed with an undue air of wonderment. How else to explain her erratic choice of lovers? With the most unlikely of names, one such undeserving cad was Casimir de Coeurs.

He had a line of baloney some girls found irresistible, giving as it did an existential twist to the limits of romance. His oft repeated spiel ran something like this: "Love affairs are like carousels what with their lovely music, their colorful steeds, and their magical unicorns. Still, try as you might to grasp the golden ring, the best you can do as a prize is just another ride. That's why," Casimir would cajole in a whisper, "the Asbury Park Tillie smiles. Truly sad but - sweetheart, darling girl - it's all we have."

Even as a horny youngster, he couldn't help but overplay his hand. In the eighth grade Marsha Winslow lured him into the clothing room between classes with the promise of sexual favors. Whilst he blithely waggled his appendage in Marsha's face, Eva Marie Elfic sprang from one of the wooden cubicles and closed an enormous geography book (opened to a chapter on the Panama Canal) upon his pecker. Howling unmercifully, Casimir zipped up just in time for Miss Koch, his homeroom teacher, to haul him off to the principal's office. Needless to say, his tormenters had fled through the rear door of the cloakroom and then into the classroom proper without so much as a by your leave, swallowing their laughter as best they could. Never again, Casimir swore, would he be so bamboozled.

Later that same year while at the YMCA's Camp Tamaqua, he acquired a nickname he bore for life: The Sheik, a moniker he acquired after he slipped into the sleeping quarters of the only female working there that summer, the cook, a rosy-cheeked Miss Esther Shaekles. No shrinking violet, she promptly boxed his ears and insisted he be "sent home in disgrace." Deeply chagrined, his poor father had to come fetch him, but other than a cuff off the back of his skull, Casimir enjoyed the ride home. Envisioning himself as Christ entering Jerusalem on a donkey amidst the hoopla and the palms, he believed he'd become a hero of sorts, oft whistling, "…into your tent I'll creep. I'm the Sheik of Araby!"

In high school, wanting girls terribly but not truly liking them, Casimir fast became a sniffer, collecting the panties of girls with whom he had been intimate – a perversity which led his brainiac friend Libby, who was studying philosophy at the time, to refer to Casimir as a "pant-theist." When Libby (so named because he played the piano like Liberace) finished reading *Hoboken, the*

Highway to Heaven or Hell, an anthropological tome which insisted that geographic origins constitute a person's destiny, he wondered whether Casimir's Lilliputian personality could be attributed to his having grown up on Willow Terrace, in one of those wrong-way-around diminutive dwellings where Colonel Stevens' servants resided a century and a half ago. Be that as it may, Casimir was a scallywag with the outward appearance of a troubadour.

During the summer months, Fiona worked at the Monmouth Hotel along the Irish Riviera in Spring Lake. She toiled before a relentless mangle with Daisy Mae Esperanza in blue uniforms and kerchiefs like those worn by Laverne and Shirley. They lifted sheets pristinely white from the clutches of padded gears and steam ever so gingerly. They folded same by the corners in a series of lithesome steps which soon took on the character of a minuet composed by the Chevalier Jean-Bapiste Lully so beloved of Sister Marie Pierre who taught Fiona French at Sacred Heart Academy on Washington Street. Daisy Mae was a downtown transvestite, albeit an attractive one, and Fiona's only friend at work. Their nemesis was a gaggle of deaf mutes whose sly glances, hooded eyelids, and silent laughter seemed most unfair. But these handicapped girls, like the rest of humanity, behaved badly merely because they could.

Casimir had all but coaxed Fiona into the sack when he blundered. With the flimsiest of excuses, he blew off a chance to meet the family in favor of attending a fancy schmancy affair at Jersey City's Casino in the Park with a Syrian girl whose skills in the art of fellatio were legendary. Quaffing champagne at the Casino, the festive couple schmoozed for photos that appeared in the *Jersey Journal,* and, pouf, the cat was out of the bag.

Two days later, back at break time in the Monmouth Hotel, Fiona cried bitter, bitter tears on the shoulder of her loyal confidant, Daisy Mae, who, crumpling up the *Journal,* promised vengeance. In truth, none was necessary as Fiona soon took up with a real sweetheart of a guy named Sha-boom. His terpsichorean moves to that tune usually caused admirers to clear the dance floor at places like Mount Carmel in Jersey City. Nonetheless, once Daisy's sisterly fealty was engaged, karma was inevitable.

Daisy Mae journeyed to Hoboken of a Sunday night and discovered from Sal Tortorella at Luigi's Grandevous (located appropriately enough on Grand St., it was one of Casmir's known haunts) that Casimir had already adjourned to Schaefer's Restaurant to top off the evening's carousing with "eggs Benedict and a side of hash." Once there, Daisy Mae quickly maneuvered Casimir into a booth via her come-hither looks and a wisp of Coco Chanel. Never one to half step, Casimir had his hand under her skirt in nothing flat, encountering as he did so a cornucopia of 'guguzeel and manly plums. Not surprisingly, the color drained from his face as Daisy Mae lied, "'Yer sweetie pie Fiona 'tole me to say, 'Bon Appetite!' whilst you was fiddlin' with my vittles." Then seeing a fiery glare welling up in Caswell's hornswoggled eyes, Daisy Mae Esperanza warned loudly enough for all to hear, "And don't you ever try bitch slappin' me, you dipsh*t Casanova, 'cause one false move 'outta you and as sure as God made monkeys and bidets, I'll tear you a new one!"

Nellie the waitress, a raven haired Amazonian

who had quelled many an incipient riot involving Sonny Leone and the Borelli brothers, veered off towards their table in order to nip this insurrection in the bud. Both the raging souls were temporarily silenced by Nellie's baleful stare - a respite Daisy Mae broke with her parting shot, delivered with a look of utter distain, "'Shudda washed 'yo hand first, touchin' my nice clean 'underwears." Casimir seethed. Swishing histrionically to the cacophony of wolf calls and the obscene insinuations of the other diners, Daisy Mae blithely disappeared out through the front door into the susurrant night air.

Knowing of Fiona's fondness for Yeats' poem, "Leda and the Swan," Casimir vowed he'd strangle one of the aforesaid creatures on Spring Lake by way of revenge. Animal cruelty would make quite a splash in the local newspaper and upset Fiona greatly, especially as he planned to write an anonymous letter to the *Coastal Star* more or less identifying himself as the culprit. Bolstering this outlandish scheme, his buddy Libby agreed to punch his time card at Alco Gravure, the graphics firm on 9th and Monroe where they both worked.

Casimir figured this conspiracy would provide him with an iron clad alibi on the night of the gozzling. Slipping out for extended periods of time, sometimes for an entire shift, was fairly common at a union shop like Alco Gravure's.

At first Operation Swan Dive went off without a hitch. On the softest of nights, Casimir and his accomplice, Thomas Pidgeon, found a leaky rowboat loosely tied up at the water's edge of Spring Lake. Thomas, a dog catcher who dreamed of becoming a soldier of fortune, agreed to help because he deemed this mission outlandish enough to merit bragging rights - not to mention a promised case of Miller High Life. From time to time, Thomas made a fast buck delivering stray dogs to testing laboratories in western New Jersey. Always a pragmatist, he brought his dog snare along to capture the swan.

Soon oars clattered in the fuzzy stillness of the night, and a brackish smell permeated the air. The intrepid pair headed straight for a huge white bird which glided majestically across the darkling surface of the lake. Filled with hubris, Casimir murmured, "'Atta boy, you feathery 'ole devil, take your time 'cause come hell or high water, you're 'gonna get yours." Casimir had all but encircled the creature's luminous neck with the snare when out of nowhere an errant black cob snapped at his elbow and honked to beat the band, thus causing Casimir to lose his balance and capsize the boat.

The jig was up. The word was out. Approaching sirens rent the quietude of the evening air. Casimir swore that the gods were punishing him for urinating on the aspidistra plants at the Casino in the Park the week before. Drenched to the skin, he fled through unseen accumulations of pond scum, cursing the swans and the moonlight.

His Devil-may-care companion Thomas merely guffawed, for bitterness was not in his nature- knowing full well folly was but man's due. To himself he recited a verse of doggerel from his youth: "Bathed in lunar silver the privy was still / when the peccaries carried him off / maddened by the excremental swill / bubbling in the trough."

Almost simultaneously, totally unbeknownst to either of the aforementioned adventurers, Fiona finished reading an Irish fairy tale which ended as follows: "... and somewhere off in the starlit twinkling night, the Cosmic Joker showered His blessings on all His children, even the fools."

Gilt Edged Guilt

Georgie Fadeen possessed a certain disarming simplicity few took advantage of, though they might easily have done so. His eyes were of the clearest blue, and it seemed as though he could see into eternity - especially when he was slurping up the creamy residue of a chocolaty soda at Ray's, though many of his betters favored the neon green lemon lime seltzer at Schnackie's. OLG's Father Gilhooley claimed Georgie was something of an idiot savant when it came to religion, as he evidenced an uncanny ability to connect the ordinary and the sublime. For instance, Georgie viewed his beloved egg cream as a symbol of the Holy Trinity: God the Father as the water, Jesus as the effervescent bubbles, and the Holy Spirit as the Bosco flavoring. Together, he claimed, they were something magical indeed.

A restless soul, he wandered about Hoboken in search of tasty soft drinks like Briar's birch beer, a Hawaiian Punch, and Yogi Berra's Yoo-Hoo - sometimes even West of Willow (considered another country by some) to exotic storefronts like Migaleen's where that proprietress was forever stirring a pot of pasta 'vazool. Anything but a scholar, he went to what detractors called the Yap Yap School although he always learned as much as he could. He especially loved baseball, what he could understand of it, and he helped Crazy François set out the bases for umpire Joe at the Little League Field. Unfortunately, he couldn't play a lick, but from time to time he'd doll himself up in the catcher's equipment and beg someone like Ducky Fontanero or Sonny Tyrell to take his picture.

Lovely Nora Gough, one of Georgie's neighbors in the Yellow Flats, was in a terrible quandary. She had inadvertently diddled her fiancé's look-alike co-worker at an Elks Halloween party. At first she'd begged off going to the club, causing her Al, who sported a two-toned mask as the Phantom of the Opera, to leave in a huff. Round about ten, Nora had a change of heart and tagged along dressed as a modern day Dogpatch Daisy Mae - in a black bustier, a garish wig, and stiletto heels. Entering the hall, she never made it downstairs as the Phantom scooped her up in the dark and ravished her on the wooden chopping block in the kitchen. Still masked, he then vanished without a word. Nora was so flustered by this erotic encounter with her beau that she hurried home before ever joining the party below.

The next morning, she learned that Al hadn't attended the party at all. He'd gone instead to play poker downtown at a social club where a fellow teamster, who had lost a bundle, borrowed Al's outfit to scout out the party. They'd just swapped clothing. To make matters worse, Jimmy Roselli's *Mala Femmena* was everywhere on the radio just then. Naturally, Nora feared her farcical affair would see the light of day and, on another level, she just felt unclean.

Such were the thoughts that tortured her heart in the obdurate night. So when next she spotted Georgie sauntering off on one of his jaunts, she detained him, for she had heard he was touched by God. Wanting to believe, she asked, "Have you ever unknowingly done something very bad?" He replied, "Yes, Miz Nora. Scouts honor, I only thought of it today. When I was little, I found a new born kitten asleep in a woodshed. Figurin' the kitty was dead with its eyes shut so tight, I buried it alive in a cigar box lined with satin. Me 'n my friends said prayers. And even though I 'dint mean no harm, I still think of the worms and death from time to time. But then there's baseball and a lime rickey at Abel's. Did you ever see Willie Mays play?"

Nora grinned from ear to ear and said, "No, but maybe I should. Georgie Fadeen, you're sweeter than cotton candy. How 'bout you and me goin' to Gold's for an ice cream sundae?" And his cerulean blue eyes opened wide with delight.

Doo Wop and Poontang's Boomerang

My ex-wife, God bless her wicked soul, used to call the bar I loved a confederacy of dunces. At other times, the Principality of Yahoos. She likewise contended that I was twice blessed because, as the old adage goes, God takes care of drunks and fools. To give the devil her due, it was true that a normal person would be an odd duck in the Horny Porcupine - a bit like tossing a rainbow trout into a school of mesopelagic viperfish, those toothy, bioluminescent denizens of unfathomable depths.

Take Titus Epps. Though 100% old school, he was by far the squirreliest inmate at the Horny Porcupine. That's saying something as this gin mill was, as I indicated earlier, a magnet for twisted souls. A garrulous raconteur when sober, Titus was given to pronouncements of religious profundity when he was in his cups - which was often. One afternoon just as an uninhibited trollop named Cindy scampered up onto a table and stripped to the Dells' recording of "Nadine," Aldo Vercelli - who fancied himself, amongst other things, a poet - chimed in with, "Oh, lithesome lass, wouldst that I could sink my teeth into your gladsome ass. Paradise lost, alas."

But Titus reminded the goggle-eyed throng that "seeking the kingdom of God was serious business with precious little room for deviant frivolity and triflers."

His bushy moustache and his penetrating stare gave him the appearance of a latter-day John the Baptist. The nonplussed ecdysiast continued to wriggle, but Titus's righteous interjection put a damper on the wanton spontaneity of Cindy's pelvic thrusts.

To most he seemed downright spooky - a presence best left unruffled. Occasionally, though, some intrepid wag would expose the comical aspects to his swivets. For example, Titus was inordinately fond of doo wop music, a generous selection of which dominated the jukebox. So, just to inspire yet another of Epps's tirades against hussies and harlots after Cindy's performance, Aldo Vercelli played the Belmonts' "Runaround Sue," calling out as he did so, "Hey, Tight Ass (for such was an alias patrons used for Titus, usually in his absence), this one's for you!" Aldo then poked his tongue in and out of his cheek in a salacious manner as though a phallus were being shoved into his maw. At the propitious moment, he warbled forth an altered line from the tune, "… she goes *down* for other guys."

Apoplectically Titus bellowed, "You miserable scumbag, if there's a God in heaven, you'll be dragooned by sodomites and diddled thrice daily in a cell festooned with mementos of your degenerate past." Smirking, Aldo told him to go f*** himself. Titus responded, "If I could, I'd never leave the house," a riposte that resulted in guffaws and applause, even from Aldo.

Selecting appropriate music as a backdrop for the asininities that occurred at the Horny Porcupine was a specialty of Aldo's. Whenever Cosmo Doodles (nicknamed Cheese) came in to cash his welfare check, Aldo would play the Silhouettes' "Get a Job." But Cosmo had a sense of humor, countering jibes about his unusual name with, "Just call me Quasimodo 'cause you're my ding-a-ling." A playful rapscallion, he'd often tell Aldo to play something by "that divine black chanteuse Elephants Gerald" instead. Nonetheless, Mr. Gilday, the tavern's elderly sage, averred that Aldo was possessed of a fine, iridescent streak of malice - one exquisitely suited to the times.

Oddly enough it was Aldo who introduced Teofilo Ortega, one of the few exceptions to the overall lunacy of the place, to the crazies at the Horny Porcupine - in part because Teo lived right next door to him on Garden Street. Teo, Aldo, and I played for the Hoboken High Redwings football team. Teo was a soft-spoken a guy, but steely and unrelenting if crossed. His father had escaped Castro's Cuba, and Teo inherited his storefront factory for rolling cigars in Union City. Teo was a straight arrow family man with a daughter Vinita whom he pampered shamelessly. Teo's wife, Heidiricia (a makeshift name combining Heidi and Patricia) was Puerto Rican, which didn't endear her to Teo's parents. But she was very attractive - a mercurial woman in whom passions ran deep. She worked at a beauty parlor for dogs and cats on Washington Street. Yuppie dog owners loved it.

Where the trouble between Teo and Heidi began, I can't imagine. Offhand you'd say it had to be something tragic or profound. Truth be told, it could have just as easily been something trivial or absurd. But we'll probably never really know.

Teo and Heidi tried to start the family car which they kept in a small garage on 9th St. between Willow and Park. No go. Only a month ago, Heidi had left an interior light on, which drained the battery. That involved pushing the aging

Buick out onto a narrow street and jump starting the car via another vehicle, which, of course, blocked traffic and caused considerable agita. Now he had to do it again. As the lumbering sedan rolled backwards, Teo cried, "Jesus, woman, shut that door before 'ya screw that up, too." As it turned out, the battery had died on its own with no one at fault.

Hours later, home after their chores, she dissolved in tears, her entire body aquiver with rage and shame. "You'd never speak to any of your friends or family like you did to me. When we first met it was all sweet talk 'n charm. Now I'm dirt under your foot- a lowly handmaiden to my lord and master. But we'll see about that." Teo was shocked by the intensity of her wrath and fell silent, bowing his head because he knew he was wrong – or, at the very least, unwise. He slunk away ostensibly to check on the store in Union City.

A swirl of emotions, all of them negative, took hold of Heidi's imagination. Stranger still, fed by snippets of catechism recalled from her days as a child with the nuns, she somehow convinced herself that Teo would enter the gates of Heaven but she would not. Irrationally, too, she recalled a domineering drake amongst the ducks she raised as a child in rural Puerto Rico – a nasty, curly tailed male named Buttons that pretended to be chasing her when her back was turned for the benefit of his harem. Airing her quaff in the here and now, Heidi sat naked before a full length mirror, lit up a Tiparillo, and smiled. After exhaling a puff or two, she murmured, "I'm not taking this lying down. On second thought, maybe I will. We'll see who's the big man then." She bristled with anger and her coat was glossy and her eyes shone much brighter than any of the pets she groomed.

This much we do know, however. Late one August afternoon so sweltering that the air conditioner over the lintel at the Horny Porcupine leaked out onto the sidewalk like a wounded robot, Teo and I were knocking back a few cervezas when two new guys who worked for old man Trifficante, the Italian roofer, swaggered in during the Mets game on TV. One of them was Uwe Tor, a handsome Aryan drifter, did all kinds of jobs when he wasn't in the hoosegow. They soon got to bragging about their sex lives. Uwe crowed that only last Friday he'd banged a "Rican broad" he met at the Latin Lounge in lower Jersey City." Someone - quite by accident, for Aldo was at home nursing a migraine - played the Corsairs "Meeting in Smoky Places." Bold-faced, Tor continued, "She told her jerkoff husband she was going to Bingo. She got that right. Had a cute little tattoo on her ass, too - a mermaid and the words, 'Todo lo vence el amor.'* Whatever the f***that means."

Teo saw red, and after shoving Uwe's moosh into his own beer, he rocketed out of the tavern with a twenty still on the bar. Couldn't have been anyone else with that tattoo. I'd seen it peeking out from Heidi's bikini on a Belmar beach back in our high school days of suds and surf. Desperate to catch Teo, I accidentally barreled into Uwe, who was already pissed off by Teo's push from behind. We got into it pretty heavy. Uwe bloodied my nose, and he had an ugly mouse under his eye before the regulars tore us apart. I then slipped in that puddle outside the bar and jostled the selfsame Mr. Trafficante, a burly curmudgeon who often stopped at the Porcupine on his way home.

Outraged, he shouted, "You scifoso 'Merigan, a 'fongulo tua sorra!" and flung the cover to a nearby garbage can at me like Oddjob hurling his razor sharp derby at James Bond. Luckily, the battered circle of metal sailed over my head and clattered harmlessly onto the pavement up ahead.

Farther down the street, Mrs. Van Everdingen's bulldog Xerxes escaped her clutches and tore a huge hunk of my gabardines from my calf before I was able to extricate myself from his slobbering jams. Loping along wildly, I then dashed out into traffic on Garden Street. A wild-eyed Hindu on a Honda motorcycle took a dive trying not to knock me into kingdom come – his curses echoing, I'm sure, in nirvana. Suddenly the entire chase seemed a comedy of errors.

However, what I saw when I turned the corner was anything but funny. A blinding sun shone overhead, cutting the hard edges of the street sharper still. Teofilo sat on the stoop his hands covered in blood. Beside him lay a cell phone. Approaching police cars screamed. Across the street Teo's daughter Vinita slung a book bag over her shoulder on the way home from school. Teo looked up at me whispering, almost tenderly, "I slit Heidi's throat with a steak knife. Now I can go straight to hell." With my hand on Teo's shoulder, I counseled, "Would that it were that easy, Amigo"; and the Clovers' "Devil or Angel," wafted forth from Aldo's open window next door.

* "Love conquers all."

CHRISTMAS

A caryatid upholding the topmost facade of an apartment house at 720 Adams Street, a sculptural figure not unlike the impish Pucklike character Hoyt Scheuffler in Hoboken's version of Charles Dickens' "Christmas Carol."

Christmas Tails: Cats, Dogs 'n Rats

Hoboken's Donald Hodle, aka Dipsy Doodle, was mentally challenged - willowy joe from the Projects with concave shoulders and a furtive demeanor even though, as his poor mother often declared, there was no harm in him. He was forever bumming cigarettes, and his fingertips were jaundiced with nicotine from smoking butts down to smoldering nubs. He did odd jobs for pocket money, like staking out the bases for the Little League, burning leaves in Church Square Park for Tony Mike, running errands for miserly shopkeepers, and delivering groceries for old ladies. He came from nothing and often depended on the kindness of strangers. When happiest he would shout, "A fireman's balls!" and he was inordinately fond of Dalmatians.

One day, picking up litter in the park, he found a lovely Celtic brooch with an emerald in the middle. He was going to stick it onto the odd hat he always wore, the one with the jagged edge like Max's in the children's book *Where the Wild Things Are*. But instead he stuffed it into his pocket along with a small box of matches, a stubbed out Lucky Strike, a bent penny, and a dime.

At a rare get-together with her mother and her older sibling Cecelia, Sister Veronica decided to say nothing of the lovely brooch she'd just lost - partly because mentioning it smacked of self-pity and partly because the brooch had been a gift from her father whom her mother, Mrs. O'Flaherty, usually referred to as "a nasty little weasel weaned on booze." True to form, he had upped and left Mrs. O'Flaherty shortly after their son Lawrence was born.

Most times Veronica hid the brooch in the hollowed out pages of an old missal. On special occasions she wore it under her habit - one of the few indulgences she allowed herself against the austerity of her every day existence. As a lit major, this mini-rebellion always made her think of the Prioress and her golden brooch in *The Canterbury Tales* on which the words "Love conquers all" were engraved.

Humorously, Veronica dismissed such indiscretions as "a mere whim in the wimple," not all that different from *The Wind in the Willows,* which she often read to her students at St. Ann's. Cecelia, also a nun, often chided her sister about her vanity, but good-naturedly so.

To lighten what was at first something of an uneasy reunion, Cecelia, a grammar school teacher like Veronica, told a funny story. " 'Yes,' I told my first graders, 'Christmas is when we celebrate the birth of Jesus our Savior.' Then quick as a mongoose, that irascible tyke Rufus Brown added, 'And Halloween is when He rose from the dead!'"

Picking up on that note of levity, Veronica repeated a rumored tale currently making the rounds about their younger brother's posse at college. "Returning from a Seton Hall basketball game in his ramshackle Dodge Dart, Lawrence and his madcap hooligans stopped to purchase beer in the Oranges. Esteban Montoya, who I'm told is as hairy as an ape, shoved his naked buttocks out the window with a cigar protruding from his rectum and asked some old geezer for a light. The caper backfired, though, as the elderly gent, not in the least taken aback, obliged with a Zippo lighter. In the process it set the ample furze on Estaban's posterior aflame - a conflagration which took several painful moments to extinguish."

To which Mrs. O'Flaherty replied, "Honestly, Veronica, sometimes you take things too far. And no matter what you've heard, those boys have good hearts even if their gonads get the upper hand from time to time - much like the *Ginger Man* and *Barry Lyndon* in Irish literature." Veronica rejoined, "Holy mackerel, Mom, I had no idea you enjoyed randy stuff like that." Said Mrs. O'Flaherty, "There's a good deal you two brides of Christ don't know about me, and that's probably just as well."

There was, however, much they *did* know about their mother and about her willingness to bend the rules for her family's sake. For instance, Mrs. O'Flaherty ran numbers back when they lived in Hell's Kitchen. In fact, Sister Cecelia had taken action for her at a nursing home in Far Rockaway where she worked fresh out of the novitiate. Who, after all, the reasoning went, would suspect a woman of the cloth? And, Mother of God, did those *alter kockers* at death's door enjoy a game of chance!

Fatman (Lawrence) O'Flaherty's merry pranksters were called the Horror-ba-loos because of their motto stated, "What the deuce, always shed horror wherever we be loose." One of their early escapades involved barging onto stage, quite unbidden, just before intermission at a Jersey City Teachers College talent contest in order to debut their theme song, a ribald ditty that featured the following refrain: "Take off your clothing attire / And we'll make love by the fire / For the glory of a Saturday afternoon."

Some of their shenanigans bordered on the criminal as when Buffalo McBride hurled a beer can from the upper regions of the Palestra in Philadelphia in order to register his displeasure over a referee's errant call at a basketball game against Villanova. Said can of Schaefer missed the zebra's head by a whisker and exploded, *ka-plat,* midcourt to gasps of dismay from the crowd.

The ride back home to Seton Hall was non-stop, for the bus driver wanted no part of the drunken carry-on prevalent amongst those still conscious aboard the chartered Greyhound bus. Accordingly, wide-mouthed Opici bottles had to suffice as urinals. The ever obliging Buffalo emptied these receptacles onto the cars stopped at various exits along the N.J. Turnpike. For some, the hilarious vision of those windshield wipers displacing a deluge of renal fluids compensated for the hell that the Horror-ba-loos caught back at Seton Hall the Monday following the Villanova debacle.

The Horror-ba-loos were definitely an unusual assortment of humanity as evidenced by Joey "Ratso" Montefusco, so nicknamed due to his facial resemblance to a rodent – that is, a large nose, pronounced teeth, and a receding chin. Which is probably why, subconsciously at least, he organized a ring of dog owners who, as a lark, periodically drove into the City with their terriers and hounds to hunt rats in darkened alley ways.

The snarly curs harried the furry little devils and then gleefully tore them asunder. Joey named this informal coterie of urban stalkers RAT, an acronym for Ravenous Avengers Trencher-fed. Oft times Joey and his comrades bribed the bums they met with a six pack for info as to the beady-eyed vermin's likely haunts. Bemused police looked on suspiciously, but strictly speaking, the practice was not illegal.

Rats were one thing, cats quite another. Years ago when the Horror-ba-loos were known as the Hobos, they ostracized Vasily Poliakoff for burying two stray tabbies up to their necks and then running a lawnmower over them, "just to see the fur fly." Vassi, a Rooskie transplant from Brighton Beach, was much sought after as a goalie when the Hobos played hockey on roller skates in the abandoned tennis courts down by the cricket. But his diabolic cruelty quickly used up whatever good juju his talent had earned him. He became a big Ozzy Osbourne fan after the Black Sabbath star bit the heads off a live dove and a bat, but his name was forever mud with the Horror-ba-loos.

Sammy the Shambling Polynesian, a swarthy imp of a fellow, lived in lower Jersey City. He was drawn to Hoboken because he loved Cal's hotdogs on Observer Highway. Like Dipsy he was "slightly touched" and for a while reigned as the official mascot of the Horror-ba-loos. But Dipsy took over that honor after Sammy proved himself unworthy. Sent out to fetch three meatball heroes from Fiore's, Sammy showed up at the Horror-ba-loos' clubhouse on Madison Street hours later, his faced smeared with marinara sauce. Lamely, his furtive gaze darting left, then right, he taradiddled, "Cump, they jumped me in the park and stole the 'sangwidges." Exile followed a beatdown along with considerable wailing and the gnashing of teeth.

Sammy's banishment was, however, only temporary. Despite the purloined meatball parms, Fatman saved Sammy a possible stint in jail last Memorial Day. Insatiable when it came to food, Sammy had shoved a large Citterio pepperoni down what he called his "skeevy 'underwears where no one wouldn't 'wanna pat 'ya down anyhow" at Rocco Facendola's deli, the Muffi Mart.

But Rocco, a no-nonsense paisan with a body like Hercules, searched him and, pepperoni in hand, called the cops – though not before Sammy, secretly shaking in his boots, got off a wisenheimer line, "'Yo, bro', you sure you got the one you really want?" – this while messaging his crotch suggestively. Nettled by Sammy's snarky tone, Rocco vowed to press charges, but Fatman intervened and got Rocco to change his mind by fixing him up with a secretary at city hall whose shapely rump and bodacious breasts had earned her the code name Abbondanza. Blessedly, the compromised pepperoni went unsold – as a thanksgiving of sorts for favors granted.

Recently at F.I.T. as part of a term project, Francis Singer designed and sewed miniature costumes for several of the figures in the crèche maintained the by Horror-ba-loos – outfits dazzling in their color and gilt. Francis was gay and completely unapologetic about it. For instance, back in high school a snippy classmate named Shaniqua was miffed that he was monopolizing the newest, fanciest sewing machine during Home Ec class. So she waggled her head disdainfully and up in his face asked, "Hey, Sweetums, 'whaddia think you own this thing?" He replied back up in hers, "Well, Missy, it's got my name on it, doesn't it?"

His razor sharp tongue kept many a spiteful bitch at bay. Eventually his feisty outbursts garnered him status as an honorary Horror-ba-loo, sponsored as he was by an older brother Phineas, a Horror in good standing famous for having spirited several white pigeons into Mr. Kolb's piano before an assembly at Demarest High School back in the day. Just as Mr. Kolb opened the piano prior to the National Anthem, the birds flew out to tumultuous applause from both students and teachers. Francis had little truck with the Horrors' bacchanalian escapades, but he liked gussying up the club and its exterior on special occasions.

Sister Veronica had a busy afternoon on her birthday, December 23rd. First she read her best ever Christmas stories to her elementary school students - *The Little Drummer Boy, The Juggler of Notre Dame,* and her favorite, *The Gift,* in which an orphan girl, Maria, nurses a sparrow with a broken wing back to health and then slips into to church with her pet as an offering on Christmas Eve. Maria does so while no else is there, fearing her meager gift unworthy amongst so many packages fit for a king. But when, at the Lord's command, the lowly creature is released from a homemade cage of rushes and twine, it trills the first ever nightingale song and, by way of a miracle, ascends into heaven utterly transformed.

After school Sister Veronica had to deliver Communion to Vincenzo DePasqual, an elderly parishioner who used to set off the fireworks at the St. Ann's Feast until most of his fingers were blown away. Later still, she was scheduled to meet with the Mary and Martha Society to decorate the church altar. But her brother, Fatman, waylaid her on her way back to the convent and practically dragged her to the Horror-ba-loos' haunt on Madison Street for a surprise birthday party.

On display was a gorgeous quilt Francis Singer had embroidered with the covers of such children favorites as *Goodnight Moon* and *Caps for Sale* – an undertaking Fatman bankrolled from his part-time labors at UPS. Several huge, colorful gifts, like a fire truck pedal car and a super deluxe pogo stick, had been purchased for those students who Sister Veronica was sure would have nothing come Christmas morn.

Lurking in the shadows with nothing so grand to offer, Dipsy pulled forth the brooch he'd found and told Lawrence, "Here, Fats, give 'er this." Overwhelmed, Veronica kissed Dipsy on the forehead. After pinning the brooch to Mary's cloak (where, she admitted, it truly belonged), Veronica wiped Dipsy's face with her tears.

Then the Horror-ba-loos, including Sammy, hoisted Dipsy up onto their shoulders and hollered, "Budweiser, Coors, and Miller Lite / Dipsy Doodle's 'gonna drink all night." Veronica said the look on his face was nothing short of beatific. While still aloft, Dipsy bummed a cigarette and exclaimed, "A fireman's balls, this makes up for waking up nights as a kid with rats nibblin' at my toes." And Ratso Montefusco shouted, "Hot diggity dog, Dipsy, have I got a road trip for you!"

A Hoboken Christmas Carol

"The miser hordes gold
like an aged whoremonger
sans testosterone."

- anonymous haiku scrawled upon a Court Street wall

Roddy Mulvany, one of Hoboken's most eligible bachelors, awoke Thursday the morning before Christmas with a woody, which was hardly surprising as his upwardly mobile mistress, Addison Tine, parceled out sex like water in the Sahara - barely enough to keep him alive. Born in Austria, she was, however, quite beautiful in a severe sort of a way and, though of meager origins, very ambitious - the ideal social companion for a small-time Wall Street broker on the rise.

Roddy had inherited his seat on the stock exchange years ago from his father, now deceased, and was doing well enough to vacation in the Hamptons. His spacious apartment had long ago gone condo, the ownership of which he scooped up after shrewdly exploiting his rights as a long time tenant. To those who'd listen, he boasted that if you looked up the word "savvy" in the dictionary, you'd see his picture there.

Such scallywaggery notwithstanding, he retained a genuine affection for his childhood friends, the closest of whom had died only a year ago to the day - Aloysius Finn, an older, larger than life figure who played fullback for the Demarest High Red Wings and then served with distinction as a Marine during the siege at Khe Sanh.

He was more like an uncle than a brother. The war stories he let slip from time to time were for Rodney much more vivid than Hollywood's harum-scarum movies about Vietnam like *Full Metal Jacket*: "Oh, Roddy boy, how that Vietcong artillery made the earth tremble as it sent shrapnel whistling hither and yon, hellacious explosions that made you to grovel in the mud cursing God even as you demanded to be saved." He even wrote some poetry about helicopters and the war:

"...the whirling blades of invisible silver
spewing forth sinuous ribbons of liquid death
downward and dancing in the primordial solitude of Orion's night;
wingéd dragons
scorching the unseen jungles below."

Eventually Aloysius moved to La La Land to cash in on his notoriety as a Medal of Honor winner *a la* Audie Murphy, whereupon Roddy nicknamed him Finn MacCool. Sadly, though, all of Finn's jostling for publicity, his orgiastic marathons, and his battles with double-dealing agents led but to drugs and a lethal overdose of some very high grade heroin. Be that as it may, Finn's advice to eat liverwurst, because it put hair on your balls, still warmed the cockles of Roddy's heart.

Freshly shaven, Roddy listened contentedly to Sal Minella's comical revision of "The Night Before Christmas" on the *Imus in the Morning* radio show, a routine during which St. Nick gets whacked "bidda bing 'wit a pipe." Oddly enough, this bit of seasonal folderol made Roddy think of a tongue-in-cheek jingle Finn had composed during the Sixties race riots in nearby Jersey

City:

"Oh, little town of Hoboken
how still we see thee lie
just shy of that bedlam
where the righteous brothers vie."

However, Roddy soon wearied of such urbane tomfoolery and scampered downstairs to the vestibule to fetch his morning newspaper. He perused a story about members of the Amalgamated Brotherhood of Real Bearded Santas - portly, ruddy faced entrepreneurs who plied their trade at prestigious holiday gatherings for sums that would make hussies blush. *When you've got it, flaunt it,* thought Roddy instinctively turning his attention to the financial page. It mentioned some unsettling possibilities for several stocks he owned - items to keep an eye on as the woods were filled with wolves.

After a breakfast of steel cut oatmeal, boiled to perfection the evening before, and a few cups of expertly brewed Kona coffee, he fussed with the Christmas tree that twinkled merrily, straightening best he could a favorite ornament he'd named Migliacci, an elfin doll in purple satin with a hooked nose, a pointed head, and a sinister mien. Miggi kept matters from becoming overly sentimental. Roddy then donned his Peruzzi full length leather coat and a pair of Louis Vuitton sunglasses and descended the narrow stairwell in stately fashion in order to bustle anew in the town he loved so well - but not before noticing a profusion of sodden newsprint, broken glass, and cigar butts outside the bar that occupied the bottom floor of his building.

Indeed, Muldoon's Shebeen had become the

bane of his existence – what with the noise, the litter, and the rowdy behavior. Such was why Roddy had put in a bid to buy the entire building, ultimately with an eye towards ousting this unruly pub whose lease would soon expire. In its place he hoped to install a cutesy eatery run by his paramour, Addison Tine, one that served crêpes suzette, blintzes, and croissants in the AM and various homemade local favorites for late night boozers in the PM. Its eclectic menu was already in the planning stage, choices that included codfish cakes prepared according to a recipe long ago stolen from O'Grady's delicatessen on Washington Street – not to mention a soupçon of, relatively speaking, peace and quiet for himself. All in due time, coaxed a voice within.

Meandering north, Roddy purchased two Arturo Fuente Cameroon Perfecto cigars on 11th Street and, a block later, ducked into the Elysian Café wherein Giancarlo (aka Gigi) Azzellini, a scrawny codger with rheumy eyes, quaffed a heady draught of Heineken's green death as he perused the *Hoboken Reporter* – a newspaper he once described as "the perfect liner for my parrot's cage." Roddy waved the bartender off as he perched himself on a stool next to Gigi. He gazed at his watch in a pointed fashion by way of emphasizing that, damn it all, he'd have to vacate the premises well before by noon. That's when a horde of Yuppie feminazis descended on the place in their running togs pushing 'Rolls Royce' baby carriages containing creatures named Rex, Skylar, Dakota, and Cokie."

In Ginacarlo's opinion, these Harpies had irrevocably poisoned the reverential atmosphere of a tavern once viewed as a bastion of male camaraderie. A connoisseur of such, he viewed the gilded tin ceiling at the Elysian on a par with the Sistine Chapel. "A shame, damn near sacrilegious, 'cause the devotees who imbibe here after midday are f*** all insufferable." Militantly Italian, the ever-irascible Giancarlo liked to flavor his comments with Celtic obscenities while in Roddy's company - by way of an ethnic jest. "Ah, 'me boyo, stay here too late and 'ya don't know what manner of shite you'll encounter."

Only yesterday, he continued, some Yuppie harridan had pitched her "soon to be patented" invention to him: a whirling gizmo, attached to the lavatory wall, that would wipe your arse lickety-split, no fuss, no muss. Piled one atop the other, scented tissues adhered to a plastic core, the soiled items of which were easily peeled away via a small vinyl tab. "Straight-faced, the aforesaid bimbo shows me a prototype of this monstrosity all ready 'ta go like she 'wuz unveiling the Holy Grail or the missing link," explained Gigi. "So all dramatic-like, I 'axskt her didn't she maybe think deviant types just might put this bung hole plunger to some perverse use instead. See, that was my way 'a tellin' her (did she think I had money?) to shove this egg beater fiasco back up where the sun never shines. But she looked at me like I had two heads and inexplicably smiled. Speakin' of which, what I wouldn't give for a little head right now."

"Don't look at me," said Rodney

"Ah 'fongool, paisano, relax; you ain't my type. As to the 'resta these portfolio-happy douchebag Yuppies, I wouldn't shtupp 'em with someone else's dick." Roddy laughed and pushed away from the bar.

"On another matter I'm sure is 'nunna my

business," Gigi digressed almost apologetically; "I think you're makin' a big mistake dumpin' Heidi Rütschmann, the barmaid at the Shebeen, for that ice maiden you've been seein' lately. Not for nothin', but Heidi's still sweet on you. Yeah, I know she's been around the block once or twice. But it's been my experience, however limited, that girls of easy virtue are often the ones with the most generous hearts - despite prudish bastards like you and me.

"Fair is fair, I'll grant 'ya your Addison has a *really* nice ass, a derrière I figure she 'oughta insure for a million bucks with 'Rhoids of London. Mind you now, I ain't no connoisseur - specially after I stumbled upon my parents when I was only twelve that time the old man was on the vinegar stroke howlin' like a hootchie-coochie man. Guys like you, on the other hand, get an erection just watchin' Shop Rite's can-can commercials. Come to think of it, though, back in the day all things bein' equal, the White Rock Girl used 'ta get me hot."

By then Roddy was long gone without so much as a "bye," and Gigi nodded in the manner of a sage. He finished his beer and headed for Walsh's, a quiet pub where most days a man could savor a drink whilst observing an almost Talmudic sense of protocol and convention.

Gregarious by nature, Roddy fancied himself a roving boulevardier, greeting acquaintances as he did from one end of town to another - especially on the Avenue when sunlight speckled the puddles and the trees, even on a chilly day in December. So bedazzled, he stopped in front of Ziggy Heimlin's pawnbroker shop as the dangling balls of gold, long ago established by the Medici as a symbol for the trade, swung gently overhead. Artistically arranged in the store window was an assortment of gaudy loot people had once prized beyond happiness itself - pocket watches, a flugelhorn, several Pentax cameras, a Waterford vase, and various pinky rings set with diamonds - bodacious booty that enchanted the curious until it was sold for a haggled pittance to some misguided romantic. An emerald stick pin caught Roddy's eye.

Just then Ziggy himself, a classmate of old, emerged from his lair, his hair slicked back and parted in the middle. Rumor had it that Ziggy sported three testicles from birth and was thus fated to become a pawnbroker.

"Word up, mein dude," Roddy greeted Ziggy. "Gotta tell 'ya, 'cumpie, I always love your displays. They're like the glittering flotsam of human existence washed up onto the shore. In the background I half expected to see the tattered garments of the shipwrecked survivors hung up as a tribute to the gods for their deliverance."

"Too deep for me, partner," answered Ziggy, thumping Roddy heartily on the shoulder. "Even so, do you remember the Shakespeare line from *The Merchant of Venice* in high school: 'All that gliltters is not gold; Often have you heard that told'? Well, the Bard got that right. 'Gimme health, a faithful woman, and good tax accountant any day. 'Anyways, I'm goin' over to the Village on the Path to see a revival of *The Sweet Smell of Success* in 'wunna those artsy-craftsy movie theaters and then onto Katz's for a pastrami on rye - a Jew's prerogative on Christmas Eve. 'Wanna join me? The wife's holdin' the fort."

"Nah," Roddy declined, "but I'll walk 'ya part of the way. If he's not too crowded, I'm 'gonna get a haircut at Papito Lindo's. I hate these feathers over my ears." Both strode forth with vigor until they encountered television cameras outside the Sugar Jon-Don Bakery, headquarters for Giovanni Minervini, better known on his reality show as the Prince of Tarts and Layer Cakes. Sugar Jon-Don's wedding cakes were architectural wonders but tasteless. Nonetheless, the line of those wishing to be photographed within stretched almost to the corner.

Amidst all this glitzy hubbub, Aldo Vercelli, an employee of the Hoboken Heritage Society and the author of a reactionary blog entitled "Born 'n Bred in 'Boken," swaggered up and down the avenue bearing a sign which read, "The Prince of Tarts 'n Cake / likes to strut about 'n wiggle his swarthy tush / but I'd just like to see 'im bake / a croquembouche." Envious in the extreme, Aldo found the limelight every bit as irresistible as did the Prince of Tarts.

Roddy and Ziggy tried to sidestep the commotion. But suddenly, with the cameras whirring, Aldo buttonholed Ziggy and Roddy, both acquaintances of his, and exclaimed, "'Yo, Wall Street and the pawn star, better 'youse should get 'yer *pastry* from Joey De *Maestri* down on 'Fort *Street*. It can't be *beat*. 'Jeez, I 'shudda worked on Madison Avenue."

Then *sotto voce,* with a gnarled hand held up to the side of his mouth, he continued, "Really, though, if you're lookin' to impress someone with stuff from the Prince of Tarts, he's got a kiosk over in Penn Station. Give the Rican broad a buck for a box on the sly and then get some really good 'gonnoles from Joey's later on. Best 'a 'bof worlds, you know what I'm sayin'? I mean, the people these 'cavones interview never talk about the *sfogliatelle,* just their photo op with the 'star,' that nebbish in kitchen whites."

Roddy gave him a courtesy chuckle and moved on. But Ziggy proclaimed aloud, largely to set things straight with the TV crew, "And for the record, I'm not a *porn* star. I run a respectable *pawn* shop, not a house of ill repute!"

"Just so, just so, my bad!" Aldo agreed enthusiastically, in an attempt to mollify both his pals and a gaggle of interested onlookers.

"'Jeez, that guy'd give Mother Theresa a case of the ass." observed Ziggy as he and Roddy headed east on First St. to avoid the throng.

"Knows a lot about Hoboken, though," offered Roddy as he stopped to admire Papi's rotating barber's pole. "And I'm in luck," he added peering within. "No one's waitin'. Happy Chunnakah, anyhow, mein Zigzagitude!" Hobokenites prided themselves on off-the-wall nicknames. Mildly amused, Ziggy shook Roddy's hand, wished him a merry Christmas, and disappeared into a maze of bleary-eyed hipsters and disgruntled seniors.

Thus unencumbered, Roddy sidled into the tonsorial parlor of Evaristo Montez, aka Papito Lindo, a time honored establishment that glittered in the prismatic splendor of mirrors, tiles, and porcelain. Papi had just returned from a smoke break out back on his patio, a refuge he'd supplied with ceramic ashtrays and brass spittoons. During the summer months this outdoor area was like a mini-grotto adorned with a fountain and draped with vines and hanging plants, a place he encouraged his customers to use while they waited their turn in the chair.

In no time at all, Evaristo whisked a freshly laundered cloth around Roddy's neck and began snipping away like Edward Scissorhands, all the while commenting on the news of the day. "'Yo, Señor Mulvany, you seen this business 'bout the 'mulanyon rapist yet?" Roddy looked up at the TV to behold the Neanderthalish countenance of the aforesaid thug on the television. "A real *hijuéputa,*" Evaristo continued, "he 'simonized some poor crippled girl for hours in a limousine. That's what straight razors are for. They 'oughta sew 'heez severed huevos up in 'heez mouth." Of diminutive stature, Evaristo struck a pugilistic pose that belied the panache of his pencil line moustache and the snow white tunic he wore.

Once Evaristo tidied Roddy up, he urged him to have a Christmas drink. He had bottles of Bacardi's rum, Jameson's whiskey, and Hiram Walker's anisette all neatly arranged on a serving table with glasses, spoons, and ice - a Hoboken tradition stretching back for ages. Roddy sampled the whiskey and was about to saunter out back to smoke one of the cigars he had purchased earlier, but his cell phone rang.

It was Addison who was visiting relatives in Detroit. Her younger brother Carson had wrecked the family car late last night, and there was no easy way to get to the airport. Besides, her mother was a basket case worrying about Carson, who, thank God, was pretty much okay except for a nasty cut on his chin, poor dear. Bottom line, would Roddy be an absolute angel (she just hated not being with him for Christmas) and put off their reunion for a day or two? Roddy agreed, though without much fervor, and shut off his cell phone in something of a huff.

Looking up at the TV, he observed that his most volatile stock, Paradigm Prophylactics, a Dusseldorf pharmaceutical company that specialized in genetically engineered antibiotics, was having trouble warding off corporate raiders. He mused: panic and sell or stay the course, as in "faint heart fair lady never won." Wondering, too, did disasters really come in threes - the anniversary of Aloysius's death, Addison's phone call, and now this financial tremor? Still undecided, he took a City bound 126 bus by way of a Yuletide diversion. After all, he reasoned, a lot could happen before the closing bell and his interests were covered by a trusted colleague.

But the fat man next to whom he sat stunk like a rutting caribou. On the other side of the river, the Port Authority Terminal was astir with migrant zombies, goose stepping every which way with their eyes fixed straight-ahead. Roddy fled the gathering tumult and wandered over to Fifth Avenue to view the fanciful displays in the windows of Bergdorf Goodman's. The best tableaus featured Jack Frost whose heart melted each time a sexy Tinkerbelle kissed him on the cheek. Ages ago, Roddy's Aunt Agatha gloried in these sidewalk pageantries after she'd bought him a Christmas present at FAO Schwartz a little farther uptown.

Underground on 51st and Lex, a scabrous bum wheedled three bucks out of Roddy for the use of the tramp's Metrocard as the vending machine dispensing transit ticket had been conveniently sabotaged. Later, on the # 6 train headed downtown, a wandering busker played "A Hard Rains Gonna Fall" on a mandolin. When no one coughed up any money, he hollered, "Balls said the stuttering castrato; if I had 'em I'd be B.B. King." Roddy gave him a dollar - for the one-liner, not for the song.

Shortly thereafter at McSorley's Old Ale House, Roddy sat next to a roaring potbelly stove into which a narrowback waiter hurled a sheet of doggerel he had snatched from the hands of a bearded poet who was haranguing customers with his deathless vitriol. "Now it belongs to the ages," bellowed the spunky garçon. A cat meowed in the sawdust underfoot. Moments later Roddy, nearly sated with crackers, cheese, condiments, and ale, read the following carved into the wooden door of the lavatory's single stall: "*Time wounds all heels*. Achilles." Indeed, the fiery mustard seemed to have singed the hair in Roddy's nose, but he knew the like would pass.

Eventually, though, all such amusements palled; and Roddy soon found himself sitting in a rocking chair back home, savoring a hot toddy made from the last few swigs of Tullamore Dew he'd rescued from a cabinet under the kitchen sink. He fell asleep to the rollicking carry-on of the Shebeen below, though his slumber was anything but restful - interrupted as it was by Aloysius Finn in the form of something more than a dream.

Aloysius appeared in a red zoot suit and a pair of blue suede shoes bearing wings just like the sandals of Hermes, the Greek messenger of the gods. Aloysius put his forefinger to his lips, signaling silence and said, "Because I squandered my chances through excess, Zeus sent me here to caution you against a tendency to repress. Obviously, the Greeks are big on irony. Be that as it may, my little Schnibble 'n Bits, we'll travel back and forth in what you mortals call time. Hopefully, along the way, you'll drink from the Pierian Spring,..." Roddy looked bewildered, and Aloysius continued, "...the source of all wisdom and knowledge." Aloysius chucked Roddy under the chin and pinching his neck said, "Like in the old day, 'lemme give 'ya a little 'labitz!"

With that they whizzed through a silvery wormhole in the space/time continuum back to the past. In the process, Aloysius transmogrified into Puck from Shakespeare's A Midsummer Night's Dream – *divine energy and devilment rolled into one. Suddenly, too, Roddy and Aloysius were like smoke drifting above the cuckoo clocks and the silver-capped beer steins in Eric Frobel's Wunderbar, a rustic tavern with a Germanic flavor that catered to the Dutchies whose freighters were docked along Hoboken's Barbary Coast. It was 1959.*

This stretch of unruly bars could be quite ominous at night since young toughs sometimes rolled seamen as they staggered riverward to their sea-going berths. Just then, however, in the early afternoon, all was tranquil and gay. Eric, the proprietor, lumbered about the kitchen tending to a brace of succulent geese, both of which Roddy's father had provided. The Beck's and the Liebfraumilch were flowing freely. Roddy, in this family spectacle, was only sixteen, clad in jeans and PF Fliers. But since it was his mother's birthday, somehow the ABC rules did not apply. As to underage drinking, the rule in many a Hoboken tavern was if you could see over the top of the bar, you could be served.

In any case, Mr. and Mrs. Kaiser, friends of the family, had hung their toddler twins, August und Helmut, from coat hooks on the far wall – suspended via the sturdy Lederhosen they wore. Blond and blue-eyed, the chubby little boys amused each other like mischievous Hummels yammering away amidst the beer, the wine, and the tasty viands. Sheathed in a greasy apron, Mrs. Frobel sang "Der Treue Hussar," and Roddy was sure the Rhinemaidens etched into the mirror behind the bar were winking just at him.

Slowly, though, like the exhalations from his father's Chesterfields, Roddy and Aloysius exited through an overhead vent. Suddenly the wormhole became the Lincoln Tunnel circa 1965; and Aloysius, in a madras shirt and chinos, was at the wheel of a decrepit Dodge Dart, the driver's side mirror of which hung from a cable and flapped along like a metallic goiter. A banged-up Caprice pulled up beside their car with Giancarlo at the wheel. Gigi honked twice and his girlfriend Tina, a go-go dancer at the infamous Meadowlands Inn, performed a maneuver right out of the Kama Sutra, one which planted her bare ass and snatch up against the car window like a Westphalian ham under glass.

Aloysius and Roddy dissolved into an ecstasy of laughter, a distraction which, however, caused their vehicle to bounce off the tunnel's curb and tiles once or twice. Luckily, the cop who zipped by on a catwalk cart chose to ignore the noisy carom. Hours later, after devouring vast quantities of linguini and calamari smothered in hot sauce at the Limehouse on Mott St., the motley foursome retold and embellished the story of their outing in raucous, dimly lit Hoboken gin mills like the Porthole and the Chatterbox until their odyssey rivaled the legendary antics of Greek mythology. "Ah," back in the wormhole, Aloysius asked, "but wasn't this wondrous fine? Much better than the sports bars and the bistros of the Yups where uppity 'slutinas curse like longshoremen. And," he added with a smile, "I hope 'ya noticed how classy that last joint was. They had ice in the urinals."

Safe and sound at home, Roddy awoke with dry

mouth and a pain in his chest. He drank a bottle of mineral water he kept in the fridge. It helped. But the Christmas Eve festivities at the Shebeen were just peaking. In an attempt to banish the attendant noise and the Technicolor visions he had just experienced, Roddy switched the TV onto Channel 13 just as Scrooge was bellowing about the need for more workhouses. Roddy's eyes fluttered, and, in the twinkling of an "I," he and that flamboyant spirit named Aloysius flitted through floors and walls as spirits into the Shebeen below for a taste of the present – not unlike the ghosts that romped through Ebenezer's bedroom.

Above the clack of balls upon the billiard table, they overheard snippets of conversation – some of it, oddly enough, bordering on the profound. For instance, a toothless codger philosophized to an ageing biddy down at the end of the bar, "Harriet, I wonder how many people, knowin' what they do of themselves, would risk an eternity of pain if God said, 'Here's the deal: on the one hand, your soul erased forever with neither the fires of hell nor the hope of heaven ***or,*** *number two, Judgment Day – with endless misery or joy in the balance.' Think about it. Who'd really have the stones to take a chance on that?" Bleary eyed the woman cooed, "Can I have another Harveys Bristol Cream?"*

Towards the middle of the bar, apropos of nothing, Willy Contreras sang a ditty he'd learned on the loading docks of Yellow Freight last Cinco de Mayo, "My name it 'eez Pancho / and I work on 'dee rancho. / I earn two pesos a day. / Then along comes Lucy. / She 'geevs me some pussy / and takes my two pesos away!"

"The story of mankind," rejoined his amigo, Jesus Petulante.

At a table near the door, Tony Lubeck, once a teamster now a luncheon aide at Public School #2, reminisced about days gone by, "Yeah, the first wife left me 'n the kids. She burned her bra and became a feminist. Now she lives in Seattle, tit loose and fancy free." Illogically Gussie Poirot, responded, "You 'wanna know how come all us firemen used 'ta have Dalmatians as mascots?" When no one ventured a guess, Gussie replied, " 'Cause they 'cud always find the hydrants in the snow."

Timmy Peps, a wiry black kid in a pork pie hat, entered the tavern toting his shoeshine box. Only sixteen, Timmy was making money hand over fist in Hoboken shining the Florsheims of Yuppies for whom an itinerant bootblack was a novelty. A crafty beggar, he pocketed more on tips than he did for the shine itself.

The regulars at the Shebeen always treated Timmy as someone special because he was seen as something of a rapscallion taking rubes for a ride. Whenever anyone at the Shebeen ordered up some spit and polish, Heide Rütchmann, the barmaid, played "Chattanooga Shoeshine Boy" or Johnny Cash's "Get Rhythm" on the jukebox. Given such inspiration, Timmy really gave himself over to his work, making every shine into something of a foot massage, tapping the customer's toe half way through to change tootsies on the footrest. Oh, smiling broadly, how he made that boogie-woogie rag pop, even louder than the din of the revelers roistering about.

Meanwhile, knowing he'd be flattered, Heidi, the barmaid, pumped Aldo Vercelli as to what he thought of the quasi cookbook, quasi memoir the Prince of Tarts had written about Hoboken. "Little more than the strained conceits and the anecdotal frippery of an unrepentant recherché popinjay!" came Aldo's learned appraisal.

But, just to stir the pot, Aldo added, "I seen Roddy earlier today." Heidi pursed her lips. "Word is he's squirin' around that witchy woman Addison," Aldo averred, filliping a bottle cap from a puddle of beer out onto the duckboards behind the bar. "She thinks who she is," he concluded.

Heidi glared at him and shouted, "Aldo, you dickwad!"

"What?" Aldo queried. "On 'accounta me dissin' Ms. Athena of Vienna or flippin' that tiny 'bitta metal on the floor?" As no reply was forthcoming, he went on in mock surprise, "Don't tell me you're still pining over Money Bags upstairs!"

"Hey, poopsie, the heart wants what the heart wants," Heidi purred. "Plain and simple, he's still a sugarplum to me. Even so, 'lemme buy you another Sambuca. It might sweeten your disposition."

Grinning like a Cheshire cat, Aloysius asked Roddy, "You gettin' the picture, Poindexter? Despite its asinine crudities and the sinful excesses, despite the shambling rummies and the belligerent yahoos, an unmistakable 'je ne sais quoi' runs through this particular gin mill – the last of its kind in town."

"Je ne sais quoi?" questioned Roddy unbelievingly.

"You know, real, special, authentic! And, oh, that Heidi! What a set of maracas. Even a ghost like me gets a certain frisson."

Such glories notwithstanding, this insubstantial pageant also faded, and the focus changed to the Grill Room at the Elks. The barkeep, Buzzie Perneau, Hoboken born and bred with hands the size of ham hocks, dabbed dolefully at some imaginary droplets on the bar while Ziggy Heimlin cursed the college kids from Stevens who had once again painted the testicles of the bronze Elk blue."

"Ruins the curb appeal for sure," offered Buzzie dispiritedly.

"They should suffer a similar fate, blue balls I mean, and their girlfriends get the 'syph," Ziggy continued. "And only last week, Jerry Moran had a run-in with those dingbats from the Society Against the Beastly Treatment of Animals. Their goggle-eyed president rented the great hall for a meeting and tried to hide the herd of antlers we got up there under sheets – dirty ones at that. The mashuggeneh 'bastid, what'd he think he'd find at the Elks – taxidermied cauliflowers? Jerry threw 'im out on his ear."

Buzzie chuckled in spite of himself just as Alfredo Tortorella, all 115 pounds of said Inner Guard, scurried into the bar from the back room where the Association of Rarefied Teachers and Parents from the local charter school was running its annual Christmas Eve Trivial Pursuit Tournament amidst an ungodly din. "Holy 'schagit, get a load of this. Comin' back from the 'bockhousa, I zigzagged through these yammering assholes and this one four-eyed geek asked a question 'bout the mating habits of seals as part of some freakin' game called Sexual Prosciut'."

*"Jesus, Alfredo," offered Buzzie after he wiped tears of laughter from his eyes, "you 'cud f*ck up a wet dream."*

Ziggy agreed, and gazing at the smorgasbord of cold cuts on the sideboard opposite the bar he mused, " 'Ya know, 'fellas, that liverwurst and sliced onion make me think of Aloysius, God rest his tortured soul. What a pisser that guy was for all his faults." Buzzie, a lugubrious butcher for a meat market downtown, nodded wistfully.

"And look around this rag 'n bottle shop of the heart,"

Ziggy maundered, waxing eloquent – his third Wild Turkey having taken hold. "'Whatta we got? 'Cept for the old timers, mostly shysters, realtors, and tin pot politicians. Nowadays seems these young guys join the club just as a business strategy – soulless mercantilism, if you asked me. God help us all, some day these jackals will be in charge."

Drumming the fingers of his right hand on the bar, Buzzie answered, "Yup!"- 'mercantilism' notwithstanding.

Further up the bar near the pinball machine, Giovanni Minervini, the Prince of Tarts, discussed civic pride with Xavier Lopez, an attorney with the city who served as an usher at Our Lady of Grace Church on Sunday. "Take, for instance, that cake sale I organized to raise money for the St. Mary's Hospital last Mother's Day," boasted Giovanni. "It went viral and raised a fortune, 'kinda like the mustard seed in the parables." From afar Ziggy could smell self-aggrandizement wafting in the air.

Said aromatic metaphor made Ziggy aware of the barber, Evaristo Montez, whose aftershave, even three stools away, was coming on rather strong. This wily Lothario put his arm around Geraldine Agusto, a cheerleader gone to seed twenty years his younger. Nudging her to the door, he whispered, "And as to you, my 'lee-til Bo Peep, we have a domicile to defile before we sleep."

"Better be the York Motel, you Rican sugar daddy," she cautioned, " 'cause my parents'll be home from A.C. pretty soon. I can't get tossed out before I find another job, and your wife sure don't 'wanna see me come the bewitching hour"

Cigarette smoke, though forbidden, drifted through the triangle of light poring forth onto the pool table towards the rear of the room. Dr. Kressler, soused beyond belief, pushed the glasses back onto the bridge of his nose as he lined up a bank shot in the corner pocket. Swaying left and right, Doc waited until he achieved the apex of his pendulum-like movements and struck the cue ball right as rain.

Whispered Xavier to Giovanni, "Doc always stuffs his winnings into that School for the Blind Box behind the bar. That's how come no one wants 'ta play 'im. Shames 'ya 'inta doin' the same. Shouldn't be smokin' in here neither. Believe it or not, he fell down the stairs to his office a week ago but got only that bump on his forehead."

Giovanni replied, perhaps a tad too loud, "God takes care of fools and drunks, so he was twice blessed."

The eight ball zipped into the corner pocket as planned. Smiling wryly, Doc grabbed the Prince of Tarts by the throat and would have throttled him soundly had not Ziggy and several others finally gotten the elderly physician calmed down – during which struggle the doctor's pants fell to his ankles. Xavier looked for skid marks but found none.

In the twilight zone where they hovered, Aloysius observed, with mischief shining in his eyes, "Not bad for a Christmas eve. Too bad the place is open only three days a week. The camp of the saints gets ever smaller." During a lull, Owney Mahone, a retired stevedore, sang as sweetly as he could, "...what more diversion can a man desire / than to sit him down by a snug turf fire / upon his knee a pretty wench / and on the table a jug of punch.'

And before the clock ticked eleven, "the golden hour of recollection," Roddy resurfaced gasping for reality through the mists of sleep around his rocking chair. The cable had gone out, so there was nothing but static on the TV. Roddy peered out his second story window, and across the street a thin tracery of snow spread across the sidewalk like the tattered hem of a wedding gown. So cold were the darkened streets, it seemed the errant sheets of newspaper tumbling about hither and thither would shatter rather than tear.

He hadn't felt so desolate since that Christmas Eve in the drafty, dimly lit billets of a German kaserne during his stint with the 4th Armored Division. Back from maneuvers, he and his buddy Rogulich heated *Glühwein* in a canteen cup atop a hot plate while they gazed out into the dreary motor pool where the wind whistled through the assault vehicles and half-tracks languishing there.

Switching off the TV, Roddy took half an Ambien. The cobwebs of sleep, those gossamer threads of what seemed to be inevitability, enveloped him anew.

Once again Aloysius rousted him, and they flew into the future as a pair of dusky seagulls, kiting through the bluster and the flurries unto Failla's Funeral Parlor on the corner of Sixth and Willow where the Elks were conducting a solemn funeral ceremony for Roddy. In the cloying stillness of a wake, the Exalter Ruler bade the Lecturing Knight to call the roll. Slowly the Lecturing Knight read the names of several Elks who answered, "Here," in muted tones. Then he called Roddy's name three times – pausing after each attempt. As per the ritual, the Exalted Ruler proclaimed, "He does not answer."

"If he does, I'm 'outta here," whispered one of the pallbearers to another. Both stifled their mirth, just barely. Such buffooneries were not altogether heartless since none of the Elks present had known Roddy. All his friends were dead or in nursing homes.

Seeing Roddy cringe, Aloysius cautioned, "It doesn't have to be this way, you know. Nothing's writ in stone. It's just what you might call a logical progression."

"You call any of this logical?"

"Good point, but you know what I mean. A stitch in time obviates many a crime."

"My God, Aloysius, I just 'wanna go home."

"Ah, there, too, is something to be learned," Aloysius volunteered as they whooshed off in that direction, a bit farther into the future. They sailed past Roddy's apartment house which was transformed into a multi-tier parking garage complete with faux windows and shutters designed to make the place still look like a dwelling. An ominous hum emanated from the structure like that of a robotic Minotaur. Roddy groaned.

With that, they headed off east across the Hudson even as below white caps leapt into the slurried night. In nothing flat they perched upon a ledge of Rockefeller Center peered into the on-going merriment of the Rainbow Room. Within, a childless widow named Addison Mulvany mixed among politicians and machers at a $1,000 a ticket meet-and-greet cocktail party. Martini in hand and dressed to the nines, she sashayed over to an elaborately decorated casement and looked down at those milling around the lighted Christmas tree. To a boy-toy dancing attendance upon her like a page at King Arthur's court, she burbled somewhat cynically, "Oh, Austin, how magical are life and humanity when viewed from afar."

"Do not despair, Bunkie," urged Aloysius, "only one more stop in our futurama journey through time - gruesome though the layover may be." They landed in a garden behind a luxury home in South Hampton on Long Island. The door to a lonely shed creaked open, and Aloysius's appearance and his demeanor changed. Maggots wriggled about in his eyebrows, and his breath was earthy strong. Wrapped in a

shroud, Aloysius put his hands together as though to pray while bits of desiccated flesh came away like papier-mâché. Crowlike, he croaked forth a single word, "Behold!" and with a long bony finger pointed towards a neglected workbench. Thereupon, barely visible, a tarnished urn containing Roddy's ashes stood next to a jar of rusty screws. Roddy collapsed.

But when he awoke the next morning spread-eagle on the couch, the living room was filled with brilliant sunlight. Church bells echoed in the distance. Roddy turned on the radio, and the Drifters sang, "...dut-dadutta-dut, I'm dreaming of a white Christmas..." Across the street a dusting of snow remained. Strangely, Roddy was elated. Fiddling with his smart phone, he learned from an insider that Paradigm Prophylactic had actually benefitted from takeover attempts of the previous day. He kindled a blaze in the fireplace, and white smoke flew up the chimney as though a new pope had been elected. Amidst the needles of the Douglas fir, even Migliacci's sardonic smile seemed to have softened.

A week later of a chilly evening, Roddy strolled along the avenue with Heidi on his arm. They had just purchased a Christmas Pyramid at a crafts fair in Lambertsville earlier that day. This Yuletide fixture, much beloved of Germans, was an eyeful what with its colorful candles, its revolving tableaus, and the cutesy heat-driven propeller at the top - an ornamental device made all the more bizarre by the addition of figures like Mighty Mouse to those of the angels and the Three Kings. Heidi thought this bit of folk art wonderful, pronouncing it "surrealistically Christian." They got it for a steal because Weihnachten was *vorbei.*

Roddy had cancelled all plans to eradicate the

Shebeen. He told Heide about some of his Christmas Eve experiences with Aloysius - concluding that, ultimately, what Aloysius had wanted most out of life was to get laid and watch sugarplums dance in his dreams. "You could do far worse, *Schatzlein*," Heide murmurred.

As the couple reached the Shebeen, they watched a local thug, Hoyt Scheuffler, being frog-walked out of the tavern amidst a cacophony of obscenities. His face was lumped up considerably and his nose bled profusely. Suddenly, Roddy sensed deep from within, as might a juju man, that like it or not he had bequeathed the rowdy city of his birth a splendid remnant of the past - a gin mill in which you could still savor a Slim Jim, shoot a game of eight ball, and have a pool cue cracked across your back. Hoyt, whose face looked like a ripped softball, was hurled out into the night. But through a film of phlegm and spittle, he vowed, "You ain't seen the last of me!" Just then Timmy Peps happened by, hollering in his spritely fashion, "Shine 'em up, mistah?" Hoyt's was a visage upon which you couldn't tell a grimace from a grin. As Benny Hill once put it, "How do you define the 'intangerine?"

Pygmalion and the Chestnut Tree

Two weeks before Christmas, a spate of thefts involving all manner of outdoor religious statuary - plastic, ceramic, and metallic - inspired the following letter to the editor of the *Hoboken Dictatorial*: "What kind of a *sfacim* steals from a crèche? Whoever it is, I hope they make room for him at the inn - the Rahway Pris-inn, right next to a guy named Ben Dover. *Rafaella Streganona.*"

In the same issue, Zack Flackhart's Mr. Tattletale column likewise drew attention to the aforesaid stolen effigies, deeming such iconoclastic thievery "the perfect distillation of the loathing many feel for the gaudy exploitation most religions foster." Usually, however, his column was devoted to nettlesome gossip about fellow Hobokenites, earning him the unofficial alias of Charlie Bubbles, a nickname possessed of more than a little irony as Zack was anything but effervescent. His caustic, skeptical nature rendered him a trifle glum.

Nonetheless he enjoyed a wide range of acquaintances and friends, one of whom was Cicero Minervini who spent much of his free time maintaining a chapel down on 5th & Adams, one which housed a rare statue known as the Black Madonna. Deeply religious, Cicero was immersed in Catholicism, but this fervor didn't blind him to the spirituality of others.

For example, he cherished his friendship with

Rabbi Lionel Ziprin, the Jewish mystic and poet of the lower east side, whom he met by chance after WWII. This hipster Talmudist, who looked like Walt Whitman on leave from a shtetl, was purchasing inexpensive underwear in Brodie's clothing store after visiting Hoboken's United Synagogue on Park Avenue. Cicero took the rabbi's words of wisdom closer to heart the older he himself became: "It is one of life's paradoxes- as our bodies falter and decline, one's spirit can become radiant like a taper flickering in some dank cellar and then soar like the Phoenix." Departing Brodie's, the old man gave Cicero a handful of Noble chocolate coins, which Jewish people often hand out around Hanukkah. Cicero never forgot it.

Childless, Cicero took many poor souls under his wing, among them Lazlo Jugovitch, a mildly retarded boy of sixteen whose mother died of MS and whose father had run off to drown his sorrows in booze and despair. Lazlo lived with an aunt who had three children of her own to raise. Cicero paid Lazlo to help in the upkeep of the chapel. After he made the altar sparkle, Lazlo loved to view it from the tiny loft that housed the organ. Then he'd treat himself to some Italian pastries from Scarpulla's Bakery next door - or next store, as people from Hoboken are wont to say.

To the untrained eye, Cicero seemed to be a run-of-the-mill guy. In truth, however, he was a bundle of contradictions. For example, he was an avid reader, but this did little to offset his Hobokenese, referring as he did to 'burgulars, 'the viadock, and his 'prostrate gland. Though a skilled handyman, he nevertheless earned his living as a stooper, someone who collects discarded tickets at racetracks and betting parlors in the hope of retrieving winners. Technically this is against the law, but racetrack officials look the other way as long as the stooper doesn't cause any trouble. Cicero had a deal with several OTB agents who would run his tickets through their scanners for a percentage of the profits.

Occasionally, too, spending as much time as he did at the track, he would stumble upon a reliable tip or two. Such was the case with an impossible long shot named Howsyerbraciole, due to run at Aqueduct that weekend. Surprisingly, this flighty thoroughbred enjoyed some local notoriety - through Mr. Tattletale. As a matter of fact, its trainer, Artie Biancosino, swore that his horse thrived on artichokes, of all things. Biancosino's friends, Luigi and Carlo Ascolese, dispatched several bushels of this unorthodox feed to Artie from their produce store on First Street. Charlie Bubbles played the whole thing up in his column- all of which piqued Cicero's interest in the horse. On an impulse some might have deemed borderline insanity, Cicero put a hundred down to win on Howsyerbraciole with Joe Bush, a local bookie.

Several days before the race, Cicero made a disquieting discovery. It was Lazlo who had stolen those decorative Christmas statues. By day he had hidden them in the sacristy, and by night upon the altar he mingled with Mary, Joseph, the Magi, and a much beleaguered shepherd who looked like death warmed over. Jesus was absent because Lazlo reserved that role for himself, playing make-believe just as he used to with his teddy bears and other stuffed animals in the rear room of his parents' apartment, on the very same bed his mother later withered away forever.

Cicero made short work of this dilemma, one he

called "the innocent gone awry." Using a jigsaw, a drill and a rivet gun, he hinged the back portion of the life-sized plastic Madonna and positioned her near the altar but behind a narrow wooden stand on which he had placed a single votive candle. He then convinced his niece Febronia to impersonate the Blessed Mother since she had already been tricked out to appear as the Madonna in a tableau to be staged at St. Anne's during Advent.

Early the next evening, Cicero and Lazlo entered the chapel, which was dark but for the lonely candle. Dressed in a diaphanous costume of blue and white, Febronia stepped out of the plastic statue and murmured, "My poor banished children of Eve, say the rosary and sin no more." With that, poof, the candle went out. Febronia vanished like a phantom of delight.

Cicero switched on the overhead lights, and Lazlo's eyes bulged in amazement. Cicero patted Lazlo on the back and explained that although the Blessed Mother knew Lazlo meant no harm in assembling the Holy Family, he was sure she wanted people to have their statues back in time for Christmas. Lazlo nodded, indicating that he understood.

Together, in the still of the night, they carted all the Nativity figures to Fifth and Bloomfield Street. They stowed them beneath an enormous chestnut tree, perhaps the only one to have survived America's chestnut blight and still bear fruit. Naturally, the newspapers had a field day with the anonymous return of the prodigal icons – especially Mr. Tattletale, who had an inside track via his buddy Cicero. Just a week and a half before Christmas, Howsyerbraciole came in at twenty to one.

Temporarily rich, Cicero bought his nephew, Maurice, a Keuffel & Esser self lubricating log-log duplex decitrig bamboo slide rule at Sorkin's so he could shine in Max Clemkeit's after school tutoring sessions and thereby one day gain admittance to Steven's Institute on the hill. Never one to hold back, Cicero also purchased a Hohner Chromonica harmonica for Lazlo because he imitated Johnny Puleo of the Harmonicats so well, using just the el cheapo mouth organ his father had given him ages ago.

On Christmas Eve, Charlie Bubbles joined Cicero for a celebratory drink at Duke's House, opposite the Lackawanna Train Station. Cicero showed Charlie Bubbles a blurb about Hoboken's "miracle" chestnut tree in a back issue of *National Geographic*. The magazine sharply contrasted this tree's remarkable immunity to the blight with the untimely disappearance of Hoboken's ginkgo bilobas on Garden St., trees which had been imported with great fanfare from China.

These arboreal revelations appeared right next to an article about the Major Leagues' use of Lena Blackburne's Baseball Rubbing Mud – a primordial, near magical sediment harvested from a secret location in New Jersey. True to form, Charlie disputed whether the chestnut tree really constituted a *miracle*. After all, even Dresden and Hiroshima boasted of survivors. He emptied his jigger of Cutty Sark in a single victorious pull.

But moments later, noting how often Cicero dabbed at his eyes with a handkerchief, the Tattler asked what was the matter. Cicero replied with muted sadness, "My ophthalmologist, Dr. D'Alfonso, says I have 'immaculate degeneration." Despite Cicero's malapropism, this was more or less true, for the blessings and the woes we humans experience this side of Paradise are often quite mixed. Cicero quaffed his Chianti and silently recalled the doctor's oft repeated paean to the importance of one's eyes: "Not only are they windows to our souls, they are the searchlights of our reason- our most reliable means of understanding the world around us." Pondering the like, Cicero suddenly found the doctor's observation quite unsettling, for saintliness aside, he was still very much a creature of this realm.

Shortly thereafter Cicero regained his good spirits even as he sat in Dr. D'Alfonso's waiting room beside an obstreperous octogenarian who wore a patch over his right eye. From time to time this grumpy old man paced about the crowded office in a restless manner and complained to his wife about the endless delay. Apparently inured to the like, she steasfastly ignored his peevish grumblings. In desperation the *alter kocker* then turned to Cicero and kvetched, "For an hour, can you believe it, I've been poked 'n stroked by assistants for tests - collecting data, collecting data. But I still haven't laid eyes on the doctor.

Perhaps unwisely, Cicero replied, "I believe in your case that would be eye." Thus embittered, the irascible codger glared at Cicero as best he could, just as the Cyclops might have stared at Odysseus before that intrepid wanderer and his shipmates gouged out the giant's single orb with a glowing timber. But Cicero smiled serenely, and somewhere Odysseus sailed homeward under Athena's watchful gaze.

MISCELLANY

An aerie at 260 Eighth Street between Park & Willow from which vantage point Methuselah Oblongadavita's Zen Bowmen slew evil avian creatures sent to kidnap little girls in the fairy tale "Gryphons 'n Hillies."

Losing Face

"The Irish are a race of people for whom psychoanalysis is of no use whatsoever!"

- an assessment commonly attributed to Sigmund Freud

Knobby Hufnagel's head, ghastly with eyes turned heavenward, sat neatly on one of the ball returns at Adams Lanes. Detective Harvey Quatsch had examined the other somewhat squishy remains of Knobby earlier that morning on Court St. where they had been stuffed into a fifty-gallon drum and then covered over with potato peels, coffee grinds and an assortment of crushed soda cans. The blood trickling forth from a puncture near the bottom of the container was a dead give-away.

By lunch time, word on the street had it that poor 'ole Knobby, both homeless and harmless, was a sacrificial lamb of sorts. Everyone knew who his killer was, Yoriboy Escalante, a low level drug dealer who often used his own mildly retarded sister as a carrier in his transactions. Her innocence made exchanges less intense, and she liked to be useful to her brother, whom she adored. Sadly, one evening in March she was robbed before she ever reached Yoriboy's client.

Word travels fast in these circles. She was then held hostage by Eddie "Big Man" Obote well before she could once again nestle safely beneath the protection of her brother's wings. Obote was Yoriboy's supplier, an untouchable drug lord from that Byzantine Empire known as Jersey City who decreed that if Yoriboy wanted his beloved sister back unharmed, he would have to produce either the purloined loot or the head of the son-of-a-bitch who'd stolen it. So, at wit's end, Yoriboy decapitated Knobby in an abandoned garage, figuring nobody'd much miss the bearded bum anyhow. In his haste, he paid a drifter named Horace Boits to get rid of the body as best he could. Yoriboy then delivered his grisly ransom, nicely ensconced in a shoeshine box, to Obote behind the bowling alley at a pre-arranged time, whereupon his sister was released and both of them wisely fled to parts unknown.

Later still, one of Obote's lackeys slipped into Adams Lanes and deftly deposited Knobby's cranium on the return just as the afterhours janitor was stowing his mops and such. Obote suspected that one of his operatives, an employee at the bowling alley, was jacking up the price of his coke and pocketing the difference. As Obote saw it, Knobby's bloody visage might well put an end to that - thus killing two birds with one stone, as it were, intimidation serving as a powerful incentive to straighten up and fly right. Eventually, Knobby's head was reunited with his body in the Essex County Morgue.

As anticipated, newly elected Mayor Hortense Quimby cancelled Hoboken's St. Patrick's Day Parade, a decision bolstered by the deluge of urine emanating from the vestibules of residents during parades in the past. Not to mention the flower pot that was hurled down upon Fireman Gus Koschig whose manly contingent was responding to one of many emergency calls during the parade last year. Fortunately, as a lark, he was wearing the spiked helmet his great grandfather had worn in Germany during WW I, and the damage was minimal. Be that as it may, the cancellation edict so infuriated an Irishman nicknamed the Tam O'Shanter that he published an open letter to the mayor in the *Hoboken Pictorial* denouncing her decree. In it he wondered aloud (for he later read the letter in city hall) what mayhem would have transpired had the mayor dared to redline the St. Ann's Feast, "Hoboken's other ethnic extravaganza." In response, a group known as Garibaldi's Downtown Carbonari sent the Tam a bag of sardines at the Elks along with a note that read, "Finn Mac Cool sleeps with the fish."

Undaunted, the Tam finalized plans for the Elks to stage an "impromptu" parade of their own. After all, preparations for the outlawed procession were already afoot: Vinny Wassermann's Gaelic marauders would provide the music and the Cunning family from Willow Terrace, founders of the original parade, would lend the march an air of authenticity. Moreover, Jeremy Fay, a cosmetologist for Failla's Funeral Home, who also dabbled in haute couture and porcelain figurines, had just spent a month fashioning a life-sized representation of St. Patrick to be seated upon a cathedra he had purchased at a local antique store. Fr. Manente, an honorary Elk, provided Jeremy with a chasuble (green in color) and an alb - priestly garb well past their prime. These Jeremy draped over a jointed mannequin he used for his numerous sewing projects. A perfectionist, he also created a porcelain head and porcelain hands, complete with stigmata - even though St. Patrick never suffered the like. Attaching them was a painstaking affair.

But the effort was worth it, for the saint's countenance exuded an ethereal quality - Celtic, otherworldly, and beautiful in its own right. Ricky Geppetto, carpenter par excellence, had weeks before cobbled together a litter painted gold with sturdy handles for carting the statue about. Fr. Manente smoothed things over with the slightly less offended Societa Madonna dei Martiri - so much so that they agreed to carry the statue of St. Patrick for the Elks on St. Patrick's Day. The way the Tam figured it, their participation would provide the renegade parade the imprimatur of widespread public support.

Witnesses had seen Horace Boits skulking about Court St. where Knobby's body had been found. Because Quatsch considered hobos a superstitious lot, he planned to swipe Knobby's noggin from the morgue in Newark and use it to spook Boits into testifying against Escalante, assuming they could ever locate said killer. Doctor Alphonse Genovese, Quatsch's longtime acquaintance, afforded Harvey access to Knobby's remains as a matter of course, resting as they were comfortably in a refrigerated vault.

Luckily for Harvey, Genovese, an unkempt, albeit vivacious member of the medical community, was easily distracted by the sports page on which Harvey had circled his selections for the Freehold races that weekend. Quatsch's expertise in such equine matters was legendary. Shortly thereafter Harvey departed the coroner's facility with Knobby's head in a bowling bag that he had filched from the lost-and-found bin at Adam's Lanes. None too soon for Harvey since the aromas of formaldehyde, death, and liverwurst sandwiches that permeated the otherwise antiseptic environs of those morbid chambers in Newark, were overwhelming.

Thirsty after his unsuccessful efforts to find Boits, Harvey ducked into the Elks where Jeremy was beside himself. Last night some drunken yahoo had accidentally shattered his magnificent porcelain visage of St. Patrick. "And the parade's tomorrow!" Jeremy screeched to all in the Grill Room. Quatsch took Jeremy aside and showed him the contents of the bag. Jeremy was aghast. "Tell me you're not suggesting...?" he whispered. "Oh, but I am," answered Harvey, "and if you can pull this off, in years to come, you'll become an underground cosmetological *legend* - just like me with the horsies!" Vanity was the way to Jeremy's heart. After fetching his maquillage materials from Failla's, he afforded Knobby's face a celestial blush not quite alive in any earthly sense, but most assuredly not dead. Harvey then affixed the final product to the wooden mannequin using shuriken spikes pointed at both ends, items from his martial arts collection.

The parade went off without a hitch. An Irish wolfhound whose testicles were lathered green with greasepaint set a lively pace for the marchers behind. (The dog's owner, Oney O'Shaughnessy, told reporters the dog looked forward to it every year.) Characters abounded, Quatsch included (but no officials). Tam O'Shanter, his crown derby tilted rakishly over one eye, strode manfully along Frank Sinatra Drive despite the uneven cobblestones underfoot. Confronted by a *Jersey Journal* photographer, he straightened his green bow tie with one hand and gingerly grasped his blackthorn stick with the other, a bit of ornamentation which was thick enough at its apex to pass as a cudgel. His sartorial splendor stirred approval amongst those disinterestedly watching Hoboken's hurling team, the Guards, who charged up and down the grassy field to the left of the parade in a match the mayor hoped would appease the Irish.

Suddenly, however, it seemed out of nowhere, a leathery ball called a sliotar sailed towards Tam O'Shanter with murderous intent... that is, until someone cried, "In-coming!" and Tam, supple as a hooligan at the Donnybrook Fair, struck the sphere an ungodly thwack with his gargantuan stick and sent the menacing sliotar whistling back through the uprights for a point. Both those in the line of march and those assembled on the pitch roared bright-eyed approval – though the umpire failed to raise the white flag. Tam O'Shanter barely broke stride, blithely twirling his blackthorn as he hummed a few bars of "The Wild Colonial Boy."

The parade was, of course, not without a modicum of unruly carry-on. A rerouted bus bearing a huge advertisement for Meryl Streep's movie about Margaret Thatcher, *The Iron Lady*, turned the corner on 11th and Hudson. Seeing the like, Roddy Mc Feeley, even more toothless and inebriated than usual, dropped his trousers (already at half mast), shoved his genitalia rearward (his motto being: "Semper commando"), and bellowed, "Here's an Irish fruit bowl for 'ya Majesty's high tea." Puzzled onlookers were nonetheless appalled, and Roddy was promptly arrested (albeit not pummeled) – none the wiser for having confused the prime minister with the Queen. Except for this mishap, the parade was a fairly dignified outing, especially since the Societa Madonna dei Martiri proved so adept in the transportation of the Blessed. However, as though to set matters straight ethnically, riverward the remnant of an old Todd Shipyard's drydock sign read, "No wake." Beneath it someone had spray painted, "Not even Finnegan's."

Immediately following the parade, Quatsch spirited Knobby's skull into the boiler room at the Elks where under lock and key he spruced it up using cold cream, exfoliates, and some good old soap and water. After which he departed the club in hopes of snagging Boits. However, once outside he ran into the mayor, who buttonholed him in an affable way and purred, "I have to admit, although unsanctioned, your parade was a first class affair. But, if you do it again next year, I hope you'll give me a heads-up." Harvey, still gripping the bowling bag, grinned from ear to ear - just long enough to allow the words of his redoubtable grandmother, Siobhan O'Sulleabhain, to permeate his memory like the sound of Angelus bells. "The Irish harbor an abiding sense of tragedy which sustains them through brief periods of joy."

Bah Bah and the Larcenous Yahoo

Back when the following events took place, Hoboken was still in its golden age, one perhaps best typified by the joy attendant upon the pigeons which flew out of Mr. Kolb's piano when one afternoon he started playing the National Anthem at an assembly in A.J. Demarest High School. For many the music, the laughter, and the flight of those birds served as a metaphor for the plebian delight that seemed to abound in a city some called the Mile Square Miracle.

Admittedly, it was a community with more than its share of egotistical hedonists. But one which somehow made a place for such misfits as Crazy François, Powerhouse Arnold, and Bah Bah, the janitor at the high school, that burly dwarf with the thick Coke-bottle eyeglasses and a profusion of jingling keys - a macabre bundle of energy who could neither speak intelligently nor hear but made himself understood via a face aquiver with emotions and a voice alive with wordless approval or dismay. To the rabble he was a real life Hunchback of Notre Dame - a creature who had no existence outside the edifice in which they found him. To his parents Vito Rosella was a blessing and a son.

A Baby Boomer heaven, the city was, of course, awash with children - many of them hungry for adventure. Accordingly, these daredevils zoomed down Murder Hill into traffic on sleds, swam in the moonlit caffeinated brine that lapped up against the Maxwell House pier, and fetched rides on the freight trains that rumbled along Hoboken's western fringe. As an initiation into this gang or that, they clung white-knuckled to a hawser tied to a girder and swung from a dusty cliff beneath the viaduct to a stone pillar some fifteen yards away. Letting loose over such a gaping void and alighting on the ivy covered stone was what Gypo Lynch, the leader of the Giddy-o Rangers, called a Kierkegaardian leap of faith. Gypo's older brother was a divinity student. So Gypo was way ahead of the others in philosophy – though he bore, like Everyman, his share of bestial impulses from the nether realm. When the moon was right of a summer's night, he and his band of adventurers hunted cats with sticks and cardboard tubing. Such was their connection with the ancient Greeks and the Bacchante.

Bah Bah, like many handicapped people, took his job quite seriously. Having swabbed the little alcove that fed into the main corridor on the third floor, he stood aside grasping his mop and admired the glistening expanse of octagon tiles. The whiff of ammonia seemed to cleanse his senses. As he propped open the corridor door, he caught sight of someone with a long wooden window pole under one arm and a metal garbage can cover over the other. Galloping towards this knight errant was a wild-eyed combatant brandishing yet another window pole. As the two collided just outside the corridor door, the second jouster glanced off the other's shield and stumbled out into the alcove where Bah Bah stood dumbstruck and befuddled.

Not surprisingly, this second warrior slipped on the gleaming floor. His lance stuck between the wrought iron spokes of the railings and then snapped in two as its bearer lunged straight ahead and tumbled headlong down the steps. The remaining delinquent whizzed by seconds later, dropping his armaments as he slid down the banister to the landing below. Bah Bah was beside himself in apoplexy, waving his arms above his head while he cursed in tongues. Both the offending miscreants barged down the stairwell howling laughter Bah Bah could not hear. The yahoo who broke Bah Bah's window pole was Luddy Gore.

Luddy, christened Ludwig, was a natural born hard ass. He was shaving when he was twelve, clearly an heir to the Teuton's penchant for recalcitrance and mayhem. His father's strap did little to tame his ways. Luddy quickly graduated to rolling Dutchies down along the Barbary Coast and other nefarious activities. High school for Luddy was but a hothouse where juicy tomatoes (girls) ripened and where tomfoolery was one big merry-go-round.

The previous summer Gypo's father had taken him to the greyhounds in Florida, and Gypo was determined to produce something comparable back home. Using a lasso and a bowl of Alpo as bait, he captured five stray dogs of varying sizes and spirited them away in the Lynch woodshed, accessible from an alleyway of garages behind his home. He kept the dogs well fed for a few days. Because Gypo's parents drank and hollered all the time, the extra noise was barely noticed. Gypo and his Giddy-o Rangers put the word out that the race of the century was afoot down by the railroad tracks. On St. Patrick's Day he led the mutts on leashes up onto the palisades at the city's edge.

Overlooking the industrial section of town, the slobbering dogs all wore soiled handkerchiefs with numbers inked upon them. A mob of some twenty youthful punters placed bets with Gypo before he reached into a burlap sack with a gloved hand and extracted a black cat spitting and hissing like a busted radiator. Naturally, the dogs went berserk.

Gypo promptly hurled the sputtering grimalkin onto the steep slope leading back into town, and the handlers released the hounds - two of which somersaulted ass over teakettle half way down the palisades completely out of the running. Many of the spectators fell down laughing, several of them rolling downhill as had the motley canines before them.

By the time Luddy wandered into the Clover Leaf tavern on St. Patrick's Day he was broke. Most of the revelers were crowded together in front of a hot plate inhaling the aromatic steam rising off the roiling waters of a pot in which swamp dogs, the poor man's corn beef, were simmering. Jackie Hannigan stabbed at the tube steaks with a greasy fork even as ashes from his dwindling Marlboro fell into the unseen morass below.

On the TV, Jack McCarthy, already well oiled, redoubled his dubious brogue as he narrated the Paddy's Day Parade in New York City and fawned over the likes of Carmel Quinn. Closer to home, the lascivious carry-on in the now bolted ladies room was noisy and considerable. The barman crouched behind the mahogany dousing several beer-encrusted mugs in an elixir of hot soapy water.

Figuring the coast was clear, Luddy glommed the

donation box belonging to St. Joe's School for the Blind, a box that stood behind the bar next to the Cheese Doodles. He vanished, à la Claude Rains, into thin air, his heavy boots sounding out the distances he covered on the macadam with a measured certainty.

However, Bah Bah, who had been drinking with his pals Joe Puzo and John Covellini, never took his eyes off Luddy in the mirror and lit out after the thief like the Hound of Heaven, his companions in tow. The sprightly Lully easily outpaced Bah Bah as he raced down Ninth Street past Sonny Garrett's forest green candy store, Columbus Park, and the bamboo factory - running backwards now and then just to show off. But as he neared the railroad tracks, he encountered several huge drainage pipes in storage, forcing him to make a detour the long way around. Bah Bah, on the other hand, merely lowered his head and sprinted straight on through. Out of nowhere, a dog wearing a kerchief numbered "3," upended the unsuspecting Luddy, sending the money box up into the air and into the arms of Bah Bah. Bah Bah and his buddies calmly headed east to celebrate the return of the Holy Grail, and Richie Exxon of Weehawken reported seeing a much dispirited Luddy limping about in the Shades of Weehawken later on in the day.

Across town near the river, John bought a six-pack and Joe brought six more hot dogs from a stand manned by a shapely blond in hot pants - since there was zero chance that the passel of cavones and schnorrers at the Clover Leaf had left even a morsel behind. Quite contented, the trio rested on pilings and watched seagulls sail over a barge next to the Holland American Line - the very same floating shack where

Marlon Brando and Johnny Friendly duked it out in the movies.

The sun shifted from behind some cloud and the river flashed its fiery scales. Just as suddenly, a rainbow appeared overhead. Bah Bah sat with the St. Joseph's box glinting between his stunted legs. He grinned from ear to ear, looking for all the world like an Italian leprechaun - with an anisette-soaked stoggy clinched in the side of his mouth as he'd seen his father do in the misty days of long ago.

Brothers - Not Karamazov

It was perhaps inevitable that his friends would nickname Russell Doutz, "Bruessel Sprouts," not that he minded much – affable sidekick that he was. His older brother Wolfgang, aka Wolfie, was more the swashbuckling alpha type. As a teenager, Wolfie was the lead guitarist in a rock group called, *Deracinated Nightshade*. They played a lot of Chicago covers, which allowed Russell to deliver an occasional flourish on his marching band trumpet. Decidedly second fiddle, however, he rarely scored with the girls. He hadn't the panache.

This dichotomy between the brothers set the pattern for much that was to follow as Wolfie, though he never made it big, lived the life of a troubadour – a rambler and a gambler, so to speak. All the while, Russell stayed home with his mom, an elderly widow with a subdued demeanor but piercing blue blues. Wiry and resilient in some ways, she was fragile and vulnerable in others. Russell called her Ariel so featherlight did she seem. They lived quite peaceably next door to De Bari's Pastry Shop. Russell was partial to their sfogliatelle, disdaining cannolis as gaudy overkill fit only for undiscerning *cafons.* Russell was nothing if not subtle.

To offset his penchant for such delicacies, however, he read a sardonic blog by Woody Shimmel, a Mile Square resident who from time to time wrote a column for the *Hoboken Excremental,* a throwaway newspaper filled with gossip and a ton of ads. Shimmel liked to seize upon some ridiculous bit of actual news and then fabricate a trailer - a similar, even wackier episode with Hoboken as its setting. For instance,

Today's Star Ledger carried a story about a man from Uganda who tried to smuggle "bushmeat" past guards at Newark Airport - cane rat and antelope in a suitcase, to be more precise. Apparently the like is becoming more common of late, as African communities become more concentrated in N.J. A monkey's head, small bats, wildebeest flesh, and passion fruit were among the other contraband intercepted. These items are of particular concern in this era of swine flu because of the zoonotic viruses such exotic fare might transmit.

Accordingly, Officer Gunter Fagela, on routine patrol, stopped a dilapidated station wagon wending its way from that Byzantine empire known as Jersey City down into Hoboken via a little known byway called Ravine Road. Said conveyance was transporting a dozen live chickens, several poisonous snakes, a small pig, a baboon's brain (in a vessel so labeled), three rhino horns, a pair of elephant testicles, and a zebra's schwanz. "This shipment looked felonious from the get-go," observed patrolman Fagela, "on 'accounta it had voodoo writ all over it. 'An I might add, that vee-hicle smelled like a certain brothel in Bremerhaven. But that's another tale entirely."

Many of Russell's religious experiences were likewise tinged with humor. He belonged to the local YMCA where naked men swaggered about the locker room with their 'dondelones 'bobbilating to the rhythm of the music piped in from above. Suffice it to say, insularity was a priority in such a milieu. Nonetheless, one afternoon as Russell lathered up in the shower, he noticed a roly-poly gent trundling naked as a jaybird towards his stall with a towel draped over his arm. Russell looked fifty ways from Sunday trying not to make eye contact - "Jesus, don't let this weirdo grab my 'schlange!." Even so, the rotund interloper asked in a plaintive fashion, "Russell, don't you know me?" It was his pastor from Our Lady of Grace Church in Hoboken. Sputtering beneath the suds, Russell replied, "I'm sorry, Father; I didn't recognize you without your collar."

On the more serious side, he read widely and considered the Parable of the Prodigal Son the very essence of Christianity. But, smiling broadly, he assured his mother he wasn't fond of "fatted calf" - much preferring her chicken and dumplings. As to Thoreau's assertion that "most men lead lives of quiet desperation," Russell guessed Henry David had never rolled around in the sack with Lulu, the waitress at Rudy Schaefer's, or gotten clarinet lessons (oral sex) under the 'viadock, that balcony of ecstasy on 14th Street. Scornful of philosophers, Russell was, however, a tad superstitious. So when he opened a fortune cookie at the Som Yung Goi Chinese takeaway, he interpreted the enclosed aphorism, "Seven hymns of joy are better than luck," as a message from above.

Consequently, as something of a lark, he decided to add up the numerical designations (like # 105) for the 21 hymns sung at the next seven Masses he attended (a magical three per Mass) and then risk $10 a throw at Pick Four on the total. Russell was addicted to TV's *Game of Thrones*. He promised himself that if he won, he'd visit Northern Ireland's Dark Hedges where that show had been filmed - so fixed in his mind had this spooky stretch of beech trees, all gnarly and twisted, become.

He had his doubts about mixing games of chance with the Bread and the Wine. Nonetheless that's the way he rolled.

Seven Sundays later his hymnal total was 7,777; and, stranger still, like a clockwork orange, he won $7,777 the seventh time he played. Russell clicked his heels as best he could and declared himself the Seventh Son of the Seventh Son. A bit hinky about banks, he hid the money in a cigar box along with a several Arturo Fuente blunts. But even before he got around to telling her about his windfall, his mother, usually a woman of few words, brushed back strands of hair which had fallen across his brow and whispered, "I love you, kiddo. Your books, your games, your music, and your laughter all tell me you're no dullard - some nebbish with no dreams of his own. So I know what you've given up for me. You're a mensch, much more than tinsel and flash. Goodnight, sweet Prince - the loveliest there ever was." He was speechless. She patted his cheek and died of heart failure the next day watching *Family Feud.*

Getting in touch with Wolfie when he was on the road was dicey at the best of times. Rumor had it he'd been was lying low of late. Nevertheless, he showed up on the QT the day before the funeral. After commiserating over the death of their mother, the brothers traipsed out into a patio garden astir with butterfly bushes, humming birds, flowerings shrubs, and bees. Russell carried a tray containing the cigar box and the accoutrement of booze.

They sat a while swapping pleasantries, smoking stogies, and quaffing brandy from snifters, but Wolfie looked pretty haggard - with bloodshot eyes, blotches on his forehead, and stubble on his chin. Russell asked how he was doing, and Wolfie replied: "Do 'ya remember the time that old rummy Rooster Purcell showed up at the corner bar lumped up and bloody after he'd fallen down the front stairs to his house in his underwear? Sharky the bartender made him wait for the ambulance outside the tavern on a barstool 'cause he was afraid the Rooster might die inside and then they'd 'hafta close the place for a week or so. Well, that's about how I feel - mainly 'cause I owe pots of money to some shylock whose sadistic goons are 'gonna bust me up good 'n proper if I don't cough up a sizeable payment soon, and I just don't have it."

Russell dumped the remaining cigars onto the table and pushed the box over to his brother. The wads of money therein produced a glassy-eyed euphoria in Wolfie not unlike that induced by cocaine - a substance, truth be told, he had sampled only yesterday. Though his hands trembled, he embraced Russell. Choking back his tears, he avowed, "Balls said the Queen! Brussels, your blood should be bottled." Straightaway, Russell was suffused with joy - as though the Pope in Rome had blessed him; and he said so. The two finished their brandies quietly, and Wolfie left hat in hand through the smoke of their extinguished cigars.

Inwardly, however, Russell ixnayed his brother's praise shortly thereafter, for he realized, somewhat cynically, that the delight he took in Wolfie's funky compliment was but further evidence of a world in which Mike Jagger trumped Mother Teresa. All the same, amidst the quietude of that urban oasis Russell called his Garden of Eden, an oriole sang a snatch of some forgotten song and of a sudden took flight.

Chocolate Truffles and the Millstone

Officer Harvey Quatsch seethed. That son-of-a-bitch Billy Sipes had gotten off as a child molester. An appeals court had ruled a crucial piece of evidence - the little boy's rabbit's foot set in a custom made base of sterling silver - inadmissible, because the police had fetched it from a rubbish bin before said incriminating trash had been deposited in the maw of the garbage truck's compactor. The realization that this cretinous pedophile was walking about scot-free ignited a conflagration in Quatsch's heart that ruined his appetite for food and thwarted his desire for sex.

In truth, he wasn't a happy fellow in the best of times. His sharp eyes, widow's peak, and slicked-back raven black hair lent his visage an avian severity. His predatory gaze dovetailed nicely with a single-mindedness that bordered on the obsessive. A balding defense attorney once falsely accused him of using L'Amour color comb blue black # 19 on his sleekly coiffed do. Harvey promptly threw him down a flight of stairs in City Hall for his impertinence. Charges were filed, but nothing came of them as there were no witnesses - none willing to appear in court, that is.

Harvey wasn't particularly religious. His mother once asked him if he had gotten his throat blessed on the Feast Day of St. Blaise. He'd answered, only half in jest,

"No, on 'accounta the candles give me a rash." But Harvey was an avid reader, which afforded his imagination an antiquarian flavor. So when he heard Christ's admonition, "Better for him that a millstone was tied about his neck and he were thrown into the sea than that he should cause one of these children to fall into sin," Harvey actually knew what a millstone was.

A randy devil, he loved women, the Bible notwithstanding - especially Gráinne O'Toole, the barmaid at Kelly's who was forever trying to hide a jagged scar that ran from the corner of her right eye almost to the ear. She drank too much and from time to time she did a line or two of coke. "'Cause," in her words, "it takes a whole 'lotta medicine for me to pretend I'm someone else." No matter, Harvey was a sucker for redheads - real ones, "not the Jezebel hussies that flew out of a bottle."

Harvey was in excellent shape, a plus he traced back to Tom Martinelli's makeshift gym run on 9th Street. Harvey still followed regimen of weight lifting and calisthenics he learned there as a kid. Even now, 20 years later, the odor of sweat and liniement, a feral combination which some women find irresistible, transported him back to the clang of iron and the voice of St. Peter and Paul's Fr. Herbert, who, pony tail and all, sometimes trained with the lads, "Yes, Harvey, life's a riot after the dances and you run up to the Flying Pizza knocking over trash cans as you go. And, better still, there's that *'paisan* in a greasy T-shirt tossing dough in the front window, looking for all the world like a clown or a fool. But he, too, loves and hates in this life where the banal and the eternal comingle. His immortal soul hangs in the balance. And that's where Satan comes in, for He'd have you believe it's all nonsense from start to finish."

Harvey drove his brother's van up to the Railway Express's stretch of low lying brick warehouses that lined Observer Highway. Within, wrapped in a canvas tarp, lay the comatose figure of Billy Sipes whom Harvey had waylaid behind Billy's ratty little apartment downtown. Sipes was bound and gagged and loaded up with Quaaludes. Harvey rang the buzzer by the office and waited until the night watchman - his old drinking buddy, Harpo Hanrahan - appeared chewing on what had once been a cigar.

Harvey fished a bottle of Tullamore Dew from his field jacket and Harpo smiled. He reached back into the office and handed Harvey an "Emergency Delivery/ Railway Express" sign to put on the dashboard of the van. Inside Harpo's lair, they soon settled into a pair of rickety easy chairs for a session. Harpo liked to talk about Beelzebub, exorcisms, demons, goblins, ghosts, bogeymen, and the Jersey Devil. Given his line of work, Harvey was well familiar with them all. From time to time he would feed Harpo a tale or two about human depravity that bordered on the infernal - just to brighten Harpo's day, as it were.

"Used to be a bartender named Dutz at the Clam Broth House who wouldn't allow women into his bar. He'd fire a starter's pistol at 'em if they tried and curse them out till they fled. Funny enough at the time, but 'ya 'gotta wonder 'bout anybody that don't like the hairs."

"Sounds like a real cuckoo midnight. Still 'n all, people from all over the world know the Clam Broth House by 'dat sign with the finger 'pertin down," responded Harpo.

"Right you are, Harpo. 'Anyways, turns out this guy Dutz was also a pyromaniac. Couldn't control himself - you know, like he was driven. The freakin' pervert torched a 'coupla places till finally we caught him red handed, so to speak, whackin' off in a phone booth watchin' the flames leapin' high like fiery tongues as they danced in the windows above. 'Dint much care who he burnt neither."

"'Jeez, Harve, that bottle was more than half full and we finished it already."

"Which is why I want you to pedal on down to Sparrows Liquors on your bike and fetch another bottle of hooch, whatever's your druthers, and a box of Slim Jims," said Harvey, handing Harpo three tens. "Next, as your reward, take this nice crisp twenty and cool your heels a while at Kelly's further on down the avenue. I'll mind the fort - mainly 'cause I'm supposed to be tailin' some douchebag *oye* B&E artist down at the White Projects, but I already know he's long gone. Much more comfortable here where I can't get into any trouble." Harpo was off in a flash.

So was Harvey who drew on a pair of close fitting gloves. Minutes later he dragged what looked like a canvas sausage stuffed with writhing snakes through the office. Then he wrestled his wriggling cargo out back into an ill-lit enclosure that abutted the train yard of the Lackawanna Railroad - a melancholy sight in the dead of night. Someone had long ago cut through the cyclone fence. Chained to one of the rusting posts on the railroad's property stood a welder's cart with pneumatic wheels - minus both the torch and the acetylene tank.

Despite the gloves, Harvey picked the lock using tools he carried in his breast pocket and hoisted his squiming consignment up onto the trolley. Wearily he inched along eastward over silvery tracks and railroad ties, past empty watch towers and overhead signals, and finally through a wasteland of broken glass, jimson weed, and several leafless trees. Heaving a great sigh, he halted at an inlet from the Hudson River known as the Long Slip.

Overhead, sooty clouds drifted past a gibbous moon like steam wafted from the bowels of Hell. A stray dog howled off in the distance. "Silence, Cerberus," Harvey whispered, "O guardian of the underworld; I have a customer for you via the River Styx."

Next to the murky canal Harvey unearthed a millstone, purchased at a garage sale in Pennsylvania, and two leather belts - all of which he had buried earlier in the week. Wheezing slightly, he slit open the canvas with a box cutter and hung the millstone around Billy Sikes' neck with one belt and secured it against his chest with the other. Billy's eyes bulged in their sockets like those of the petrified horses on the Parthenon as Harvey hurled him into the slip. Eventually, a few moonlit bubbles emerged from the iridescent bilge below, none of which had frozen due to an unusually mild winter.

Harvey locked up the welding cart all in good time just as he had found it. Harpo returned hours later, exquisitely drunk. Desperate for a snooze, Harvey trundled off shortly thereafter, leaving Harpo most of the whiskey. Suddenly famished, Harvey had, however, eaten all but a handful of the Slim Jims.

The next morning, February the 14th, Phoebus

reigned resplendent as his chariot raced across the heavens. Harvey purchased a Valentine's Day assortment of chocolates for Gráinne at Lepore's on 6th & Garden. A life size papier-mâché likeness of a character, the owners called the Truffleupagus, beckoned the assembled legions to buy even more. As Harvey exited the store, which was awash with Frank Sinatra memorabilia, he noted what a flibberigibbet was the soul of man. It seemed that all but those with a maniacal singularity of purpose flitted from the profound to the trivial in the twinkling of an eye.

As though on cue, a line from the *Memorare* ran through his thoughts, "Oh, Mary, most compassionate Mother of God, never was it known that anyone who fled to your protection, implored your assistance, or sought your intercession was left unaided," closely followed by a jingle ending, "...Melrose 5 5 3000." Ages ago it had been part of a commercial for Macy's reupholstery one heard during the frequent intermissions of the Million Dollar Movie on TV. Leaning against the candy colored fence outside Lepore's, Harvey leafed through the *Daily News* and noticed Walgreens was having a Valentine's Day special on a gross of prophylactics - reservoir tipped. It was to laugh.

Hans Dieter, No Dog in the Manger

Many will find historical discrepancies in the following tale, but as with the conflicting Gospels concerning the behavior of Dismas, the Good Thief crucified along with Jesus, minor inconsistencies do not obviate the essential truth of the tale. However, events really unfolded. Surely one hopes Dismas is this day in Paradise.

Hans Dieter leapt off a freight train on the eve of Christmas Eve near the Shades in Weehawken, one town over from Hoboken, the home of his birth. His bindle on his shoulder, he ducked into the Zoo, a neighborhood go-go dive. Hoping to put the arm on some old friends, he didn't see anyone he knew. A gnome-like little guy in long underwear, named Uncle Ralphy, was chasing scantily clad girls around the bar when he left.

Skirting back along the railroad ties, he found shelter in a makeshift hut along the cliffs on the western rim of Hoboken. The morning star shone brightly above Union City as he hit the sack on an unseasonably warm evening. Obviously intoxicated, three guys dressed as kings in silky gowns and various crowns, trundled up the path past Hans' clapboard shack on a line with the twinkling star - probably on their way to some Yuletide fare. Closing his eyes on the glittering necklaces of light in the city below, Hans heard celestial trumpets sounding in the night.

He awoke to the fabled "rosy-fingered dawn," Sapphic erotica! Sophomoric humor, indeed. But the classics are the best. He tied up his bed roll and headed for town. Though he was practically broke, he checked with the Edwards Hotel as to rooms and discovered that, due to plumbing problems, it had only one room to let and that was taken by a couple visiting from Black Beaver, Oklahoma. The Hotel Victor was full up with bums on whom the proprietor held life insurance policies – with, literally, no room at the inn.

But Schaefer's restaurant opposite the train station was hard up for a dish washer, and in the flap of a stained apron Hans was elbow deep in a bubbly sea of scalding hot grease cutting water – his feet spread wide apart to offset the tension in his back. The boss paid Hans ten bucks straight away, the rest due tomorrow when Hans was needed for brunch on Christmas morning.

Round about noon, his belly full of bacon and eggs, Hans was lounging about the back steps on a break inhaling a half-smoked cigar some customer had left behind when Simon Crean, a long lost childhood friend, stumbled by begging food. Hans gladly provided him with some scraps from within. Simon, tearful and toothless, showed Hans a dog eared photo of his lovely young dark haired daughter Veronica whose mother had died of TB. Bowing his head shamefully, Simon admitted she now lived at the Hammond Home for orphans on Park Avenue on account of his landing in an asylum in Secaucus for alcoholism about a year ago. Hans gave Simon his ten dollars. Tipping his cap, Simon shambled off over the cobblestone alleyway still wet with the water from Hans's mop and bucket.

Hans got off work around three. Once a competent draftsman, Hans sat in the kitchen and, using pens and pencils borrowed from the wait staff, he created a charming likeness of Veronica on a swatch of colored paper, along with a catchy plea for generosity towards the kids at the Hammond Home. This image he affixed to a huge jar and then set forth on a charity crusade. A bartender named Blacky threw Hans out of the Clam Broth House before he even reached the dented stainless steel urn containing free soup. Outside Hans gave the sign's downward pointing finger the finger.

But the Filipinos at the Four Star restaurant on Washington St. stuffed the jar with green even as golden slices of bread tumbled from a huge toaster. Seated at the counter, Hans chatted with a census worker who, almost as a jest, penciled him in as "having no fixed abode." Farther down the road, Hans marveled at the shrine to Frank Sinatra kept in Scalzo's eatery, cringed under the ominous gaze of a moose head in Geismar's clothing store, and grinned as an effeminate tailor lingered over a customer's inseam in Goodman's haberdashery. Hans made numerous additional stops, and by the time he stood under the clock at Kramer's he had amassed a small fortune.

Much elated, he hopped a jitney that headed back to Schaefer's. Several giggling riders called out, "Back door, Meyer!" to the driver, who in return bellowed, 'Youse know Gott damn well, 'zere is no back door on 'zis bus." When Hans alighted from this ancient conveyance, two policemen pulled him aside. Their greeting was colder than a Presbyterian's breakfast. The taller of the two, Officer Pelotti, minced no words, "Aren't you the bold little monkey, runnin' a scam on

Christmas Eve?" The smaller policeman, Jude Escarrio, reached for the money. Hans aimed a blow at his right ear, which, fortunately, missed.

Pelotti pinned Hans hard against the news stand and explained in a haughty tone, "By rights we should run you in - were that convenient, soliciting without a license 'n all. As it stands, we'll just confiscate the loot. Next time we meet, you better rise and shine and give God your glory 'cause I'm 'gonna put a foot up your ass as sure as death and taxes."

Hans twinged and wriggled beneath Pelotti's billy club. "How 'bout we deliver the money to the home - especially the $25 I intended giving to her, the daughter of a friend?" Hans suggested, pointing to his portrait of Veronica.

"Who loves 'ya, Santa" whispered Escarrio, kissing Hans ironically on the cheek. "I like your style, ballsy and direct."

The police drove Hans to the home. All three handed the money over to a matron who explained that the children were at the Fabian Theater watching *The Robe.* She promised to divvy up the money as directed-with kudos for Veronica's dad. Hans shuffled off quietly as Pelotti warned, "None of your 'ole lip now!"

That evening during midnight Mass, having left his bindle in the foyer, Hans sat in the rear of OLG whilst an elderly rummy changed the words of a famous carol to "Oh little town of Hoboken," causing considerable amusement for the jocular inebriates milling about the holy water fount. Later, exiting the church in what seemed a cloud of incense, Joey Arimetheo, a former classmate, tugged at Han's elbow. Joey handed out towels from his little cage in the bowels of the YMCA, but he held the keys to the kingdom. A paid up resident, Owney McEvoy, had died only two days ago, so Joey offered Hans the room until the end of the month.

That night Hans slept soundly beside a hissing radiator. Early the next day he joined Joey on the roof of the "Y" as that lumbering tatterdemalion fed the pigeons. Joey delighted in the frantic, moiling helix of the birds. Gazing upon the New York Life's golden dome resplendent in the morning's blaze, Hans recalled the following: "Heaven and earth are full of your glory. Hosanna in the highest." Work awaited him at Schaefer's, and he figured he'd stick around until New Year's Eve so he could hear "the whistles."*

*A Hoboken tradition: factories blowing their horns for Auld Lang Syne.

Bosom Buddy

Jamesy McIntyre, though nearly fifty when he died, was an odd stretch of a fellow, all gangly and anything but handsome. His lower lip drooped, a huge cowlick swirled about the back of his head, and a stand of elfin blond down sprouted from the edge of his ears. When it came to looks, he was a dodo bird amongst exotic roosters.

Which, oddly, reminds me of an incident when Jamesy and I were swilling drinks like a couple of toffs at the sumptuous Campbell Apartment bar atop Grand Central Station. Sitting across from us was a young guy in denims whose Mohawk-like hairdo was spiked in several different colors - green, gold, red, and blue. Not all that thirsty, Jamesy kept staring at the popinjay between sips from his tumbler of Wild Turkey. "A new take on Chingachgook," Jamesy mumbled *sotto voce*.

The youthful dandy suffered Jamesy's near-silent obloquy for a time before he finally hissed, "What's the matter, old man, never done anything wild in your life?" Jamsey's retort came right on cue, "Got drunk once and had sex with a peacock. I was just wondering if you were my son."

To his credit, the Technicolored swain asked, "F***ed a peacock. Doesn't that make you queer?" A big *Seinfeld* fan, Jamsey answered, "Not that there's anything wrong with that!" And they both laughed.

Possessed of a sly sense of humor and a gentle, disarming smile, Jamesy was inordinately fond of the clever riposte, the off-the-cuff bon mot. For instance, exchanging jests about religion with an overweight friend Sylvester Hightower, who insisted that God, like love, was everywhere, Jamsey called Sylvester a pantheist "because Sylvester worshipped the flapjack."

Similarly, Jamsey dubbed the three meatball sandwich at Joey Manganella's Italian deli "the pawnbroker." Accordingly, Joey said it came with a money back guarantee. But, in truth, if you asked for a refund, you'd be frog-walked to the door. As Jamesy liked to put it, "cast out into the darkness where there would be weeping and gnashing of teeth." Not surprisingly, Jamsey's hero was Oscar Wilde.

Unlike Oscar's, Jamsey's witticisms were often testicularly themed. Freud would have ridiculed the like, but Jamsey considered psychology a pseudoscience - a Viennese cock and bull story, one fostered by a fraud addicted to heroin. In like manner, we were both quaffing beverages at the Shamrock Bar whilst a hippie-like woman of a certain age, with long grey hair down to her arse, rhapsodized about an oft debunked branch of science called phrenology. Jamesy listened patiently and then observed, "As regards men anyway, you can learn a lot more about them by massaging their balls than their skulls." She was not amused.

Though he was happiest when matching wits and jousting intellectually, he was forever organizing unusual outings or road trips like lunch time at Callahan's hotdog stand in Fort Lee, the dog track in Bridgeport, Connecticut; a minor league baseball game in Buffalo, NY, or a leisurely cruise on a barge along the

Erie Canal. Closer to home I met him in Manhattan one St. Patrick's Day for the parade.

Half way through the roiling carry-on, we had to find a gin mill several avenues over so as to, in Jamsey's words, "drain the lizard." Best we could do was a Korean restaurant that had a small bar. Once there, we ordered Irish whiskey to commemorate the day. The owner said he had none but, quick as Jack Robinson, sent one of his minions out to purchase a bottle.

We settled for draughts in the meantime and went to the john. When we returned, most of the twenty I'd left on the bar was gone - something we both scrutinized closely. New York prices! Just then the lackey returned with a fifth of Bushmills. After I snatched up my remaining silver, Jamsey proclaimed, "That's Protestant whiskey. Catholics can't drink that shite," and we left the owner in high dudgeon, cursing: "You 'filly 'Ilish 'sunna 'bishes!"

Both of us became Hoboken teachers - not, unfortunately, the devoted kind who always wanted to do just that, as though we had a calling like a priest. Truth be told, we started teaching because we couldn't find steady work doing what we loved – me as a writer, him as a thespian. He was actually pretty good at treading the boards, but unsightly as he was, he was always cast as a villain or a nebbish in cameo roles, and precious few of those. All the same, pedagogy paid the bills. Plus there were two very good reasons for easing into our profession – July and August.

Kindred souls, we palled around together during and after school for several decades despite my family life in the suburbs and his solitary existence in

Hoboken's Marine View Plaza. In the end, poor old Jamesy wound up in lower Jersey City's Alaris hospice dying of cancer. I visited him nearly every afternoon. On his better days we swapped tales of our experiences at Brandt School; and being an inveterate scribbler, I kept notes. The following is a compilation of those reminiscences - tidied up here and there, I admit, in keeping with a belief that if a story isn't worth embroidering, it isn't worth telling.

Jamesy: Before you joined the staff, a math instructor, Hymie Goosch, fell out of favor. He was relegated to teaching sex ed and hygiene. The students knew this class counted for nothing as regarded promotion or graduation. So, naturally, they behaved accordingly. Returning his grade book during class one afternoon, I witnessed a brazen hussy, Shaniqua Pottle, call out, "Yo, 'Misser 'Goose, like in this book how come 'wunna 'a man's nuts always hangs down lower 'then the other?" Undaunted, Hymie took a seat beside his desk and, hiking his right knee over the left, answered, "Cause otherwise a guy couldn't cross his legs." Nonplussed, Shaniqua waggled her head defiantly and sat down.

Me: He was a legend alright. But my favorite was Hughie Deverone. As you probably know he was something of a fop - always duded up. One day he spilled the remains of a latte onto the crotch of his elegant trousers and quickly retired to the lavatory in the teachers' room to dab up the mess. So happened right about this time, Vice Principal Julia Rätsel wanted to speak to Hughie about some minor matter. Newly appointed, a disciplinarian, she was determined to establish herself as a non-nonsense administrator. When she called upon Hughie's classroom, she found it in an uproar with only a monitor in charge.

Incensed by this dereliction of duty, she stormed off to the teachers' room. There, with the lavatory door ajar, she observed Hughie splashing water on the front of his slacks. Aghast, she remonstrated, "Mr. Deverone, whatever, in God's name, are you doing?" Without missing a beat, Hughie replied, "Ah, Ms. Rätsel, this time of day it gets overheated and I have to cool it down." She left abruptly, none too pleased, but she never bothered him again.

Jamesy (laughing heartily between intervals of shallow breathing): The higher-ups were always a curious lot. I don't know if you ever heard of this carry-on down in Connors School? Because it provided both sunlight and a modicum of privacy, Augie DePalma and his posse liked to have lunch in a basement alcove that gym teachers sometimes used for volleyball. From time to time, however, this space - located as it was in the bowels of downtown Hoboken - would flood, causing unspeakable offal to flow hither and thither. Naturally, these teachers complained and for a long while to no avail.

Finally, however, Mr. Ferrante, as business manager and director of school buildings, decided to assess this unsanitary condition, but not before Augie got wind of it. Augie, a madcap of sorts, dashed off to Apicella's fishery and purchased a porgy, a mackerel, and a ling.

Later that afternoon Mr. Ferrante arrived and, viewing the ankle deep stagnant water, exclaimed, "What the heck is that volleyball net doing in that muck?

Get it out of there." Augie hauled in the net, which, of course, contained the porgy, the mackerel, and the ling. Mr. Ferrante smiled and asked, "Come on, who put those fish in there?" Augie answered, "See Cosmo Ciani. He's 'muffi-taise!"

Augie's humor always had an Italian flavor – like his sexual advice: "If it smells like provolone, leave it alone!"

Me: We had some interesting students, too, like Ramesh Patel, that lovable Hindustani kid I dubbed our "Regimental Beastie." A gutsy pupil, he later became a well-to-do pharmacist. He won the Brandt School spelling bee before he could even speak English properly. Returning from summer vacation one September, he stopped by my classroom. Brown as a berry, he enthused, "Mr. Tyrone, my family spent nearly the whole summer in the islands!" I asked which ones – Bermuda, Tobago, or maybe Saint Croix. He replied, "No, Coney and Staten."

Jamesy: Yeah, great stuff. And remember Pigs Balls who got his name after he told a gaggle of teachers, loitering in the corridor, about the nocturnal vampire bats that feasted on the testicles of his uncle's swine in rural Puerto Rico? Out of the night when the full moon is bright! To this day, I can't recall Pigs Balls' real name, but I know it wasn't Zorro or Lawrence Talbot.

Me: Jean Paul Duvalier` was another of our prodigies. Went on to Steven's Tech and made a bundle in engineering patents. But a science fair at Brandt School was always something of a three ring circus under the best of circumstances. It was an event inevitably beset with electric buzzers, erupting volcanos, and a consortium of ant farms. Intent upon winning his second straight best-in-show, Jean Paul bugged me for weeks about the ins and outs of a hot air balloon he was perfecting. I had my doubts about what he was planning. So I was surprised when he showed up in the auditorium looking cocky as could be with alcohol, a coffee tin, and a strange cylindrical sac of thin, transparent plastic attached to the lightest of aluminum rims.

The balloon didn't look very promising, but he got permission from the principal to fire it up on the auditorium stage with myself and another student assisting. We held the bag over the coffee can as Jean Paul ignited the alcohol, and soon we could feel the heated fumes rising into the plastic sac. By then we had attracted a crowd. As the fragile bag began to billow forth with buoyant heat, the anticipation of imminent flight silenced the din below.

At last the balloon was fully erect, and Jean Paul hollered, "Okay, Mr. Tyrone, let 'er rip!" Wondrously his contraption rose to the ceiling in one steady, graceful parabola. The rabble was ecstatic, and Jean Paul smiled from ear to ear. But as for me, his apparatus seemed to flaunt an unintentional, humorous likeness to something in the bawdier recesses of my consciousness. There was an unspoken licentiousness about this air borne plastic that made me gaze into the audience to check the reactions of my ne'er-do-well colleagues – like you, Jamesy. Several had, I suspected, turned away as if to disguise their merriment.

Nonetheless, I suppressed these inklings. I took pains to hide my own considerable glee lest I arouse some untoward comparisons in the minds of my youthful charges. It was late in the school day, so we all hurried back to our classrooms prior to dismissal. But before leaving, I announced I wasn't sure who had won prizes, but I was certain who had stolen the show. And from the throng one snaggletoothed wag cackled, "Yeah, Jean Paul and his flying condom!"

* * * *

Jamesy died pumping intravenously fed morphine into a body writhing in pain, but not before he gazed out a window filled with sunshine. Stealing a line from a Kingston Trio tune, he said, "*It's hard to die when all the birds are singing in the sky.* Harder still, I bet, in the dead of night."

Later that day, I collected his things as he had no family to speak of – only a beloved Uncle Seamus who languished suffering from Alzheimer's in a Long Island nursing home. I thought for a moment of what a lively, though lonely spirit Jamesy was; and I wondered had he ever held a sweetheart in his arms. There was a copy of *Cyrano de Bergerac* on the cabinet beside his hospital bed. I picked it up and tucked between its pages was a folded, coffee-stained sheet of paper. In a wavering hand, Jamesy had written a poem which read as follows:

"Liquor thirsty and bouncing
I heard the church bells chime
just outside the Shamrock Bar
on a windswept corner
dappled autumn bright with limp brown leaves
that lay wet in the morning's blaze;
and a puddled lively sun

I shattered with my heavy boots
as I staggered slightly by.

Incongruous is a word
my teachers used: loneliness
and golden honey flashing through the dry rustling leaves,
emptiness amidst that brilliant little world of ours;
but I remember
times before
summer-green leaves
we pressed against some Sunday street
with never the slightest thought
for the cold little drops
that fell into a rippled "O"
for my mouth was alive
with apple butter and bits of toast
and I was much too busy
watching you like some little girl
with cherry blossoms in your bright red hair.

Pigeons swirled above
cables glistening, dripping from
a midnight shower,
gossamer threads of memory;
and, yes, once,
how she stroked my ruddy face
with her slightly, very delicately freckled hands
as though she'd always care.

Jesus, what an awful taste
that whiskey leaves.

And 'ya think 'ya know someone.

Sean and the Fantastical Fish

"An old man returns to Paris as every old man must... His dreams have turned to dust."

–Excerpt from a Kingston Trio song

The doctors were certain, Sean Shaughraun, though but sixty, was dying - something to do with the heart. Peering out at the summertime hustle and bustle of the pavement below, he decided his railroad flat on Clinton St. was too dreary a lair in which to breathe his last, so he headed for the Erie Lackawanna railway station with Belmar as his ultimate destination.

Valise in hand, he stopped at Presto's on Washington St. to get his shoes shined, if only to luxuriate one last time in those padded cubicles with the heavy wooden doors at the rear of the store. As usual, the proprietor, Mr. Trevi, sat rotund and serene in the front window as he gazed through a jeweler's loop at the inner workings of a golden pocket watch like a philosopher delving into the meaning of life itself.

Overhead fans whirred, and Marvin Misculin, the store's bootblack and Hoboken's unofficial raconteur - a story teller who threw every ounce of his being into his tales - delivered a litany of the city's latest cock-ups for all to hear. His speedy shoeshine rag punctuated the pauses.

"Any 'a 'youse know that muscle bound guy Emil Seven Rooms 'a Gloom? Well, a 'coupla days ago 'outta the blue his sweetie gave him the gate. Emil was so bent 'outta shape that he 'laid down in the middle of Willow Avenue durin' rush hour and begged 'a angry UPS driver to put 'im 'outta his misery. What a 'maroon!" Pop. "And 'da cops 'tolt me that last Friday Nelllie, the dark haired Amazonian waitress who works the graveyard shift, 'hadda quell a riot in the Town Lunch after Totty Wilson deemed it necessary to hurl yet another trifler through the restaurant's front window." Pop.

"Think that's something? Tuesday evenin' that cuckoo midnight Dennis Hogan tried to swim across the Hudson again, this only a week after he rode a horse into the Hoboken House and hitched the skittish filly to a Ballantine tap as he downed a frothy mug of beer." For a while at least, Marvin's folderol made Sean's spirit shine even brighter than his newly polished brogues.

Shortly thereafter, Sean passed under the golden balls of the Hoboken's only pawnbroker (the extra ball or testicle necessitated by the prices charged) so as to purchase a fishing rod complete with reel. Odd, he thought, how in moments of distress or joy, a single item can transport one back in time. Standing before the pawnbroker's ancient cash register, Sean watched, through the gossamer veils of memory, anglers along River Drive cast weighted fishing lines out onto the gentle waves that summery Memorial Day decades ago when Mario "Buckwheat" Menaggia, clad in a tricolored hat, and his buddy Holofernes Hillibrand, swaddled in an American flag, set out upon the waters in a huge rubber raft trying to parody George Washington's crossing of the Delaware.

Inevitably, the intrepid duo drifted past the serpentine cliffs where a coterie of the aforementioned fishermen and accompanying merrymakers were barbecuing chorizo and gyrating to the sounds of the Baja Marimba Doo Wop Band. Ever mindful of a potential audience, Buckwheat pulled down his sweats and, to the tune of "Sealed with a Kiss," mooned the assembled sybarites who, by way of vengeance, hurled rocks and obscene epithets Buckwheat's way. Stirred by such attentions, Buckwheat shoved his genitalia rearward, thereby transforming his ribald presentation into a classic "fruit bowl," even as the music shifted to "I Only Have Eyes for You."

Overhead, ominous clouds obscured the sun. Popito Lindo, a feisty Latino with a moustache as silvery as the studs on his motorcycle boots, cursed the licentious punchinello and rummaged through the archery equipment he'd brought to entertain his teenage nephews. Still glaring at his tormenter, he soaked the colorful bandana he had been wearing with lighter fluid, bound the sodden cloth to the shaft of an arrow with a bit of wire, and set the whole shebang aglow.

Popito's flaming arrow then zipped out over the olive drab waters of the Hudson, narrowly missing Buckwheat's pale white posterior - its hiss and sizzle causing the bare bottomed mariner to duck and curl. Just as Buckwheat hit the water, the sun reappeared and set the oleaginous soup of the Hudson ablaze with its shattered rays. Sean, watching from a bluff behind the partiers, dissolved into paroxysms of laughter and hurriedly scribbled the following lines on a Dunkin Donuts receipt, "Across the murky river swells / I heard the cacophony of the harlequin's bells."

The vision dispersed and Sean purchased the rod and reel even as the cho-cho train beckoned.

With few exceptions Sean Shaughraun had spent his whole life in Hoboken, summering at the Jersey shore. Both of which realities seemed to have been foretold by a fortune teller named Madam Chi Chi Garcia-Luna in Spanish Harlem where his spinster Aunt Fionna had taken him at the age of seven. They went after a visit to the Central Park Zoo because Fionna, something of a free spirit despite her virginal ways, was a great believer in such things. Permeated with a sense of *other* via its chimes, incense, veils, and candles, Chi Chi's creaking hovel was located above an OTB parlor on 101st Street.

Sean well remembered a blue macaw squawking, "Que sera, sera!" even as the clairvoyant, in flamboyant attire, stroked his slender hands with a fragrant lotion and then peered, it seemed, into his very soul. Her breath was sweet, ambrosial even. Closing her eyes, she murmured that, yes, water was rippling everywherein his aura - rivers, lakes, and the great oceans beyond, an observation she later confirmed dealing out a spate of Tarot cards associated with Aquarius and Pisces. Naturally, Fionna explained, his life was to take many a watery turn.

To a large extent this was true. Oddly though, as a kid, he rarely saw the Hudson because a string of shipyards, factories and warehouses along city's shores blocked its view. But Sean was nonetheless keenly aware of its murky waters flowing swiftly by - in the sense best captured by Marvell's famous line, "And at my back I always hear Time's winged chariot hurrying near." After exams in high school, he treated himself to ferry rides to Battery Park. Upon his return, as though they were kindred spirits, he waved to the indifferent seagulls standing idly upon the slimy pilings of the Lackawanna Station, its green patina walls glowing in the afternoon sun.

Remnants of the Hoboken's past - like its trolley car tracks and its cobblestone thoroughfares, now since macadamed over - forever anchored Sean to the past, to the way things once were. Not surprisingly, books like Thomas Wolfe's *Of Time and the River* were among his favorites. After high school, Sean sailed as a scullery knave on the Holland American Line. Later, as an adult, he worked as a deckhand on a tug toting barges up the Hudson, during which time he spent many a moonlit evening below deck in the galley reading about Irish mythology and Cuchulainn, the Celtic hero who in the midst of battle tied himself to pillar stone so as not to die lying down.

Similarly, while on leave from the Army in Germany, Sean cruised as many waterways as he could- the Mosel, the Elbe, and the Saar. More importantly, his troubled relations with women mirrored Heinrich Heine's story of the Lorelei. For periodically, it seemed, Sean's restless heart crashed upon the rocks like those German sailors on the Rhine.

Thus it was hardly surprising that within several hours of his "end game" decision to desert the city of his birth, he was down the shore in a beach chair fishing for stripers. A lump of clam skillfully bound to the hook via a bit of sewing thread - just as his buddy of old, Bilge Filth Bob, had taught him a lifetime ago - his pole held lightly between his legs. Sean'd caught one already - a magnificent fish which periodically thrashed about in a bucket of ice beside his chair. Nearby, a couple of swarthy teenagers eyed the fish from time to time.

Enchanted by the tourmaline pink of the setting sun, Sean's mind wandered back to a time when he and Bilge Filth mooched a slew of blow fish from a fisherman in pince-nez glasses and waders - a grouchy sort who considered the then numerous puffers an outright nuisance. Seniors in high school, Bilge Filth and Sean made a feast of the unwanted fish and purchased hootch with the money they had saved on vittles - a mistake. Bilge Filth, ripped on tequila, later tore the wall paper from their clapboard room at a boarding house, behavior which, in effect, banished them from Belmar for a year. Both of them were considered incorrigible by all the landladies who kept in close contact.

The surf tugged at Sean's line. Startled back into the present, Sean spied a tramp strolling the water's edge with a decrepit dog whose single testicle dragged in the sand. As the pair approached, Sean could see that the elderly drifter had a cesta, the basket-like scoop used in the sport of jai alai, attached to his right arm - a device which the vagabond employed to gather up his pet's turds, subsequently hurling them into the ocean or onto some exclusive patio as his mood required. Seeing Sean's appreciative smile, the gnarly derelict stopped and exclaimed, "Off the wall, I'll grant 'ya, but stuff like this helps me deal with the shit life keeps puttin' in my way." Then the hobo and the hound ambled on.

Sean closed his eyes, and the would-be youthful thieves sidled closer. He could have given them the fish- but it was more fun this way - for them and for him. Suddenly, however, he felt something give way within as though existence itself were dissolving. Letting loose the rod, he envisioned himself a much younger man hauling a gargantuan fish up alongside a glistening jetty.

The fish sported massive dorsal humps, one of which bore a tattoo reading, "Born to Booze." Surrealistically, the creature whispered between pitiful gasps that it was the veritable Abraham of his species, one destined to spawn offspring as countless as the stars - a claim illogically substantiated by the cruciform discolorations on its fins.

Deeply moved, Sean heaved the leviathan back into the moiling surf. Moments later, out on the darkening horizon, the monstrous fish somersaulted into a crimson spray just as Cuchulainn in one of his salmon leaps might have done. For an instant, experience and imagination fused. For such was the final earthly image to flash among the dying synapses still sputtering in Sean's skull, that living chalice which served as a reservoir to his soul. The striper on ice beneath his chair was gone, and so was he.

Graffiti, Tats 'n Rats but No Unicorns

His mother knew she had a handful when Esteban Encarnacion, aged only four, renamed a cartoon character "Caspar the Douchebag Ghost." An impressionable lad, he quickly transmogrified into an angry young man who sometimes took things a bit too seriously. For instance, soon after a group of corner boys tagged his father's barber shop with aerosol paint cans, he became what was later dubbed the "Graffiti Vigilante," stalking these so-called artists during moonless evenings several times a year.

Equipped with infra-red glasses, he peppered them on high with a paint gun. Most notably, a vandal fell to his death one Halloween while he was desecrating a Hoboken landmark, a dilapidated water tower which listed on its rusty uprights, the container itself resembling a barrel constructed of vertical wooden staves and bands of steel. The "artist's" opus, wild style and neon bright, resembled consecutive frames of an animated movie - like a reel slipped from the lens of a projector. Esteban left him dead on the pavement and outlined him with his own paint spray - all this on the qt, sans any boasting or notoriety.

For Esteban graffiti spelled evil, as did tattoos. As he knew well, the Catholic Church viewed the latter as "defiling the Temple of the Holy Ghost." Hence, for a time, Esteban avoided girls with tats, even those with big maracas. As he put it, he wasn't going to date "anyone some else had scribbled upon." Eventually, however, he spent a fortune covering much of his own body in tattoos, many of them in hues of orange and a purple even darker than his soul. Often, it seems, the thing which we hate in others is but an evil spore waiting to explode within ourselves, giving rise to Christ's parable cautioning us to remove the beam from our own eyes before noting the mote in the eye of another.

True, Esteban seethed with guilt after each such flamboyant colorful indulgence. But he comforted himself with the justification that, unlike the graffiti artists, at least the canvas was his own. Then, too, he reserved a rectangle of unsullied flesh for where his gold crucifix lay.

Originally from Philadelphia, Esteban returned every so often to see his beloved Phillies and to devour an authentic cheesesteak sandwich at Mama Luke's. Early one spring, he arrived at the stadium for a day game which was actually scheduled to be played that night. Hoping to kill some time, he scouted out neighborhood tattoo parlors in search of a new ink master. On a secluded side street, he stumbled upon a place called Indigo Gold. The logo once emblazoned on the storefront window had faded to but a ghostly outline of its former glory.

Within, a mustachioed practitioner was hunched over a burly middle-aged man who was having a pair of all-seeing eyes tattooed on the back of his balding skull – presumably to ward off bad juju from someone else's mal de ojo. Steam rose from a nearby autoclave. Amid the smell of rubbing alcohol, the persistent buzz of tattooist's machine, and the "flash" on the further wall, another artist, Shax Duvall, strode forth from shadows in a sleeveless shirt. A jagged scar on his left cheek marred an otherwise handsome visage. Noting Esteban's presence, he smiled wistfully and turned ever so slightly, the better to show off the tat on his left bicep- the startling depiction of an angel and a demon deadlocked in battle over the words: Born to Choose. The tattoo was done in American traditional, and the craftsmanship was superb.

Esteban removed his Phillies jersey to display the images enveloping his torso, and Shax's gaze was drawn to the empty rectangle on Esteban's chest. "These tattoos are exceedingly fine but disjointed," said Shax as he traced the flow of some of the dominant lines with a forefinger. "Oh, yes, my little droogie, in a flash I see how these components can be fused into a masterpiece using but a single letter- a "Z" for Zarathustra, Nietzsche's anti-hero. No ordinary Z either. I'd gussy it up to mirror the illuminated text in the Book of Kells." Esteban paused.

In the background, the middle-aged man talked a blue streak to distract himself from the pain caused by his tattooist's needles - like someone speaking in tongues. As though mesmerized, Esteban removed his crucifix and murmured, "Okay, Zorro, do your thing!"

This adornment was a dazzling success, but weeks later it itched whenever the crucifix fell upon it - in the manner of a psychosomatic twinge. Perhaps, too, this spooky phenomenon had something to do with the fact that Shax, who also bore a filigreed "Z" on his sternum, had only a month ago raped a girl in the City of Brotherly Love. Unbeknownst to Shax, the victim's blindfold had slipped long enough for her to spot amidst a jumble of other images an ornate Z on his chest. A week following the assault, a detective, all gruff and businesslike, questioned him about "possible customers sporting such a design." So, when Esteban fell into Shax's lap like a present from Beelzebub, Shax promptly framed his customer via the aforementioned zed. After a few anonymous phone calls to the police he fled to Seattle where his criminality and eccentricity found a ready home.

Esteban, on the other hand, was convicted of rape and sent to prison. By then, obsessions being what they are, he already looked like Ray Bradbury's Amazing Illustrated Man.

During the thirteenth year of Esteban's incarceration, Eastern State Penitentiary instituted a rehabilitation effort entitled Transformation Through the Creative Process, a program developed by a charlatan called P.T. (Percival Timothy) Smithers. Accordingly, the painting of murals was supposed to sensitize the participants to beauty - whilst simultaneously developing skills ex-cons might be able to market on the outside. As though in a fever to succeed, Encarnacion executed a slapdash albeit eye-catching work even more bizarre than the monstrosity that once enlivened the southerly wall of Bamberger's Department Store in Paramus, NJ. One morning in 1992, Esteban stripped naked before his creation of lively splashes and swirls, many of them orange and a purple even darker than his soul. He disappeared into the surface of the mural forever, utterly vanishing into that non-existent aesthetic universe depicted by abstract flimflam artists like Jackson Pollack and Willem de Kooning.

The guards were astounded. For instance, Wilfredo Alvarez, a sergeant at Eastern State Penitentiary, exclaimed, "Ain't no one escaped from this lock-up since Willy Sutton in 1945, but black 'n white photos of Encarnación pop up on the walls of the prison from time 'ta time, 'prolly the work of the demented jokers we 'gotta deal with here. Funny thing is, though, the 'pitchers all turn to color 'fore we 'kin take 'em down - like some demon with magic markers filled 'em in. Downright miraculous, the way I see it, 'kinda like Our Lady of Guadalupe in reverse. But maybe, since in here, Satan's devotees are already legion, don't nobody make much of a fuss. Besides, the warden likes to keep stuff like that on the down-low, if you know what I mean. Low profile's definitely the way to go in this racket." Some claim Smithers, who was sweet on Esteban, sprung him. But this was little more than folk lore.

This much was known, however. A newspaper columnist with an eye for the sensational publicized a makeshift diary found under Esteban's bunk. Entries proclaimed Esteban's innocence in the case of the rape but admitted his guilt in the Hoboken murder of a graffitist, a crime for which he had never been charged.

"Thus, regardless of whither he has disappeared," the journalist concluded, "Esteban's spirit lives on." Suddenly, vigilantes all over the country were out hunting graffiti artists, shooting them down from their aerial heights - some with paint guns and potato bazookas, others with sling shots and crossbows. Outlining deceased victims where they fell became *de rigueur*, but the use of legitimate firearms was anathema.

Indeed, Esteban had become an instantaneous legend, a Technicolor avenger striking down the despoilers of the urban landscape even as some misguided bleeding hearts tried to turn the spray-painting yahoos into martyrs. After all, for some, nothing's ever just black and white.

Northern Gothic

Early in the day on the western fringes of Hoboken, Hindustani worshippers, dressed in saris and dhotis, thronged in and around the Ganesha Temple as part of a consecration ceremony. The temple was, in fact, a refurbished warehouse. A bare-chested priest held aloft a huge multi-colored, tasseled parasol as he dismounted a live elephant bearing a gold-studded shield on its forehead. Beautiful dark haired girls greeted the immense creature with melons and incense as it was ushered into the temple. On scaffolds high above, priests in flowing red garments doused the temple's ornate statues of deities with holy water - the fertility goddess Bhoodevi among them. Below, the faithful rushed forward to catch the abundant droplets amidst the chanting and the bells.

Later, elsewhere in town, the intoxicating aroma of Italian sausage wafted through the crowd at the annual summertime feast sponsored by the Church of the Immaculate Conception. The zeppoles, sprinkled with confectionary sugar, bordered on the miraculous. Dusk hovered like a halo above the garish lighting of the musical festivities onstage directly opposite the church. The statue of the Madonna, back from a twilight trek through the byways of the city, was hoisted up the church steps. Out of respect, the makeshift church band accompanying Our Lady's cortege fell silent. Shifting from foot to foot beneath the gentle glow of the street lights, the ragtag musicians exuded reverence and satisfaction despite their baggy uniforms and tawdry epaulets.

However, as though on cue, the evening's professional entertainment known as the Mellifluous Swine (a popular cover band of some note) began acting out in erotic fashion the pulsating lyrics of the Village People's "YMCA"- a performance which quickly devolved into a wanton, bumping, grinding, crotch-grabbing, Bacchanalian, priapic free-for-all. Across the street elderly, devout Italian women, dressed in black, reached over the railings to touch the image of Our Blessed Mother one last time before she slipped quietly into the sanctuary of her foyer. The huge wooden doors closed behind her.

Thus abandoned, Piety wept as the Beast cavorted in the fullness of the darkening air. Standing in the eaves of the church, Fr. Dante Pontrelli seethed, for rarely had the chasm between the secular and the religious seemed more fraught with danger - or more obvious. Viewed from an Old Testament perspective, someone, he concluded, would surely catch hell. Profits from the feast were a blessing, but this was an *infamita.*

Much, much later a downpour lashed the dusky alleyway behind Ralphy's garage, which at that hour was closed for business. Buzzing dangerously, a lone street light out back made the raindrops look like atomic particles in a reactor. A jagged streak of lightning jumped from one invisible cloud to another. For a moment a fire escape across the way stood out like a gallows, the ladder clanging in the wind like a toneless bell. Jenks had been working late on his brother's car, adjusting the clutch which was slipping. Jenks stopped for a smoke and listened to the deluge drumming on tin rooftops, cars, and dumpsters. The dank smell of garbage wafted in through the rear door left ajar, and an enormous freestanding fan wobbled and whirred.

The headlights of a truck lit up the crumbling backstreet macadam. The engine was missing badly. A black face, all smiles and eyes opened wide, peeked around the door. "Brother, you'll pardon the intrusion. I know this seems 'outta place; but I got an assortment of items for sale real cheap: shell steaks, fresh lobster, and some really good tools - Stihl. Stuff hasn't even fallen off the truck yet. Just about sold out before the heavens opened up - down the gutters 'n out the spout. Then I seen yo' light though dim," said the interloper in preacherly tones, "and figured I might make a sale within."

Jenks waved the swag man in out of the rain and tossed his cigarette to the floor. Dripping wet, the rhyming hustler wore combat boots, a torn yellow slicker, and a porkpie cap, which had fallen down around his eyebrows. "Much obliged," acknowledged the salesman redoubling his grin. "Interested? The steaks are frozen and the lobsters're alive and kickin'."

"If the price is right, I could use an electric drill - a big one. And several steaks. One lobster'd do me fine."

"Comin' up, boss." The man in the pork pie hat disappeared snapping his fingers amidst a clap of thunder and then reappeared in a flash- literally, for lightning crackled across the sky again. Jenks bought an enormous drill, a dozen steaks and one fulsome crustacean- all for a song.

"Anyone else you know might be in the market

for such?" the hustler asked in an accent Jenks couldn't quite discern.

Jenks dumped the lobster into a white plastic bucket and filled it half way with water from a hose. "This time 'a night, maybe the Four Star diner, three blocks up on your left after your exit the alley. Guys in the kitchen might make you a deal - especially for the food. But, see, cops like to eat there sometimes, too."

"'Somma them are my best customers," answered the man in the yellow slicker, carefully folding the greasy bills into his existing roll. A rustling just outside the alley caught the attention of both. "'Lotsa rats astir on night like this," he laughed and slipped back out into the glare of his headlights. The truck rattled angrily and then trundled off like a tinker's caravan.

Jenks shut the rear door. He was nearly done, but he didn't want to take the car for a test run in the dark and the rain. He sidled over to the slop sink and washed up using an orange smelling soap called Goop. His washed his face several times, but the grime seemed to take refuge in the ginger-hued stubble that covered his visage. Gradually the storm abated, though the wind and a irksome drizzle continued. Jenks shoved the steaks, already encased in cardboard, into a cheap vinyl bag and stowed the drill, still in its box, behind a stack of worthless tires. The lobster, however, was, it now seemed, perhaps more trouble than it was worth.

After locking up, Jenks slung the vinyl bag over his shoulder and toted the plastic pail to the bus stop a block away. An oily residue trickled down his neck and behind his ears as the bus, all fogged up, stopped beside an illegally parked car. Two elderly blacks sat behind the driver, their furled umbrellas feeding an unsightly puddle of rain water and filth. Jenks sat opposite them with the plastic bucket and the lobster between his legs.

Moments later a Hispanic woman in a cloche hat, sprinkled with moisture, and a little girl in pigtails stepped towards the front of the bus – careful to hold fast to the hand grips on the seats as they proceeded. Peering into the container, the child squealed with delight when she saw the creature's antennae and claws. "Momma, look, the 'cockaroach got muscles," she exclaimed. Smiling broadly, Jenks hauled the pinkish monster from his lair. The sprightly tyke hid behind her mother's considerable girth. "'Neber mind that nonsense, Magdalena; and go find the 'brella 'jew left behind." Jenks plunged his dinner back into the pail. "Truth be told," said the matronly passenger shaking her head, "she ain't 'afraida nothin'."

"Amen. I can well believe it," replied Jenks. The bus halted and the woman and her child vanished into the mists and shadows outside. The elderly couple across the aisle looked on and grinned. A half empty soda can rolled from the rear of the bus where a 'skeevy white guy in dreadlocks slept fitfully, his unshaven cheek vibrating against the Plexiglas window.

Two noisy teenagers in sodden sweats, a couple, got on at Prescott Boulevard. The girl, in flip flops, ran off a skein of obscenities after she nearly tripped over the lobster bucket. Jenks loathed the type – greasy hair, a fat ass, and a foul mouth. 'Rid hard and put up wet, he thought. But, to be fair, he moved the container even further out of the way. The bus pulled past an idling police car, its lights like those of a psychedelic carousel, reflected eerily in the oily black streets below. Jenks got off at the next stop and, hobbled by the encumbrance of the lobster barrel, splashed the smelly water onto his fatigues.

His apartment was just around the corner, several floors up over a bodega. Jenks ascended the stairs past Mrs. Rosella's baby carriage, through the vaporous remains of Mrs. Rapcienski's cabbage soup, and around Mrs. Vega's armoire, which she was storing for her sister Inez who was looking for an apartment. At last his door swung open wide; the lights were already on. He set the sluggish lobster down in front of the stove and shoved the steaks in the freezer with little room to spare. Humming snatches from "Maxwell's Silver Hammer," he washed his hands at the sink and set a large much-dented pot of water on a back burner to boil. Rooting around in the refrigerator, he found some left over macaroni and cheese in a Corning Ware bowl and placed it near the microwave so as to be handy once the lobster "whistled."

Jenks then latched onto a can of Bud and hurled himself into a rump sprung easy chair. He turned on the dusty little radio that stood upon an end table cluttered with books and an ash tray full of butts. "Run Around Sue" was just about through, when the pot began to rattle about on the stove. Time for the lobster's swan song. Jenks remembered, as part of an artsy-craftsy literature class in high school, having read a Samuel Beckett short story about some alienated soul boiling a lobster. He recalled little about the story itself. But somehow the accompanying commentary stuck in his head: "The comic effect stems from the mixture of the squalid and the profound." Jenks gazed about the room and, sliding the frantic crustacean into the cauldron, observed, "Well, at any rate, we're half way there."

He added a bay leaf to boiling water. A fly buzzed about the fragrant haze emanating from the roiling pot, and Jenks swatted the noisome creature as it alighted on the counter near the stove. He set the microwave in motion for three minutes. Then he melted some butter in a frying pan and sautéed a spoonful of minced garlic. Shortly thereafter, seated at a rickety Formica-topped table, that was suitably scarred with cigarette burns along the edges, he feasted upon the buttery lobster and the macaroni.

After dumping all the dishes into the mangled pot with some liquid soap in order to soak, he reheated some day-old coffee in a Pyrex percolator, which over time had attained a beige patina. Jenks relished a moment or two of utter silence even though he often felt the soreness of the day at this point in the evening. He noticed the rain had ceased entirely, but the married twosome next door was at it again. "You 'guinnie scumbag makin' googly eyes with that big-titted bimbo at my sister's birthday party no less. If there's a god in heaven, you'll wind up in a gutter with your own cock shoved up your ass."

Jenks turned on the TV. The Mets were shelling the San Francisco Giants, and lunatics in kayaks out upon McCovey's Cove paddled pell-mell to retrieve another homerun ball. Jenks rarely got to see the Giants, his favorite baseball team. There was a pitching change, and he had to urinate. One of the bulbs was burnt out in the john, lending the tiny room a sinister air. He peered out through a narrow window across a web of clotheslines and backyard paraphernalia on the odd chance that the chocolate doll on the top floor opposite his building had left her shade up again. No dice. Instead, he let fly at the Lucky Strike clincher which floated about in the commode. Despite the half light, the steady stream of urine tore into the fag's hull, spewing forth its cargo of tobacco.

Back in the living room, the Mets had added four more to their lead. Jenks switched the TV off and tackled the dishes. The citrus scented dish soap offset the funky smell of the lobster leavings. Jenks dried his hands on his T-shirt and slid back into his easy chair. He picked up a comic book - a parody called *Captain Dip Shit* in which a hero with the brain of a squirrel somehow accomplishes serendipitous rescues and derring-do good deeds - acting, in the words of the back cover's blurb, as a "catalyst for grace" despite the Captain's *commedia dell'arte* carry-on.

The Reverend Francis Montefusco, Jenks' confessor, deemed the Captain a modern day Crusader Rabbit. Catholicism and lunacy were, Jenks had discovered, quite compatible. But this evening even the colored pictures weren't enough to keep him awake, so he tied up the garbage and took a walk.

Out on the street, the darkling storm had cleared the air. A taxicab honked and a dog yowled off in the distance. Jenks deposited his trash in one of the galvanized cans within the gate. A chalky gibbous moon appeared behind the art deco frieze of the tenement across the street as clouds, ebony and gray, sped off into the void.

Rounding the corner, Jenks found a wooden flag pole leaning up against a fence. It didn't fit into the trash barrel, out of which peeked a gasmask with cracked lenses along with a set of kids' shoulder pads - materials which would come in handy this Friday evening.

Every other Friday Jenks and about a dozen of his friends participated in what they thought of as a live action video game on a roof top about a block from his apartment - something along the lines of Hieronymus Bosch meets the punk rockers. Basically, during these madcap sessions, dubbed Boom Boom Khartoum, three shooters or "archers" fired pneumatic spud guns at ten "wankers" (for such they were called regardless of sex) - decked out in ridiculous costumes including assorted goggles and outlandish masks, skate boarders' knee guards, outsized jock straps (complete with catcher's cup), brassieres fashioned out of stainless steel bowls, weightlifter's belts, opera length evening gloves, elaborately designed T-shirts, and a weird array of hats- the best of which was a multicolored beanie with a propeller spinner on top. Jenks liked to think the accoutrement reeked of movies like *A Clockwork Orange* and *Roller Ball.* As part of this folderol, "archers" shouldered leather mail sacks filled with red potatoes- their ammunition. Thus supplied, the archers served as marksmen for the entire night, transmogrifying back into wankers at subsequent gatherings known as "jousts." Jousts were subdivided into three periods called "sorties."

As with dodge ball, the object of the game was not to get hit. Heeding the caution of safety in numbers, most wankers pranced about within the prescribed boundaries in front of a wall painted white. They then crouched or dove or sought protection behind another wanker once the action began. Only wankers could score points, but the winner wasn't necessarily the last one standing (a "four"). Prior to elimination, wankers could amass credit by striking certain poses- thumbing his nose in profile (a "one"), double Popeye bicep flex (a "two"), and a triple pelvic thrust with hands interwoven behind one's head (obviously a "three"), all at pre-designated, highly exposed spots on the roof- in front of the skylight, on top of the exhaust fan, or beside a stanchion bearing a no trespassing sign. Kathleen O'Shaunghnessy, a girl with a clubfoot, served as permanent judge and score keeper. She was inordinately fond of Irish Mist, which was provided free in exchange for her services. Oddly enough, her tallies were impeccable.

The game had evolved to the point where a photographer's equipment was used for lighting and Warner Brother's cartoons were projected as a backdrop on the wall painted white. Tomfoolery between sorties was often hilarious as with Sarah Jane's in *medias res* exposure of her naked derriere during a showing of *The Little Mermaid*. The positioning of Sarah Jane's posterior was such that Sebastian, the solicitous crab, seemed to be exiting the fissure twixt Sarah Jane's formidable buttocks. The frequent author of such hijinks, Sarah Jane considered herself a star.

Needless to say, copious drink was involved – each supplying his own poison. Though modest, the dues allowed the Boom Boom winner of a joust to drink free at the El Coqui tavern for about a week with enough left over to purchase the good will of the police, who oddly enough were rarely called. Surrounded by empty lots, the tenement hosting the jousts was badly run down and only partially occupied. Two of the players lived there. The festivities were done by 10:30 so the complaints were few in number, and the two tenants were in good with the superintendent.

But that would be then and this was now. So Jenks hung the shoulder pads from the end of the flag pole, the better to tote this equipment, and shoved the goggles in his pocket. He positioned the pole over his shoulder and shambled along chanting, like the Wicked Witch's castle guards in *The Wizard of Oz*, "O-Ee-Yah! Eoh-Ah!" Perfectly balanced, the shoulder pads seemed to be floating on air.

Suddenly a growling schnauzer, quite possibly the one Jenks had heard earlier, charged Jenks from behind a Roto-Rooter van. Timing the charge perfectly, Jenks swung the flagpole and struck the snarling creature upside the head. The pads went flying and the dog rolled into the gutter. Despite an angry looking welt below its ear, the disheartened cur made another half-hearted attempt at belligerence. But when Jenks advanced brandishing the pole, it slunk off into the night, alternately whimpering and baying in misery. *Mondo cane*, thought Jenks. Mongrels love to harass the bedraggled, hence the unpopularity of postal workers. Singing "Shuffle Off to Buffalo," Jenks resumed his stroll.

Keeping an eye peeled for the dog's return, he picked up the pace. Moments later, he spotted the huge psychedelic eye which adorned the basement window of the Voodoo Temple of Sister Seraphina - an all-seeing Day-Glo orb atop a logo which read: The Spirit vanquishes all, especially complacency. "Hallelujah," murmured Jenks and turned the corner. Nearer home Jenks encountered two shifty dudes arguing bitterly on a stoop - the one with his hand raised above a nappy hairdo, his forefinger pointing in a menacing manner like a snake gauging the distance to its prey. The other, in a pork pie hat, was exclaiming, "You *pendejo maricone,* get 'outta my face before I rip your head off and piss down your neck." Jenks recognized the guy in the cap as the lobster man, though magically speaking another lingo. Nonetheless Jenks hurried on. The walk had been an eventful one, and it seemed like you could hear trouble comin' even before it arrived.

Vernon Terwilliger, who operated a newsstand only blocks from Jenks' abode, lived simply with his aged mother Myrtle in a wooden frame house within walking distance of his tiny place of business. A raspberry colored birth mark bespattered his face and his balding pate. Minute ink spots speckled the white shirts he invariably wore. The cuffs and the collars were dingy except at Easter or Christmas when his mother, who still wore gloves and a veil to Mass, bought him new. A diminutive, gnome-like man, he toiled endlessly at his meager enterprise though pain racked his turnip-shaped body, hardships he endured without complaint, for he had long ago resigned himself to this existence on earth as a vale of tears. Except for his mother and a very few friends, his pilgrimage was a lonely one.

Well he knew, his faith counseled that he oughtn't count the cost. But when he tallied up how matters stood, as he sometimes did, he was, all things considered, comfortable enough - better than some, worse than others - a clean, self-sufficient recipient of the grace of God. On Saturday evenings, before the deliveries to the stand began, he sat on the screened-in porch and watched the eastern goldfinches, their tiny yellow bodies so lithe and spry, flutter about a feeder packed with thistle as he feasted on a king-sized Snickers bar. He closed his eyes. It was as though the incense of Benediction filled his senses, as though he were bathed in the Blood of the Lamb.

Vernon was what some called an old school Catholic because he still ate fish on Friday, still bowed his head at the mention of Jesus' name, and still prayed that America would turn its back on abortion as a means of birth control. Despite his limited means and his mother's reliance on his income, he was very generous to the St. Vincent de Paul Society- so much so that he could have claimed to have tithed; but he made no such boast.

What little free time he possessed he often spent helping Pietro Percione, a pastry chef, maintain a tiny chapel on the outskirts of town. It was a haven for the Statue of Our Blessed Mother which was, once a year, paraded through the streets of town during the Feast of Madonna dei Martiri. To help carry the Madonna was a great honor. Doing so required some skill as one had to learn a little stutter step resulting in the rocking motion of the Statue for, according to a Twelfth-century tradition, an icon of Mary was found miraculously floating on the Adriatic Sea near Molfetta. Vernon, however, was far too short to serve in such a capacity. Instead, organizers allowed him to clear the path of the Madonna by chasing cornerboy ne'er-do-wells who frequently infiltrated the devout observers. He did so with a long baton topped by a golden cross, sometimes swearing in his indignation and exuberance - something, however, he also confessed.

He read a monthly magazine called *Recalcitrance*, which looked askance at the changes inaugurated by the

Second Vatican Council. Whenever he could, he attended a Latin Mass. His mentor, Fr. Dante Pontrelli, eschewed the role of the avuncular pastor and employed the rhetorical eloquence of bygone era to urge his parishioners to perfect their lives in the imitation of Christ. To do so meant to follow practices already well established through the ages – through the development of Christian virtues, the avoidance of the seven deadly sins, and the practice of corporal works of mercy. In Fr. Pontrelli's view, the aggiornamento of Pope John equated piety with hypocrisy and empty form, and in doing so badly misread the hearts of the faithful. Moreover, Fr. Pontrellli insisted, the changes brought about by the Second Vatican Council needlessly alienated millions of loyal Catholics and furthered the secularization and the dumbing down of Holy Mother Church, especially in America.

Vernon didn't always understand all the permutations of these ecclesiastical skirmishes. But the "widening gyre" (Fr. Pontrelli's favorite phrase) of hedonistic sin and wanton savagery seemed obvious even to someone as simple and trusting as Vernon. His fervent prayer was not that his unsightliness be transformed, but rather that his sufferings, though minor, be put to some greater cause. Vernon often attended novenas. *Tantum ergo* he understood.

The previously mentioned Pietro Pericone, the sacristan at the Madonna's chapel, was one of Vernon's few friends and something of a comedian. Pietro once published a hilarious glossary of Italo-American terms, some of them a trifle obscene, like *sfacime, menza 'dah 'gush, facia bruta, 'bockhouse, strunz, mamaluke, kaputz, chiacchierone* and *'geeta mort* in the newsletter he put out for his chapter of Unico – ostensibly for the "benefit" of Yuppies whom he considered an alien presence. "Vern, my *familia* in this city goes back to before the War of the Worlds. I call it that because monsters like Hitler and that *'gobba 'dah gotz* Mussolini were involved. So I have a little fun with these modern day *'cavones*. And if they don't like it, they can take it up with the law firm of *Gotz 'n Ghool*." Though he understood but half of what Pietro sometimes said, Vernon smiled, for Pietro was, despite his prickly jests, a sweet tempered man.

Horseplay aside, it was Pietro's homely "theology" which fascinated Vernon most – utterances like, "The messianic complex seems to be most prevalent in those who don't believe in One." Or, "Sometimes I think God Himself laughs at the less deadly follies His beloved humans embrace. Ergo, my friend, you can't take yourself too serious or no one else will."

That said, repentance still counted for much in Vernon's religion – witness the Prodigal Son for whom the fatted calf was slain and the sins of the man who wrote "Amazing Grace." But Vernon had no grand Luciferian deeds to repent. Thinking it a compliment, a Jesuit once told him God could have a compliant soul such as his with but a tug upon the string. Much chagrined, Vernon wondered was he worth the trouble.

Kathleen awoke in tears when ordinary sounds were heard from afar in the still of the night – the scraping of a door upon a lintel, someone clearing his throat, the hissing of a cat. Vivid dreams, involving sex and retribution, troubled her sleep. A light breeze caused the curtains to flutter, and the headlights of an occasional vehicle threw ghostly shadows on the walls – wordless meditations in gray. Her mouth was dry, so she wiped her eyes on the pillowcase and drank from a tumbler on the night stand. She glanced at the alarm clock which glowed in the dark. Silently, she thanked God it was ages before she had to rise. Unseen pixels reconfigured existence even as humanity dozed. Confused and quite forlorn, Kathleen loitered in the anteroom of despair. Above her breast she bore a tattoo- roses, shamrocks and thorns intertwined. Grasping the bedclothes like one sinking away, she realized her thirst for love and affection had led her very badly astray.

A month ago in the seedy little downtown club, Baffo Profundo - the music of a bluesy gospel quartet called Dynaflow Trans - coaxed her spirit to gambol. Above the tawdry clutter of booze and sodden coasters - in what seemed a timeless realm where pain and joy were, through the prism of imagination - somehow all fused. Her deformity had fallen away like the cocoon of a butterfly, and she listened to the earthy lyrics and the gruff but sensual patter of the lead singer. "This German dude Nietsche 'sed Christianity was but an assembly of weaklings 'n cripples. But I ask you, couldn't as much be 'sed 'bout any 'buncha men or 'wimmenses gathered in His name or otherwise?" Then guitar, sax, and drums launched into a rendition of number called "Don't That Cross Gouge Your Shoulder Some?"- closely followed a saucy ballad entitled "Tear My Heart Asunder."

Irish Mist dissolved the ice in Kathleen's glass. A sweet-talking black guy named Nettles in a porkpie hat laughed at her stories and spoke to her with eloquence and conviction about futility of mankind's shoveling shit against the tide, about the myth of Sisyphus, and about a coterie of enlightened souls who understood Dostoyevsky. Nettles had a curious accent and made animated use of his hands. Because, he explained, hadn't God, as the aborigines claimed, set the willy-willies, and thus the entire universe, aspin by twirling just His little finger?

Later in Nettles' tidy apartment, Kathleen, slightly tipsy and suffused with her suitor's aura of gentle manliness, listened to his humorous tales of conquest and defeat, as she gazed about a front room painted mango and decorated with folk art from Africa, Haiti, and Brazil. Shouts and murmurs from the street below wafted through a window opened wide. Nettles whispered her eyes were pools of the purest blue. A line from a Bette Midler tune banished her wary sense of foolishness. "It's the one who won't be taken who cannot seem to give" as they drank mojitos enlivened with fresh mint as a nightcap. Afterwards in his bedroom, which was scented by patchouli and a touch of ganja, she savored the smoothness of his ebony skin and the tangy sweetness of his mouth. He was vigorous but not demeaning, and, for a spell that could not be measured in time, she was quite outside herself.

But now she prayed for the curse that was counted out in days. Though few would say so aloud, she knew eight months hence how harshly she would be assessed. "So desperate she shtupped for a tutsoon." Then the muted anger of family and friends, served up in small lethal doses, the tainted child as her rightful penance. She remembered her Irish grandmother saying about the famine, "A troubled soul is like the hungry grass - all consuming." The brutal clarity of truth and consequences overwhelmed her defenses. Once again, she was awash in tears.

Another session of Khartoum resumed and One

Bite Valente, so named for his ability to consume a sandwich in just that, proposed that the scoring system be expanded to allow for some athletic moves – a split, a back somersault, and a pirouette – showoffy stunts to be tacked onto the already incorporated goofy poses. Despite his girth, One Bite was surprisingly limber. Kathleen was all for such embellishments as they made her contribution to the creative mayhem that much more substantial. In a like spirit, she'd taken to decorating the score sheets with little thumbnail sketches of the more colorful wankers – sometimes adding color to the renderings later at home – this in spite of the video tape shot by dilettantes on the sidelines. Their work was kinetic. Hers was timeless in its artistry. God was in the details, she liked to say; and Jenks usually deferred to Kathleen's judgments in matters pertaining to the joust, for she had seen into the heart of their madcap escapades from the start.

The sorties that evening were especially action packed. One Bite demonstrated his proposed additions, painfully so as he took a potato in the groin for his trouble. During the second sortie, both of Night Train Lorraine's formidable maracas were struck simultaneously. Later still, Ezio Malocchio's skintight Dr. Denton's, embroidered with stars and comets, rent asunder as he attempted a split, thereby exposing his hirsute genitalia and sending fellow wankers, archers, and observers into paroxysms of laughter. One Bite asked Ezio about the chalky substance coating the coarse black hair on his groin, and Ezio replied, "Hey, you 'gotta powder 'em 'cause that's probably the best you're 'gonna feel all day." Kathleen claimed to have "wet 'em"; and in the twinkling of Ezio's beastly flesh, these extraordinary festivities came to a close.

During the aftermath at the El Coqui, Ezio and Harvey Valentine, another wanker, swapped sexcapades - erotic tales drenched in the bizarre. Until Tommy Duvall, a middle aged sot who tended to lisp when he was in his cups, launched into a gothic reverie all his own as he had heard about as much braggadocio as he could swallow in one evening. "I remember when 'zis 'Frens girl 'wif really big tits and a tiny 'lil waist - 'ashually somebody's slutty wife that worked in 'za mayor's offith, was suckin' my rubbery 'ole cock right here in the back room of 'zith bar. Moanin' 'n cryin' like an animal in heat, 'see got me all turned around. I smelled her fur and stuck my finger into her tight little 'snath all gooey 'n wet. Oh, the 'soff yellow down on her 'ath! My head was spinnnin' and I 'kithed her on the 'mouf, and sucked her titties - first 'zith one, 'den the 'ofer, till her nipples 'wuth burstin' like chestnuts 'unner my thumb, 'zat huge 'n firm I didn't know whether to 's(h)it or go blind. So finally I grabbed a 'gazunga 'wif boff hands and 'suved 'onna them rock hard, burgeoning nipples up my 'ath." An appalling silence filled the air. Not surprisingly the barman asked the trio to leave. Tommy, his dentures all aclatter, said the guy "was 'prolly queer." Nonetheless, it was getting late and they were spent, so they left without a beef or even a goodbye.

Further down the bar, in a quiet corner under a yellowing calendar that was stuck in September of the previous year, the elderly Mr. Oney Mulvaney sat at the bar quaffing Bushmills, - which, despite its Protestant origins, he considered superior to the Jameson's of Catholicity. Breathing slowly so as not to spill a drop, he chatted amiably with One Bite who, harboring something of a dark nature himself, was interested in the experiences of playful misanthropes like Mr. Mulvaney. "Modern man is an *omadhan* incapable of appreciating the miracle of life or the quintessential sadness of human existence," said Oney, "For, by and large, he's merely a cricket or a firefly – noisy and bright but as ephemeral as the will-o'-the-wisp." One Bite guffawed and asked the nattily attired gentleman if he'd ever seen a banshee or a leprechaun.

"I'm afraid not," Oney replied. "But real-life fearsome creatures are closer at hand. Only today I read giant Humboldt squid are presently swarming in the shallow waters off San Diego in search of prey. Formerly unseen in such waters, these monsters, which wield razor sharp beaks and attain a weight of some 100 pounds, have been known to attack humans. Closer to home, an extraordinary proliferation of Coney Island white fish have been reported in places like Fire Island and Sheepshead Bay. Their flaccid immobility serves for some as a symbol for modern man's tampering with the Life Force. Surf's up, you might say, mixed with *gummi* (or prophylactics) *und* milt- if I may wax Teutonic. By way of perspective, the baboon at the Bronx Zoo shows his red arse whilst whistling Dixie." One Bite gazed confusedly from beneath his tousled hair for he had long since lost the thread of Mr. Mulvaney's thought.

Jenks, a perspicacious soul when he had a mind to be, noticed a brittle edge to Kathleen's gaiety even before her vivacious chatter with a tableful of wankers trailed off into a wistful smile. Despite the banter and the frivolity, something about the way Kathleen rested her cheek on both her hands telegraphed her woe. Besides, he'd seen her moments before in what seemed to be an anguished conversation with the black guy he recognized as the purveyor of swag not a month ago.

Outside, after closing time, when Jenks asked her what was wrong, she pulled him into a vestibule and because she trusted him she told him everything - sparing nothing, least of all herself. "I know what I should do though I can't. This is so real, but I'm a pussy. Jesus, this baby ruins everything. I'll be an outcast despite everyone's pretending. Sooner or later I'll come to hate the child; and dividing his loyalties he'd surely come to hate me, too."

"What makes you so sure, it'd be a he? Or, more importantly, that everyone would turn on you so?"

"I just am. And Jenks, come on, for fuck's sake what if he has a foot like mine? Look, part of me knows squelching this fetus violates something far more basic than dogmas and laws. But, Christ, I'm no saint and it's still a zygote, isn't it, something smaller than a shrimp, and - bottom line - I haven't the courage of a genuine hero. All those knocked up Puerto Rican teenagers, who become mothers, put me to shame." Kathleen put her head down and wept bitter, bitter tears.

"Kathleen, you tremulous creature," ventured Jenks, "I have no answer for troubles like these. Though I'll help any way I can. Really. But right now, let's find a cab and I'll take you home." As though by magic one appeared, and they puttered off in silence as puffs of steam escaped from manholes and the grates. Seconds later, Mr. Mulvaney lurched out of the saloon. Mooned from a passing car, he stood beneath a real life lunar orb and envisioned first a pressed ham under glass and then of Cezanne's still lifes, "Fruit Bowl on the Credenza."

He fancied himself a gourmet, an art connoisseur, and a master of one-upmanship vis-à-vis the more bestial tendencies of man. Later Jenks, no scholar, wondered whence the word "tremulous" had come.

Vernon Terwilliger was often one of the first in the church on Sunday mornings. He picked up lost-and-found items the ushers had missed, checked the altar candles, and filled the holy water fonts. As he shambled towards the lobby where the "No Parking" signs were stored, he spied a young woman praying in an alcove set aside for the Blessed Mother. She caught his notice because she was very modestly attired and wore a veil-most unusual in that day and age. Veronica's veil, thought Vernon searching for a frame of reference for what to others would have seemed odd but trivial. Hearing his tread upon the wooden floor, she turned his way. Through the veil the bluest of eyes glistened with tears.

Vernon rolled out the heavy metal signs and afterwards found an inconspicuous spot, nearest the Sixth, his favorite, Station of the Via Dolorosa - "Simon shoulders His cross." The young lady in the veil had moved and knelt several pews behind. Though services had already begun, a smattering of latecomers sidled into a niche of empty spaces by the side doors. Because the readings were exceedingly short that day, the Mass sped forward to the Gospel - to the story of the woman at the well. Subsequently, as he preached, Fr. Pontrelli cut a resplendent figure upon the raised pulpit at St. Jude's, gesturing dramatically beneath the green fanlike canopy which depicted the Paraclete descending.

The connection between the actual Gospel and Fr. Pontrelli's comments seemed a bit vague to Vernon though he always listened intently. The Reverend's homily concluded, "For better or worse, we live in a world where the ridiculous abuts the sublime, where the farcical juxtaposes tragedy. But, such madness notwithstanding, I can swear to you now that there is nothing funny about the slaughter of unborn children in our midst- about the willful extermination of creatures as blameless as the Holy Innocents. My brothers and sisters in Christ, we must pray that this modern-day abomination is obliterated - before what our Holy Father deemed to call the Culture of Death envelopes us forever more. But prayer, my fellow soldiers in Christ, is but a beginning. Action is called for."

Sweating profusely, Fr. Pontrelli cut short his peroration just before he was consumed emotionally. Much weakened by his fervency, he uttered not another word. Parishioners stirred for the recitation of the Creed, and Vernon noticed his Veronica had flown. Sitting next to where the veiled woman had knelt was a black man whose hair, even from a distance, seemed to shimmer. Tense jawed, he stared straight ahead as though thwarted but determined still.

That evening while sleeping Vernon had a vision in which God told an angel, a fallen one enveloped in flames, "I love these misguided humans, but they can fuck up a wet dream without even trying." And Job in a Cubbies hat whispered, "That's why it's easier to believe in the Evil One than it is in Him."

The sun shone through the clouds as though painted on a fresco. Fr. Pontrelli, in a biretta, collar, and a cape, spearheaded an impromptu delegation of parishioners to protest the "sterilized slaughter" taking place at an abortion clinic located not far from the

Hindustani temple and the chapel dedicated to Mary. Directly behind him Vernon Terwilliger carried his baton topped with a golden cross, followed by eight or nine stalwart souls. A casual observer, interviewed by the daily newspaper several days, later described the motley procession of pilgrims as "something right out of Chaucer's Canterbury Tales" – a soldier in camouflage fatigues, a Franciscan brother in a tattered brown habit, a pastry chef (Pietro Pericone) in his kitchen whites, Sister Seraphina (the voodoo priestess) in a tie-dyed muumuu, two Knights of Columbus in full feathered regalia, and several others bearing posters which read, "Dismember them no more" and "A mother's love conquers all."

Fr. Pontrelli had put the word out as to their fledgling demonstration. Only one reporter showed up. He was from the bi-monthly *Gazeteer*. Much disheveled and distressed, this youthful journalist arrived by bus at the last minute only a block away from the clinic. Seeking a statement of purpose, he waylaid the pastor, who, given a chance to pontificate, sent his contingent on ahead.

Arm in arm Jenks and Kathleen approached the clinic from the opposite direction. As though out of nowhere, like Rumpelstiltskin's other self, Nettles, dressed in a crimson guayabera, appeared between two parked cars. Spreading his arms out wide, he beseeched Kathleen to reconsider aborting their child. Half-heartedly Jenks tried to intervene, but Nettles shoved him hard and screamed, "I 'akxed around. You're a great one for the parties and all. How'd your buddy Ezio put it, 'the fortnightly harlequinade.' And me? I know I'm just a petty thief, but this stuff is for real. So back off –

lightweights need not apply. This is between me and her." Jenks was not so easily brushed aside and grasped at Nettles' throat, but Nettles felled him with a single blow. Kathleen, catatonic until then, turned on Nettles in a fury, flailing at his face and calling him a thug. Though writhing in anger, Nettles never flinched. He grabbed Kathleen's bodice and hauled her towards the clinic, bellowing, "Go ahead, you dirty bitch, kill the baby nigger. No way you'd do this if the child was lily white."

At that moment, Vernon and the protesters turned the corner. He saw Nettles, raving still, drag a tearful Kathleen - the very picture of innocence - towards what Vernon subsequently called "the factory of death." So, too, he spied the seducer's hand upon Kathleen's torn blouse, thus exposing the rose tattoo, and then in slow motion as in a movie, only just a shutterful forward, the black hand upon her pale white skin.

Back beyond the synapses and the impulses of his soul, Vernon envisioned St. Michael laying low an angel adorned in red. He swung his baton with such force that he lost his footing. Even so, the crucifix struck Nettles square in face, the metal crossbeam gouging out a terrible wound just above the cheekbone. Nettles went down like a sacrificial beast, blood spattering everywhere. He lay deadly still.

Kathleen, close to fainting, fell to her knees burbling ungodly obscenities. Vernon, having performed the one impassioned deed of his life, stared into the abyss quite undone. Aghast, Sister Seraphina clutched the gaudy rosary beads encircling her neck. Amidst sirens sounding in the distance, she exclaimed:

"Saints above, Holy Mother of Jesus, like my momma used to say, it's all fun and games 'till someone puts his'n eye out withal."

Made in the USA
Lexington, KY
25 July 2018